She leaned forward and pressed her lips to his cheek, a kiss of thanks. Of understanding. And of something more…

"Stay with me." Her words whispered, featherlight, where she pressed her lips to his ear.

The secrets that swirled around Adair Acres nearly held him back. He cared for her and he didn't want to take advantage of her situation. A situation that *would* have a resolution.

Her lips moved once more against his ear. "Make love with me because it's what we both want."

When he hesitated, torn between what he wanted and what he believed was right, she pushed on. "This is what *I* want, Derek. I want you. Forget all the reasons we shouldn't. Be with me. Just because."

He'd felt himself capitulating, but it was only when she said the last that he knew he was lost.

"Yes."

Be sure to check out the next books in this ~~~ **The Adair Affairs** political family is e secrets.

SECRET AGENT BOYFRIEND

BY
ADDISON FOX

Published in Great Britain 2015
by Mills & Boon, an imprint of Harlequin (UK) Limited,
Eton House, 18-24 Paradise Road, Richmond, Surrey, TW9 1SR

© 2015 Harlequin Books S.A.

Special thanks and acknowledgement to Addison Fox for her contribution to The Adair Affairs series.

ISBN: 978-0-263-25412-9

18-0415

Harlequin (UK) Limited's policy is to use papers that are natural, renewable and recyclable products and made from wood grown in sustainable forests. The logging and manufacturing processes conform to the legal environmental regulations of the country of origin.

Printed and bound in Spain
by CPI, Barcelona

Addison Fox is a Philadelphia girl transplanted to Dallas, Texas. Although her similarities to Grace Kelly stop at sharing the same place of birth, she's often dreamed of marrying a prince and living along the Mediterranean.

In the meantime, she's more than happy penning romance novels about two strong-willed and exciting people who deserve their happy-ever-after—after she makes them work so hard for it, of course. When she's not writing, she can be found spending time with family and friends, reading or enjoying a glass of wine.

Find out more about Addison or contact her at her website—www.addisonfox.com—or catch up with her on Facebook (addisonfoxauthor) and Twitter (@addisonfox).

To Family
The ones we're blessed to be born with and the ones
we're lucky enough to find along the way.

Chapter 1

Landry Adair flipped and pushed herself off the concrete wall of the pool. The heated water kept her body
comfortable while the cool morning air coated the back
of her skin as she swam lap after lap.

Forty-four.

The words echoed in her head, a promise that she had
only six more laps to reach her daily goal.

Spring was in the air, and each time she took a breath
the light scent of alfalfa mixed with a deep, rich citrus
that wafted up from the lush valley that formed the back-
drop of Adair Acres.

Home.

Even if it had felt more like a prison these past months.

She turned off the pool wall with an extra hard push,
images of her father's funeral and the ensuing madness
since filling her thoughts. Secrets. Kidnapping. And
murder.

Her father might have been a distant man, but she'd never given up hope Reginald Adair might come to be the real father she'd always craved.

The pain she'd worked so diligently to push to the back of her mind reared up and swamped her, choking her throat and pushing her up out of the pool, gasping for breath. Hot tears spilled over her cheeks, made even hotter by the cool spring air that blew over her skin.

When would it stop? The moments of abject pain that came up and simply swallowed her when she thought of her father, his life snuffed out by the will of another.

A hard cough drew her from her thoughts, and she ran wet hands over her cheeks to remove the tears before turning. No one interrupted her morning sessions in the pool, and it was jarring to know someone was there.

And they'd seen her tears.

Whatever embarrassment that might have caused faded as she took in the large male form that stood at the edge of the pool. Long and lean, she caught only a vague sense of dark features as the early-morning sun limned his frame, highlighting an impressive set of shoulders in a rich patina of gold.

Wrapping the haughty demeanor she'd perfected through the years around her own shoulders like a shawl, she climbed up the pool ladder to get a better look at their visitor. Because of the lingering threats of the past few months, no one got onto Adair property without passing several security checkpoints.

If he was here, he was meant to be here.

But who was he?

"Miss Adair?"

He spoke first, his voice rich and deep. She ignored the outreach as she grabbed her towel, curious when a buzz of nerves lit her stomach.

Landry dried her face but let her body drip water on the Spanish tiles that made up the length of the pool terrace. Although she hated scrutiny, she knew well enough how to use her long, lithe body as a weapon, and the water would only highlight her curves.

It might have a trick as old as time, but it remained a surprisingly effective tool against the male of the species.

"Landry?" Sharper now, but with a hint of something husky and warm in that deep baritone.

"Yes?"

"I'm Derek Winchester. I'd like a moment with you."

"It's awfully early for a moment, don't you think?" She kept her gaze cool but allowed it to roam over his body. Was this the man her brother Carson had spoken to her about?

He certainly fit the bill with that long, rangy form so tall and straight he appeared to stand at attention.

Tight.

Contained.

Controlled.

Reluctantly fascinated, she continued her assessment, cataloging his features as she looked her fill. His skin was a rich bronze, set off by short black hair and deep, piercing eyes nearly as dark as his hair.

He was attractive in a wholly masculine way. There was nothing pretty about him; rather, he exuded a mix of confidence and stoicism that drew the eye.

"It's early for a swim that could fell an Olympian, too. That doesn't make my business any less urgent."

Business?

Although the urge to bait him was strong, she reached for her pool wrap and slipped underneath the thin black material. Showing off her body to gain an advantage was one thing. Sitting there half naked during a business transaction was tantamount to stupid.

And she wasn't stupid.

"Please have a seat." Landry gestured to the long glass-topped table that dominated a section of the patio. "Help yourself to whatever you'd like."

She busied herself with drying her hair and took a few more moments to assess her adversary. He crossed to the long table the kitchen staff set up each morning, filled with coffee service, an assortment of pastries and fresh fruit. When he returned with nothing more than a cup of black coffee, she was curious.

Was he nervous?

In her experience—and she had plenty with the size of her family—men ate breakfast.

She crossed to the buffet to fix her coffee, then her usual plate of fruit. The kitchen's world-famous blueberry muffins beckoned, but she suppressed the urge to take one and added a few extra pieces of melon.

"So, Mr. Winchester. What can be so urgent you needed to interrupt my morning?"

Her brother's earnest request that she play along echoed through her thoughts but she tamped it down. If Derek Winchester was the man they thought, then he should be able to handle anything she threw at him, too.

"I thought it made sense to get started."

Started?

And why did that word sound like a promise?

A shudder of awareness prickled her spine that had nothing to do with the light breeze that coated her skin. She turned away from the buffet and kept her voice light. Unaffected. "Started for what?"

"Effective immediately, I'm your new boyfriend."

* * *

Derek sat back and waited for the fireworks as a series of reactions flashed across Landry Adair's expressive face. For the first time since receiving this asinine mission from his old boss and trusted friend, Kate Adair, he actually had a moment to enjoy himself.

So the resident princess did have a bit of heat underneath that cool demeanor.

The thought surprised him as it took root and he turned the words over in his mind. Why should he care if Landry Adair ran hot or cold? She was a job, nothing more.

Even if he hadn't felt any heat—for anything—in far too long.

Nor had he found himself captivated by the long arch of a woman's neck, where it tapered down to meet her shoulder in a delicious dip just made for his mouth, in an equally long time.

Shaking off the lush images of running his lips over her skin, he shifted his attention to the valley that spread out as far as the eye could see.

Adair Acres.

Or simply "the ranch," as he'd already heard it called more than once.

A shockingly gorgeous stretch of land that spoke of money and promise, hard work and fierce ambition. His gaze drifted over the lush vista, the light scent of citrus wafting from the rolling hills full of grove after grove. Oranges and avocado, grapefruit and lemons.

It was a far cry from the street gangs of LA or the more refined—yet no less devious—minds of Washington, DC.

Which only reinforced the question he'd been asking himself since fielding a phone call from Kate Durant

Adair O'Hara, former vice president and current whirling dervish.

What had she gotten him into?

While he respected the heck out of the former vice president—and he appreciated her belief in his abilities more than he could ever put to words—he still didn't fully see how he could help her.

But no amount of skepticism had put Kate off her plan.

"What are you playing at, Mr. Winchester?"

Landry had stilled at his rash comment, and while he'd expected the hostility, he hadn't expected the cool, assessing look in her vivid blue eyes.

Or the sudden realization that fake or not, no one would ever buy Landry Adair hanging off his arm.

"Your aunt Kate wants me to look out for you."

"And what makes her so sure I need looking after?"

Whatever momentary gain he had with his opening salvo faded as she collected herself, wrapped in an aura of predatory cool.

Damn, but the woman was a looker. Tall—he'd put her around five foot ten to his six one—which gave him the unusual opportunity to practically look her in the eye without craning his neck. Her body was long and lean, lethal in its perfection.

He contrasted that perfect form with memories of Sarah's petite frame. They'd never quite fit, and he'd always felt like a giant standing next to her. He'd never have hurt her, of course, but he could never quite shake the feeling that he lumbered next to her small, pixie-like build.

Shaking off memories of his ex-fiancée—memories that belonged in the locked box where he'd shoved them six months ago—he refocused on the here and now.

And the very real fact that he needed to convince

Landry Adair that it was in her best interest not only to cooperate with him, but to work with him, too.

She brushed past him with her plate of food and took a seat at the large patio table. The morning sun beat down on her still-wet hair and he guessed at the shade he'd seen only in photographs. Dark layers, mixed with a refined blond.

The fresh scents of citrus from the groves below enveloped him while something more potent mingled underneath. Lush and erotic with the lightest touch of honeysuckle.

Landry.

Heat still sparked under his skin where she'd brushed his arm, and he lifted his coffee mug for a sip, taking a moment to right himself.

Focus on the job.

It should have been easy, Derek knew. He'd been the job for so long he didn't even remember how to be anything else.

"Surely you're not immune to what's happened here. Your father's killer is still on the loose."

Pain flashed in her eyes, electrifying those blue depths, before she laid down her fork. "You think to come into my home and scare me?"

"I'm here to protect you."

She reached for a pair of sunglasses lying on the middle of the table and twirled the frame as she kept her gaze steady on his. "I'm a big girl, Mr. Winchester. I haven't needed protecting for a long time."

A wholly inappropriate thought sliced through his midsection at her words. She *was* all grown-up, with a woman's curves and a woman's beauty. Although she'd put on a wrap, the swells of her breasts were visible through the dark V-neck, a greater temptation than when she'd worn only her swimsuit.

Steeling himself against the temptation, Derek focused on why he was here. Whatever arguments she attempted to push his way, he'd deflect.

For Kate.

And for the very real chance to earn back a bit of the self-respect he'd lost over the past six months. He needed this job. And he needed some damn sense of purpose again.

"You may want to rethink that, since you've never been up against a nameless killer or a missing-person's case."

"Ah yes, family drama worthy of a nighttime soap." She eyed him over the rim of her coffee mug, more amusement in her gaze than any trace of fear, before leaning forward. "Does my aunt Kate think my mother killed my father, too? That's the prevailing wisdom, you know."

The urge to hold back was strong, but he went with honesty. For her own protection, Landry deserved at least that much. But on a deeper level, he sensed he'd gain far more by appealing to her inherent intelligence than placating her as he suspected too many others did. "She hasn't ruled anything out. And your mother's mad dash to Europe hasn't put suspicious minds to rest."

"She's also an easy target. Kate has never cared for my mother."

"From what little I've gathered, I'd say that's a sport around here."

Derek saw the moment his words registered, her eyes going round in her face before the first genuine smile curved her lips. "Now that's one you don't hear every day."

"I'm not here to placate anyone. And I suspect I'd be rather bad at it if I tried."

Her smile faded, their moment of connection lost. "What else did my aunt say?"

"She believes you're all in danger, you especially. And she believes that danger won't pass until the identity of your brother Jackson is discovered."

Landry settled back in her seat, the aggression fading from her shoulders. "Ah yes, the missing Adair heir. It's all anyone can talk about."

If the past few days had shown him anything, it was that the Adairs knew how to keep to themselves. Yes, they had a legion of staff at their disposal, but they were a family that lived at the highest echelons of society. Babbling about their family business wasn't in their nature. And he suspected that what conversation had gone on was done behind closed doors so even the servants couldn't hear all the details.

"No, it's all you and your family can talk about. And it's the real reason Kate asked me to come."

Her gaze roamed over his face, and he fought the urge to shift in his seat under that direct stare. Before she could say anything, he pressed on. "My expertise is missing-persons cases. It's what I do for the FBI and I'm damn good at it."

Until recently.

That admonition whispered like smoke through his mind, and he ignored it. Ignored that pervasive sense of failure that had dogged his heels like the hounds of hell since his last case went unsolved. Ignored the resulting sense of loss at his failure to protect an innocent young girl.

Landry Adair wasn't Rena.

And he wouldn't fail again.

"So that's the gig? You pose as my new boyfriend so you can nose around here and dig into the past?"

"Pretty much."

Landry slipped on her sunglasses, the shielding of her eyes as clear a message as simply standing up and walking away. "I'll consider it on one condition."

"What's that?"

"We're partners on your little investigation."

"I work better alone."

"Then you can head right back the way you came. Despite what she may think, my aunt doesn't have a say in what goes on in this house. Neither do my brothers. And while I may love all of them to pieces, I'm not going to follow along like some frightened puppy."

"I'm a trained professional."

"And I live here. You'll do far better as my ally than my enemy."

Derek knew he had a stubborn streak a mile wide and twice as deep. He also knew when it made sense to step back and let the target think they had the lead. He'd give Landry Adair her head for a few days. From all the intel he had, it was easy to assume she'd get bored in less time, anyway.

"No one can know what I'm after."

"Of course."

"Not even your mother."

"Then it won't be a change from how we usually get on. I don't tell my mother anything. And as you so succinctly mentioned, she's out of the country right now anyway."

With her eyes shaded, he couldn't see any hint of emotion deep in her expressive gaze, but even sunglasses couldn't hide the subtle tightening of her slim shoulders. "So we're agreed?"

"Agreed."

She extended her hand across the table and Derek hesitated, the implied contract not lost on him. When she only waited, he slid his fingers over hers, her delicate skin soft under his calloused palm.

It didn't make sense, nor was it rational, but in that moment he knew his world had reordered itself. And he knew with even greater certainty that nothing would ever be the same again.

Her hand slipped from his as she stood, her breakfast untouched. "Well, then. You'd better get ready."

"For what?"

"We've got a governor to go meet."

Landry slipped her cell phone into her caramel-colored clutch purse and left her room. She'd already fastened on her suit—Armani, of course—and the subtle jewelry that had become her trademark. Her heels sank into the ranch's plush carpet as she moved from her wing toward the main staircase.

Although she'd been raised with the understanding that not much was expected of her beyond perfect hair, impeccable manners and a few well-chosen charities, she'd determined early on that she wasn't going to let that be an excuse. So she'd channeled the frustration born of low expectations—along with boredom and a damn fine business degree—into making life better for others.

It had been a fulfilling choice until recently.

Until the bottom had dropped out of her world and she'd been forced to wonder about the morals, ethics and basic decency of her loved ones.

And her mother sat at the top of the list.

As Patsy Adair's youngest child—and only daughter—she'd grown up with the knowledge that her mother was different. Cold and brittle, she wore both like a battle shield against the world. And wielded them equally well.

As a result, Landry had gone to the right schools. Had the right friends. Hell, she'd nearly even married the *right* man because it fit what was expected of her.

Wealth brought privileges and expectation in equal measure, and Landry had always understood that. What she couldn't understand was how her mother could live a life so devoid of warmth and kindness.

Or love.

She turned down the last corridor toward the stairs and came to a stop at the top, thoughts of her family and their low expectations vanishing as if they'd never been.

Derek Winchester stood in the great hall, a phone pressed to his ear, and she gave herself a moment to look her fill. The same impression she'd gotten this morning of subtle strength and power was still there, but she let others swirl and form around it. He was tall and whip-cord lean, but the strength in those broad shoulders was more than evident.

His coloring was dark—darker than she'd realized in the sun—and she placed his ancestry as holding some, if not all, Native American. Unbidden, an image of him on horseback filled her mind's eye, roaming the High Plains and protecting his family from harm.

Protecting what was his.

She fought the fanciful notion and continued on down the stairs, already on the descent before he could catch her staring at him. Landry fought the slight hitch in her chest when she cleared the last stair and came to stand next to him.

And she refused to give an inch by relaxing the haughty demeanor that she swirled around herself like a cloak. "Do you have a suit jacket?"

"In the car."

"And a tie?"

"Right next to the jacket."

"Then let's get them and go."

Twenty minutes later they were on their way toward San Diego in her BMW. Unwilling to ruin her hair, she left the top up all while cursing herself for the choice. She should have selected her large SUV instead of the tight confines of the two-seater.

Serious mistake.

Derek's large body filled up those confines and she could swear she felt the heat rising off the edge of his shoulders, branding her with its intensity.

"What event are we going to?"

Landry filled him in on the work of her favorite charity, the project's focus on children an ongoing highlight in her life. Although she'd let several of her other commitments lapse over the last few months since her father's death, she'd refused to cut ties with the bright and able-bodied leaders who worked tirelessly to ensure that the children of Southern California had enough basic necessities to not only survive, but blossom.

Weekend camps, tutoring and days out simply enjoying their youth were a mainstay of the organization, and in the past three years she'd seen the children who took part begin to thrive.

"Sounds like a special group. Why is the governor attending?"

"He promised some additional funding if we met certain testing criteria, and the children in the program exceeded every goal set for them."

"You're proud of them."

"Absolutely." The response was out, warm and

friendly, without a trace of her "haughty demeanor" cloak.

"Everyone needs a champion. Those children are lucky to have you on their side."

Whether it was the close confines or something more, Landry didn't know, but she sensed something underneath his words. Treading carefully despite the curiosity that ran hot in her veins, she nodded and kept her tone neutral. "All children deserve that."

"Even if there are too many who don't get that opportunity. Or a chance to shine."

And there it was.

That subtle suggestion of something indefinable. Of something *more*.

"You speak from experience?"

"My work revolves around missing-persons cases. There aren't nearly as many happy endings as there should be. Or beginnings, for that matter."

The urge to remain distant was strong, but something long dead inside her sparked back to life. "It sounds like a taxing profession."

"At times. But it's also one I'm good at. Your aunt was a part of that." She shifted into another lane, the sign for their exit coming up, and he continued on. "I was on her protection detail, but she saw something in me. She knew I had ambitions beyond security, and when a job opened on the FBI's missing-persons team she gave me a glowing recommendation."

"You must have impressed her. Kate Adair doesn't do 'glowing' lightly."

"She's a special woman."

Landry risked a glance at him as she slowed for her exit ramp. His face was set in hard lines as he stared straight ahead, his gaze set on something only he could see. Once more, the realization that something hovered just under the surface tugged at her.

The hotel came up on her right, and she pulled into the valet station. Two valets rushed to open their doors, the man on her left all smiles as he gave her his hand. "Welcome back, Miss Adair."

"Thank you, Michael."

Landry didn't miss Derek's widened eyes over the top of the car or the assessing gaze that accompanied his perusal. Annoyance speared through her at the speculation she saw there—and the surprise that she'd know the name of a hotel employee.

Whatever he thought—or whatever she believed she'd seen—vanished under a facade that was all business as he rounded the front of the car. With swift movements, he took her hand. "Come on, darling."

Heat traveled up her arm, zinging from her fingers to her wrist to her elbow before beelining straight for her belly. She kept her expression bright and her smile wide, even as she clamped down on her back teeth. "What do you think you're doing?"

His grip tightened, his smile equally fierce as another set of employees opened the hotel's double front doors. "Why, escorting you, of course."

"I hardly think this is necessary."

"Of course it's necessary. People see what they want to see, and we've got something for them to talk about. You're showing off your new love, whom you can't bear to be parted from."

While she'd later admit to herself she had no excuse, in that moment she could no more stop herself than she could have voluntarily stopped breathing. The combative imp that liked to plant itself on her shoulder—the one that regularly whispered she needed to push against convention and what was expected of her—couldn't resist putting her earlier impressions into words.

"So it's all about distraction, then."

The rich scent of lilies filled the air around them, dripping from the six-foot vases that filled the lobby of the hotel, a vivid counterpoint to the foul stench of her father's murder that had seemingly clung to her—to all of them—for the past two months.

"Distraction?" Derek's eyebrows rose over the almost-black depths of his eyes.

"Of course. It helps hide the secrets. Like a sleight of hand, it focuses attention elsewhere."

"Are you suggesting you're hiding a secret?"

"No. But I think you are."

Landry had to give him credit, he held it together, his poker face firmly intact. If she hadn't been looking for it, she wouldn't have even noticed that slight tightening of his jaw that gave him away.

"Everybody's got a few, you know. But in this case, I'd say your secrets are more present. Recent, even," she said.

"I don't have any secrets."

"Oh, no?" Landry waited a beat or two—her father had taught her the effectiveness of the approach—and watched as his attention caught, then held on her. "Then what is a big, bad FBI agent doing here on babysitting duty?"

Chapter 2

*S*ecrets.

The word whispered over and over through Derek's mind, filling up every nook and crevice until he barely knew who he was anymore.

Hell yes, he had secrets. And an endless series of questions that always culminated in the biggest query of all. When had it all gone so wrong?

Six months ago he was a man with a plan. A career he loved. A fiancée he was planning on spending the rest of his life with. And a series of cases that gave him purpose each and every day.

And now he was a glorified babysitter, living with the memories of a child who was still missing, a perp wounded by Derek's own hand and a leave of absence while the FBI investigated it all.

Did he have secrets? Bile choked his throat at the raw truth of that question.

He had a boatload of secrets, and every damn one of them was eating him alive.

"Stay with me, Ace." Landry's sultry voice whispered in his ear moments before her hand came to rest on his forearm. "I have someone I'd like you to meet."

"I haven't gone anywhere."

She cocked her head, the motion almost comical if it weren't for the well of compassion she couldn't fully hide beneath her gentle blue gaze. "You keep telling yourself that."

She turned away before he could respond, and then there was no need when the governor stood before them, his crisp black suit as perfect as his smile.

"Governor Nichols. So lovely to see you again. I so enjoyed catching up at Congresswoman Meyers's home last November."

"As did I, Landry."

Landry made quick introductions and Derek sensed the question that hovered in the air among all three of them.

Who was this man with one of California's favorite daughters?

Was he good enough?

Would he ever be?

"Derek's a friend of my aunt Kate. She's raved about him for years and simply insisted we had to meet."

The governor's handshake was firm and his eye contact direct as he nodded through Landry's introduction. "Kate always gets what she wants."

Landry's arm wrapped around Derek's the moment he was done shaking hands and she squeezed. Hard. "Don't I know it."

Derek took that as his cue, smiling at Landry before turning toward Nichols. "And clearly I'm the lucky beneficiary. A beautiful, dynamic woman on my arm and the endorsement of another dynamic beauty."

"And what do you do, Mr. Winchester?" Nichols's smile was broad, but Derek didn't miss the continued curiosity underneath the polite veneer.

"A little of this, a little of that."

"Derek's got the especially lucky opportunity to travel where his whims take him. Give of his time where he sees fit. And support the causes that are near and dear to him."

Landry's quick description of a wealthy, aimless playboy had the governor's eyes dulling, and Derek chafed at the description.

Sure, he was here on an op, nothing more. But it still stung.

He worked damn hard, for every single thing in his life. None of it had come easy, nor had it come without a price. Long hours. Endless days spent briefing and debriefing, planning and then executing to a precise schedule.

They exchanged a few more pleasantries—and Landry's confirmation of when the organization could expect a check from the governor's office as promised. Only when Nichols walked away did Derek feel Landry relax by his side, her grip loosening, even though she didn't fully pull away.

"Nice job, Slick. Even if you were gritting your teeth through my flowery description of your globe-trotting adventures."

"I have a name, you know."

She dropped his arm, but the husky register of her voice made him feel as if they still touched. Intimately.

"Yes, but then how can I objectify you in my mind? If I use your name, I'll be forced to see you as a person."

He marveled at her words and their distillation of something career abusers inherently understood. Objectify the victim. See them as something separate. Apart. If you don't humanize them, then there's no guilt over your choices—as with Rena and her captor.

"That's awfully deep. And here I thought you had a business degree."

"With a minor in psychology." She patted his arm before reaching for the slim purse she'd laid on their table.

"I'd say you understand more than a few courses' worth."

Those husky notes gave way to a lighter, airier tone. "Ah, yes. The glorious education one receives as an Adair. We can't forget that."

Derek followed her back the way they came, down a long corridor and then through the main lobby. "Sounds lonely."

"At times. Until you hit a point when you don't care any longer." The breezy socialite was back as she handed her valet ticket to the attendant.

Derek marveled at her quick and ready costume changes—the cool, refined temptress from the pool to the excited ingenue on their drive over to the responsible socialite with the governor.

Each one was undoubtedly a facet of her personality, but which one was dominant? Which one was the real Landry Adair?

And when had he begun to crave the answer?

Landry offered up a small "come in" at the knock on her bedroom door. She shoved the Roosevelt biography under her covers and opened the tabloid just as her brother Carson walked in.

She glanced up from a spread on upcoming summer

movies and closed the issue, tossing it beside the bed before Carson could see she had it upside down. "Hey there, big brother."

"Hey, yourself."

Carson limped into the room, the bullet wound that had ended his career in the Marines a permanent presence in his life. Thankfully, so was his new fiancée, Georgia.

She'd worried for him when he first came home, ghosts dwelling in the blue eyes that were a match for her own. But in the past month he'd turned the corner. Their father's death weighed heavily on all of them, but the fact that he'd found something strong and true with Georgia Mason had changed him.

And when you added how they found each other, Carson's journey back to full emotional health was especially amazing.

"I heard you were out and about today."

"When am I not?" She shifted on her bed, making room for Carson's well-muscled form. He might move a bit more slowly than in the past, but he was far from soft. In fact, in some ways, his new physical limitations had only pushed him harder to keep his body in top condition.

"Let me rephrase my point. I heard you were out and about today with Derek Winchester."

"Ah. You mean the babysitter."

Landry let the words dangle there, curious to see Carson's reaction. "The man's damn good at what he does."

"It still doesn't mean I need to be watched over."

"Come on. We discussed this and you said you were okay with it."

They had. And she was.

Until a long, lean warrior arrived at the edge of her pool at eight o'clock this morning. The man messed up her routine and her order. He made her curious. About him. About what had brought him to their door. About what it might be like to kiss him.

And to ignore the fact that their relationship was a fake and pretend for a few glorious moments it was 100 percent real.

Shrugging it off, she tossed a jaunty smile toward her brother. "A girl has a right to change her mind."

"Then if it's that easy, change it back."

"Why have we let an outsider in?"

"So he can see the things we can't. We're too close to it all. We've got absolutely zero perspective, and that makes us vulnerable."

"I'm not too close to anything."

"Oh, no?" Carson stretched out and folded his hands behind his head like a pillow. "You can honestly sit here and tell me you aren't shocked as hell that we might have a brother somewhere?"

"No." *Yes.* She averted her eyes rather than admit the truth to Carson with his all-knowing gaze.

"And you're equally *not* shocked that someone shot and killed our father in cold blood."

"Oh, come on, that's below the belt, Cars."

"No. It's honest." Carson shifted, rolling onto his side. "You know as well as I do this is not only a shock, but it's happening from the inside."

Much as she wanted to argue, Landry knew he was right. The events of the past few months had sent an earthquake through their family. While much of it was a blur at times, she couldn't deny her brother's words.

Underneath it all, everything felt personal. And way, way too close.

First her father's death, shot in his office at point-blank range. Then the discovery during the reading of his will of a kidnapped child from his first marriage. Even their mother's race to Europe smacked of personal knowledge.

Carson's voice dropped. "And you know we can't discard the questions about Noah."

Despite the large rooms and relative isolation each of them had in the various wings of the house, on some level Landry understood Carson's need to whisper.

Their cousin, Noah, had been a part of their lives forever. He was just...*there*. A part of their family. A part of them. Now they all had doubts and reservations since Carson's fiancée, Georgia, asked the one question none of them had ever known to ask.

Was it possible their cousin, Noah Scott, was really their father's missing son, Jackson Adair?

Georgia had seen an old photo years before of her stepmother's father. The old photo depicted a young man, handsome and full of life.

And a shocking genetic mirror of Noah.

Ruby, her stepmother, had lost her baby son, then subsequently her husband. Did they dare get her hopes up that Jackson might have been nearby all these years?

"Please tell me you understand why we need Derek?"

"Of course I do."

"Is that a 'Carson, I understand and will cooperate as you've asked' sort of yes?"

She shoved at his shoulder, the motion doing little to move him. "Yes, it is."

"Good. I've already briefed him. You can give him proper cover in the morning when he begins his investigation."

The words were on the tip of her tongue to argue and let him know she and Derek were going into this as equal partners, investigating *together*, but she held back. She knew Derek hadn't been all that pleased with her request, and she knew damn well her brother wouldn't be, either.

So she held her tongue and smiled. "Of course I will."

Carson lifted up on an elbow to give her a quick kiss on the cheek before rolling toward the edge of the bed. Despite his injury, he moved off the mattress and got to his feet in one swift motion.

"And Landry?"

"Yes."

His hand snaked out before she realized its destination and dragged the thick hardcover out from where she'd hidden it. "Go easy on him. He's one of the good guys."

Carson dropped the hardcover on top of the blankets where it bounced with a hard *thud*, his grin broad and cocky as his hands went to his hips.

That smile brought back memories of their youth, roaming Adair Acres and playing through the endless groves of citrus trees. He'd often fancied himself Peter Pan, his hands perched at his waist as he issued orders for how to fight pirates or manage their skyward flight to Neverland.

There had been a time when Landry thought she'd never see that smile again. And now that it was back, she could only be grateful.

She might not like her immediate circumstances.

But she was glad to have her brother back.

Derek kept his gaze on the pool from his guest-room window, Landry's morning swim as captivating from a distance as it had been up close and personal the day before.

He hadn't intended to be a pervert—and as a lawman who spent his life in pursuit of those who lived up to the moniker, he knew he wasn't—but for the life of him he couldn't turn away from the window.

She was magnificent. Her long body was a vision, the product of discipline and obvious hard work. But it was her mind and the emotions that lurked behind her expressive blue eyes that had him even more fascinated.

He'd replayed the day before over and over, tossing into the early hours of the morning as images of Landry Adair had floated through his sleep-deprived brain.

And for the first time in months, he'd had company through the long night with a memory that didn't end in blood.

With one final glance out the window, Derek pulled himself together and headed for the stables. He knew he'd made a promise to Landry—they'd handle the investigation as partners—but if the suspicions about her cousin were right, her presence would only hinder the investigation.

He slid his wallet in his back pocket, his fingers bereft when a badge didn't follow, and fought the daily swell of battered pride and bruised ego.

He was a federal agent. He knew how to do his job, and he was good at it.

Damn good.

He navigated the large house, the back stairwell into the kitchen the closest to his bedroom. The scent of coffee and fresh muffins assailed him as he hit the bottom step, and he caught a shy smile from the head cook as he stepped into the kitchen.

"Good morning, Mr. Winchester."

"Derek, please, Kathleen. How are you this morning?"

The woman blushed, her obvious surprise that he'd remembered her name highlighting her already-rosy cheeks with a warm blush. "Fine. Fine. I hope you slept well."

"Excellent." The lie tripped off his tongue, and he felt no remorse. To tell the truth would only mar the moment.

"Can I fix you a plate?"

"I'd love to, but I actually wanted to get down to the stables for an early ride. Might I swing a to-go mug of coffee from you?"

The woman blushed once more before quickly busying herself with his request. He used the moment to watch the comings and goings in the large, bustling kitchen. Two additional cooks managed at stations along the wall while a series of maids streamed in and out in the few moments he stood there.

An overall impression of efficiency and expertise pervaded the room, and he marveled at the fact that the home ran without the obvious oversight of the lady of the manor.

Interesting.

Patsy Adair had a reputation for ruling her domain with an iron fist, and the promise of that rule must have extended even to times when she was away.

Was that same personality capable of murder? And the cold-blooded killing of her husband, no less?

While he felt obligated to review every angle, something about it didn't play for him. Why would a woman so determined to keep her place in society risk that place over something as pointless as murder?

Especially cold-blooded, calculated murder in her husband's office.

The power Patsy Adair wielded came from the powerful man she'd married. Killing Reginald would have been tantamount to killing the golden goose.

Kathleen bustled back with his coffee and a wrapped muffin still hot underneath its napkin.

"You shouldn't have."

"I saw you eyeing them yesterday with Miss Landry. I try to tempt her with them every day, but that girl's will-power is greater than my muffins. Please don't break my heart and tell me you can refuse them, too?"

The rich scents of vanilla and blueberry wafted up from the warm muffin in his hand, and Derek shook his head. "No, ma'am. In fact, I was hoping to steal one from you, so getting it fresh out of the oven is an extra treat."

"You enjoy."

Derek took a moment to assess his chances with the sweet woman and decided to go for broke. "Sad things often make people lose their appetite. Landry will come around."

Kathleen shook her head, the light vanishing from her gaze. "I hope so. There's too much sadness here. I left after the holidays to help my sister and her family in Ireland. My niece got married and we made it a family reunion. They were happy times. Then I come back here to nothing but grief and pain."

"I'm sorry. I didn't mean to upset you."

"I'm not upset." The woman dashed at her eyes. "I'm angry. Someone attacks Mr. Adair and leaves him for dead. Then they come after the family. It's not right."

Derek laid a gentle hand on her arm. "The family will get answers and things *will* be right again."

"I hope you're right." She blushed once more, then pasted on another smile before she sent him on the way. Derek couldn't help noticing the smile wasn't quite as bright as when she'd handed over the muffin.

He maintained an easy stride past one of the property's orange groves on his way to the stables. It was only when Derek got closer and saw the man he was looking for exercising a horse in a large paddock that the tension he'd lived with for the past six months returned to his shoulders and stiffened his spine.

If what Carson Adair suspected was true, Noah Scott had been living a lie.

And Derek knew it was his job to uncover the truth.

Chapter 3

Derek waited until Noah was at a stopping point before lifting his coffee mug in a morning salute. "Hello!"

He willed the tension from his body as man and horse swung his direction. The last thing he needed to do was alert Noah he wasn't who he claimed to be. And if the horse got spooked by the subtle tension, Derek could kiss his cover goodbye.

Noah's comfortable smile remained in place before he directed his mount toward the edge of the paddock. "What can I do for you?"

Derek introduced himself, before adding, "I'm a good friend of Landry's."

"Ah yes, the new boyfriend." Noah's smile was friendly and his tone that of an easygoing cowboy. "It was all the kitchen could talk about this morning when I stopped in for coffee."

A strange sensation—like thousands of bees stinging

his face—worked its way across Derek's cheeks and then on down his neck before he ignored it, repressing any sense of embarrassment. "People like to gossip."

"That they do. And I can tell you it's the national pastime here at Adair Acres."

"I'll keep that in mind."

Derek reviewed his approach in his mind, working through the script he'd planned through the long hours of the night. "Landry said I could come down and ride any of the horses. Said to confirm with you who's feeling well and up for a new rider."

Noah's jovial grin grew even broader. "That's her polite way of saying I needed to pick who I want you to ride and also make sure you don't get a crack at Pete."

"Who's Pete?"

"Landry's beloved thoroughbred. Paperwork says he's come down through Seattle Slew's line."

Derek heard the words, even if it took his brain a few minutes to catch up.

Landry Adair had a horse from the same line as a Triple Crown winner? And she selfishly kept him to herself and gave him an ordinary name like Pete?

Maintaining the loose-limbed personality and devil-may-care attitude of an aimless playboy, he smiled and nodded. "I guess I'll have to work on her, then."

"Let me know how that goes. My cousin's not easily swayed."

Cousin. Or half sister.

Without even knowing it, Noah gave him an entrée to discuss the real reason he was here. "You're cousins? Landry didn't mention it."

"Sure are. My mom and her dad are sister and brother."

"So you grew up together?" Derek added a smile he

hoped conveyed a dreamy, besotted quality. "I bet she was a cute kid."

"If all knees and elbows are cute, with a side of bossy territorialism, then yeah," Noah said. "There's a little more than ten years between us so I missed her later years. The stories are legendary of her terrorizing the grooms until they finally put her up on her father's favorite horse."

"Another thoroughbred?"

"Yep. Shared the same sire with Pete."

"Damn." Derek shook his head and tried to imagine a young girl of no more than eight or nine up on a horse designed for speed and endurance, descended from a horse who had those traits in spades. "Where the hell were her parents?"

"Around." Noah said nothing more, and Derek knew he needed to pull back. Whatever loyalties were there were embedded deep, forged over a lifetime. He needed to go slowly.

"She's quite a woman. Clearly that started at a young age."

"That it did. Look. Give me a minute to get Lucky Strike taken care of and I'll get you settled."

Noah dismounted and walked the regal Lucky Strike toward a groom waiting at the edge of the corral. Derek took the moment to observe the exchange, the groom's respect more than evident in the set of his shoulders and the ready smile at whatever joke Noah told.

In moments the man was back, directing Derek toward a long barn equipped with the latest in technology. Electronic signs lit up the walls, detailing feeding schedules, medicine needs, upcoming vet and farrier visits, and general comments around exercise and well-being. The horses he passed in each stall were impeccably groomed and glowed with good health.

Noah's doing?

"You manage this part of the estate?"

"In a roundabout way. I manage most of the agriculture on Adair Acres. But the horses are my passion. So this is where I spend most of my free time."

Derek hadn't been on a horse in years, and he was surprised to find himself anticipating the experience like a kid waiting for Christmas.

"Why don't you take San Diego Sunrise out? Diego needs some time in a big way." Noah pointed toward a horse two stalls down from where they stood. The large bay was a deep brown, the color of the richest dark chocolate.

"Anywhere on the property you'd prefer we don't go?"

"Nah. Enjoy the morning and give him his head for a bit if you will. He hasn't been out for a while. And be sure to give him some time in the alfalfa pasture down on the south edge of the property."

Derek patted Diego's nose, smiling when the horse nudged his palm. "He wants me to butter you up."

"A few well-placed words never hurt, but a trip to his favorite pasture and Diego here will be yours for life."

They worked in tandem, quickly saddling the horse, before Derek pushed his last comment of the morning. "Thanks for the help. This is a beautiful place. It'll be great to see it up close and personal."

"There's something special about Adair Acres. I felt it the first time I came here."

The specific word choice caught Derek's attention, and he cycled quickly through the details Carson had provided in advance. He knew what the family believed about Noah's parentage, but if the man hadn't even been in the States, how could he be the missing Adair heir?

"First time? Haven't you come here your whole life?"

"Nah." Noah added a few notes to Diego's stall via a keyboard. He quickly tapped his way through several screens before turning back toward Derek. "I lived in Europe as a kid. Didn't get here until I was about eight. But I fell in love with this place and haven't looked back."

Was he purposely kept away from the ranch and his real family by his mother? Or was he truly the biological son of Emmaline Adair Scott, Reginald's widowed sister?

Derek reflected on the implications as he maneuvered Diego out of the barn. Noah Scott seemed like a decent, hardworking, stand-up sort of guy.

And whatever love or sense of belonging he felt at Adair Acres was at risk of breaking into a million shattered pieces.

Mark Goodnight glanced at the various materials laid out on his desk and calculated how much he'd need to use to tip Winchester off. He'd already cut out enough letters from magazine covers and newspaper headlines to make a pretty good demand note. All that was left was to glue it together and then mail the note to Winchester at the FBI office.

So damn easy.

It'd be even easier if he could just sneak the materials into the lab and run a few tests on his own, fudging results where he needed to, but a guy couldn't have everything.

Besides, he didn't need everything. He just needed Sarah. And in a few more weeks, he'd have her. He'd already been the world's greatest friend, meeting her every afternoon for coffee and letting her pour her heart out about Derek. How he wasn't there for her. How he made the job his life. And how he couldn't get the disappearance of one small girl out of his head.

What else could she do but leave him?

Mark crooned out loud, his whispered chorus of "of course you needed to leave" a litany that spilled from his lips as he unscrewed the cap on a bottle of rubber cement.

And when *he* solved the case of the missing Rena, Derek's mania would finally be put to rest.

Winchester hadn't been trying to help the girl.

He'd been obsessively destroying her.

And Mark would deliver the proof that put Derek Winchester far away from Sarah. And his job. And everything else he held dear.

Landry let Pete move at his own pace, the fresh morning air whipping past both of them as the thoroughbred thundered over the lush fields of Adair Acres.

Fool. Liar. And freaking Lone Ranger wannabe.

She'd made a deal with Derek Winchester, and a mere twenty-four hours later he'd already disregarded their agreement.

Toad.

Pete's powerful body moved and shifted underneath her, sinewy grace and unleashed speed. The ride matched her mood—wild and untamed—and she hoped like hell Derek Winchester had put on a hazmat suit this morning, because she was about to unleash a rain of fire on his too-fine ass.

She caught sight of Derek and Diego, just where Noah had promised they'd be. The horse grazed in his favorite alfalfa pasture and Derek held lightly to his reins, walking beside the horse at a leisurely pace, bridle in hand.

She applied subtle pressure to Pete's back and he

slowed instantly, the hard race over the grounds calming to a swift gallop. His ears perked up and she could have sworn she felt him begin to prance beneath her as he realized their destination.

Every resident of the Adair Acres barn loved the rich field that lay at the south end of the property. Her father had planted it for the thoroughbred he loved—Pete's brother—and it had become a sort of tradition on the property.

She slowed Pete down even more as they grew closer before bringing him to a halt a few yards from Diego and his traitorous rider.

"Good morning."

"Save it." She dismounted and held up her free hand. "I do not want to hear it."

"Isn't exercise supposed to make you less grumpy? You swam God knows how many laps this morning and just rode hell for leather over the grounds. Where are all your endorphins?"

Whatever she'd been about to say sputtered to a halt at the jovial fellow who stared at her. Where was the pensive bodyguard? Or the FBI agent with hidden, troubled depths? Or even the frustrated playboy wannabe who had to demonstrate a decided lack of ambition to the governor?

She'd seen all those personas yesterday, and wondered how they'd given way to the happy fellow standing in the middle of an alfalfa patch.

"I have plenty of endorphins."

"Could have fooled me."

She felt Pete's tug on his reins and stepped back, unwilling to tease him so close to his treat. She made quick work of removing his bridle, leaving only his halter so he could graze properly.

Or gorge, if he had his way.

As soon as she had him situated, she turned back to Derek. "We made a deal yesterday. I'd do this with you if we were equal partners. And first thing this morning you run away when you knew I wouldn't be looking to come talk to Noah."

"Yes, I did."

She was so taken aback by his words she simply stood there. Did he really think she'd calm down in the face of his honesty?

"Look, Landry. What would it look like if you were with me the first time I tried to get to know the guy?"

"It would look like I was introducing my supposed new boyfriend to my cousin."

"And it would have been polite chitchat before he turned tail and ran to avoid being in the company of the new lovers, in the throes of new, unbridled passion."

She swallowed hard at the image he painted, her mind quickly filling in the heated detail of what unbridled passion actually looked like.

And felt like.

Shaking off the bold images, she forced as wry a tone as she could muster into her voice. "Right. Because I can't keep my hands off you."

"Hey. You said it."

The sheer lunacy of their conversation struck her at the same moment she registered his shockingly huge sex appeal. A worn gray T-shirt stretched over his shoulders and chest, molded to the perfection of his body. Faded jeans followed as she worked her gaze down his body, covering his slim hips and long, long legs.

The man was a vision, and she was increasingly helpless to ignore that fact.

She'd been around the block, and hadn't lived a completely chaste life in her first twenty-six years. She wasn't promiscuous, but she wasn't innocent, either.

And no man she'd ever met made her as *aware* as Derek Winchester.

Energy flowed between them, swift as a raging river, as they stood there in the middle of the pasture. Pete tugged on his lead, pulling her back to the fact that more than a thousand pounds of horse stood behind her.

"Want me to take him?"

"No." She took a step back, the lead once again going slack in her hands. "I've got him. Focus on Diego. He's liable to race off if you don't keep watch."

"Right. Because he's found the equine equivalent of heaven and he's going to race off without getting his fill and then some."

"Just—" She broke off, not sure of what to say. The self-righteous anger that had carried her across the grounds faded in the reality of his words. Her presence would have stood in the way of Derek's initial introduction to Noah.

But it still stung.

She was more than everyone's expectations of her. And for some strange reason she'd thought Derek Winchester had understood that.

Derek moved closer, letting the length of Diego's lead out as he moved. "This field has some pretty fantastic properties for humans, too."

"Oh?"

He took another step closer, one hand closing over her hip while the other held the full extension of Diego's lead. "I'd say it's pretty amazing, actually."

"It's just a grazing pasture."

"No. It's more than that."

She tried to keep up, but the heat of his body was

wreaking havoc on her ability to form a coherent thought. "More? I don't think so."

"It's a pasture with Landry Adair standing smack in the middle of it." That lone hand on her waist pulled her until she was flush with his body. The hard lines of his chest pressed against the sensitive curves of her breasts, and a hard tug pooled low in her belly.

"And if I play my cards right, she might even kiss me."

A question formed on her lips, then vanished as his mouth came down over hers and answered it.

Chapter 4

Landry felt the rigid boundaries of her self-control slipping as Derek's arms wrapped tight around her. Long, luscious moments spun out, one more glorious than the next, as his mouth plundered hers, his hand drifting over her spine until it settled low on her back.

She leaned into the kiss—and the hard man who held her as though she was something precious—and let herself go in the moment.

The long months of fear and worry faded away in the press of a hard male body against hers. The featherlight aromas of citrus and alfalfa mixed with the more potent scents of sweat and leather, all imprinting themselves on her senses.

Life.

It was the one word that kept running through her mind as she leaned into Derek, as taken with the kiss as he was.

This was life.

Raw and needy. Necessary, even.

She vaguely registered Pete's lead in her palm before using her other hand to settle low on Derek's hip. Thick muscles bunched under her fingertips, proof the body she'd sensed lay under his clothes was as taut and well honed as it appeared.

A smile worked its way to her lips, vanishing the moment he reached out with his teeth, drawing the sensitive skin into his mouth. Hot need swirled through her, settling itself low in her stomach, tightening the muscles a few inches below.

The hand at his hips fisted in the material of his T-shirt, and she was about to drag a handful over his stomach to get to the warm skin beneath when his strong hand snapped to her shoulder.

His movements were firm—final—as the moment jolted to a harsh stop and the sensual exploration vanished as if it had never been.

Their connection lost, Landry could only stare up into the dark orbs of his eyes. She didn't miss how his pupils had gone wide with need and arousal, despite the bright sun that shone down on them both.

"That was—" He broke off.

At the increasing evidence of his embarrassment, she took a step back, desperate to get away from the heat that branded her as it shimmered off his body. With long years of practice, she swirled the anger that rose up inside her like a protective shield, cloaking herself from hurt.

"What's the matter, Ace? Cat got your tongue?"

His mouth snapped closed, whatever he was about to say vanishing at her careless tone.

She should have kept quiet. Landry knew she'd regret it later, even as the words spilled forth, but a sad recklessness gripped her with iron claws. With a soft pat on his shoulders, she shot him one of her trademark carefree smiles. "Don't worry. It's obvious we can put on a good show for anyone watching. Our fake relationship should be a breeze."

Without waiting for a response, she tightened Pete's lead in her hand and headed for the stables.

His first year in the Secret Service, Derek and his team had faced a bomb threat at a hotel while on protection detail. Despite working their way through a series of practiced maneuvers as they moved the vice president to safety, he'd never forgotten the sheer rush of adrenaline and the absolute lack of knowledge of what the next several minutes would bring.

Annihilation or safety.

The question had hovered through his mind as they escorted the VP down several long corridors toward her waiting car, a phalanx of men surrounding her in unified timing.

They'd had one goal, one mission.

And they'd executed that mission with flawless grace, their only concern the woman in their protection.

Images of that day still remained, emblazoned on his memories with detailed precision. He'd understood his job before then. He'd known what he'd signed up for and what it meant to lay down his life for another. But until that day, with Kate Adair wrapped in a tight cocoon of protection, he hadn't understood what that vow truly meant.

While Derek knew a kiss in a meadow on a bright spring morning couldn't—and shouldn't—qualify as equally dangerous, he'd be damned if the same thought didn't keep spinning through his mind as he crossed the sweeping property of Adair Acres.

Annihilation or safety.

Although the vice president was no longer his responsibility, her niece was, and Derek recognized the trust Kate had placed in him. Which meant he had no business dragging said responsibility in for a mind-blowing kiss in broad daylight, all while his body screamed with the unfulfilled need to do so much more.

He slipped in the back door of the house, Landry's parting words echoing in his ears.

Our fake relationship should be a breeze.

Yeah. Right.

The sound of voices rose up from the direction of the dining room, Landry's huskier tones mixed with the deeper baritone of her brother. Although Derek sensed the conversation was private from the muted undertones, he was in the middle of whatever was happening here, whether Landry liked it or not. With a resigned sigh, he headed for the entry to the long room, prepared to join in the melee.

"I don't owe you an explanation, Carson." Her direct words spilled into the hallway. "I said I'd go along with it and I am."

"By stomping around here like the spoiled princess of the manor?"

"Oh come now, big brother. I'm simply living up to expectations. You know that as well as I do."

Derek let out a short, discreet cough to announce his presence, and both turned as he walked into the room. Carson and Landry stood close, their similarities as siblings more than evident in their fair coloring.

But it was the matched battle stances that truly marked them as siblings, warriors down to their core.

Whatever he might have been, Reginald Adair had a reputation for being ruthless in going after what he wanted. Stubborn to a fault, he didn't take no for an answer, nor did he back down. It was a trait his children had apparently inherited in spades.

"Am I interrupting something?"

"Would it matter if I said yes?" The quick words snapped at him with the force of a striking cobra. Despite their earlier kiss and his subsequent fumbling, he couldn't quite shake the smile at the fierce expression that only served to heighten the sensuality of those bee-stung lips.

Derek shrugged. "Probably not."

Her bright blue eyes narrowed and Derek saw the light of battle as clearly as if she'd hollered "Charge!"

"Well, then. Since you're not leaving, perhaps you can explain to my brother why you felt the need to introduce yourself to Noah this morning, despite our explicit agreement that we'd manage this little deception together."

"I thought we already worked that out."

"Do I look like we worked it out?"

You look like a woman who's been loved.

The thought gripped him so tightly he was amazed the words didn't actually leak from his lips. Color still rode high on Landry's cheeks, and the faint mark of his morning stubble edged her gorgeous lips in stubborn lines of pink like a brand.

His brand.

"Why don't I get going and leave you two to figure this out?" Carson edged away from his sister, his gaze wary.

"Some ally you are. You're a traitor to the cause."

"Yep." Carson smiled for the first time since Derek

had entered the room, then added a wink for good measure. "See you later."

Landry's moue of disgust did nothing to hide the sultry sweep of her lips, and she turned on a very fine heel to refill her coffee mug.

"I didn't talk to Noah on my own to go against your wishes. I thought I made that clear earlier."

"You did."

Something faint drifted across the gorgeous blue of her eyes. If he hadn't been searching her face so hard, he'd likely have missed it. "You think I was wrong for taking the opportunity?"

"No."

"Then why the attitude?"

Her gaze drifted around the opulent room before she settled her focus back on him. "Noah's my cousin. My family. And he has no idea what we all suspect."

Landry's words stopped him and the momentary amusement he'd felt at her battle stance faded. He knew what it was to ruin someone's life with the truth. Knew even better what it was to have that truth thrust upon you without warning.

Despite that knowledge—or perhaps in spite of it—he pressed his point. "Noah can't know. Not yet."

"Why not? If we ask him, he might be able to assuage our fears. Might be able to give us answers to our questions."

Derek understood her deep desire to keep the truth at bay. Like a hovering specter that turned warm memories cold and settled fear deep in the bone, their suspicions would change the course of Noah Scott's life if they were proven true.

"Or we'll possibly create more questions. What if he

tips his mother off before we have a chance to properly investigate and make our case?"

The mention of Noah's mother, Emmaline, did the trick. Landry's open, almost pleading gaze faded, replaced with stoic resolve. "You think she's guilty?"

"I think we need to evaluate on our own before making suppositions or rushing to judgment."

Her long, slender fingers fisted at her sides. "And you haven't?"

"An investigation based on facts isn't judgment. It's what I do. What I know how to do. If you can't accept that, then maybe my initial thought to work this alone was a better idea."

"Threats, Derek?"

A retort rose up but he held it back, the urge to defend himself fading in memory of the clear hurt in her eyes when she leaped off her horse to confront him earlier.

She *had* been hurt. While he wouldn't have done anything differently, even if given the chance, he wasn't immune to the disappointment he'd seen in the set of her slim shoulders.

Landry Adair was used to being let down. He wasn't sure how he knew that with such bone-deep certainty, but he did. And he'd be damned if he wanted to be yet another person who did the same.

"I don't make threats. And I'm not apologizing again. But now that I've met Noah on my own terms, I have no interest in continuing to work this on my own."

"Oh." The admission was enough to knock the wind from her arguments, and Landry shot him a stoic gaze over her shoulder before picking up a delicate pot of creamer on the sideboard. The dollop she dropped in her cup barely colored the black coffee, and an image of a woman in fierce control of herself struck him with swift fists.

No muffin the day before over breakfast. A spot of cream that was so small as to be invisible. And a fierce battle of wills over her family that she was obviously desperate to win.

Perhaps he'd misjudged the woman who appeared to have everything.

From his vantage point, he was beginning to wonder if she had nothing.

Landry dropped her purse in the backseat of her SUV before she reached for the driver's door. Derek had kept a low profile through the rest of the morning, simply asking her to be ready to take off at lunchtime.

She'd wanted to ask where they were going, but sheer stubborn pride had kept her mouth closed. As a result, she had no idea if the light sweater set and cream-colored slacks were appropriate for their outing or not.

Especially when Derek Winchester sauntered out of the house in another one of his T-shirts—black this time—and low-slung jeans. That same heavy throb from their morning in the alfalfa pasture gripped her stomach and she fought it back, slipping her dark sunglasses quickly over her eyes.

She wouldn't let him see the irrepressible response of her body, which no doubt filled her gaze with ripe appreciation.

And she'd be damned if she worried she was overdressed for whatever outing the infuriating man had planned that he couldn't bother to share with her.

Partners.

The word stuck bitterly in her throat as she climbed into the car.

They were no more partners than her parents had been. Those two loveless souls who'd drifted over Adair Acres, perfectly content to lead vastly separate lives. Reginald and Patsy had known how to turn on the charm and lay it on thick when the social situation warranted it, but the rest of the time they seemed equally happy to ignore each other.

Functional. Cold. And devoid of any sense of passion or need or that bone-deep craving that bonded lovers together.

Was she destined for the same?

Images of her morning kiss with Derek flooded her mind's eye, the thought so vivid she could once again taste him on her tongue. Masculine, with a hint of something smoky like whiskey, tinged with dark coffee overtones. She fought the shiver that gripped her and tightened her hands on the wheel.

Derek climbed into the passenger seat and closed the door, oblivious to her discomfort. *Damn man.*

The walls of the spacious SUV grew tight as his scent surrounded her once more. She'd accepted the feeling of confinement the day before because her sports car was so small, hence the decision to take her boat of an SUV for today's little errand.

So how did he manage to eat up all the space anyway?

Ignoring the zing that lit up her nerve endings, she turned toward him and kept her gaze somewhere around his ear. "Where to?"

"Los Angeles. To my office."

"We're going to the FBI?"

"I want to look into a few things, and it gets us out of the house for a while." He kept his gaze steady on hers and she fought the urge to look away, reminding herself he couldn't see through the dark black lenses of her sunglasses.

"Can't you access your files remotely?"

"I can do it faster and quicker at headquarters. Besides—" He broke off and she caught the sense of something lying just beneath his words.

"Besides what?"

"I want to check in, that's all. I've been out of pocket for a few days and it makes me itchy."

Landry hit the button for the ignition, the high-end model she drove already registering the key in her purse, and shifted into reverse. Despite herself, she was intrigued. By their outing and by whatever else he wanted to accomplish in LA. "What are you looking for?"

"Birth records, for starters. I want to know when and where Noah was born."

The reminder that their hunt centered on digging into Noah's background took some of the wind out of her sails, and Landry couldn't help but eye the large gate that swung closed behind her car after she pulled out of Adair Acres. Two large *A*s sat at the top of the fence, their swirling script as familiar a sight to her as her own signature.

So why did they suddenly appear so menacing? Like a brand, marking the property and all the secrets that hid in its folds?

She shook off the fanciful notion and kept her eyes on the road. The rolling countryside flew by her windows as she traveled the canyon roads she'd grown up on.

"It's beautiful country."

Derek's voice pulled her from her thoughts, echoing what she already knew to be true about the land she called home. "It is. It's so vibrant and lush, and no other place smells quite as sweet."

"You truly love your home."

Heat crept up her neck at his observation. She did love her home and always had. It was a large part of why she'd never ventured all that far, even if it meant living with the stifling expectations of her family.

She'd thought about New York as a teenager, and later fantasized about a flat in London or Paris. She'd even spent a winter on the French Riviera during a college break. But no matter how blue the water, the Côte d'Azur simply had nothing on her little corner of Southern California.

Several thoughts drifted through her mind as she imagined how she wanted to play Derek's question, but in the end she simply settled for the truth. "I do."

"It's good to belong somewhere." She risked a glance at his profile as she took the entrance to the freeway, surprised to see a forlorn expression that turned his masculine features craggy.

But when he turned and caught her gaze, she knew without question there was more beneath his words. "It's good to have roots, Landry."

"What about wings?"

"Sometimes flying's overrated."

His cryptic words smacked of sadness and loss. And as they sank in, the wholly unexpected need to nurture stuck in her chest, tightening her muscles like drawstrings.

She had no right to nurture.

Or question.

Or insert her opinions in whatever had put that haunted look behind his dark, solemn gaze.

They weren't in a relationship. And despite the strange tug of attraction that had been her constant companion since he stood above the pool staring down at her the day before, she didn't know Derek Winchester.

But you do know the feel of his lips and the caress of his hands.

She tamped down the traitorous thought as her car flew down the road, the heavy traffic of the city building with each passing mile. No matter how enticing those few moments in his arms, they were the consequence of a power play, nothing more.

A battle of wills between two stubborn people, testing the other to see how far each could push.

They absolutely were not the quiet moments of a couple in the throes of early attraction, barreling down that steep slide into love.

"At the risk of exposing my deep and abiding love for gritty detective shows, TV really doesn't do it justice." Landry looked around the spacious entrance to the FBI office in LA, doing her level best to fight the mix of awe and excitement.

Derek glanced up from where he signed her in as his guest, a lopsided grin turning up one corner of his mouth. "What were you expecting? Lennie Briscoe sitting at a desk at the corner?"

His reference to Jerry Orbach's character on *Law & Order* warmed her, adding a surprising sense of fun to their hunt for information on Noah. "Maybe."

"What else did you imagine?"

"I don't know." She shrugged before getting into the game. "I guess I thought I might see a crime lord someone nabbed at lunch."

"Naturally. Because crime lords are a dime a dozen."

"Exactly."

"I'm afraid to disappoint, but it looks like we've missed today's crime lord sighting. But I happen to have something even more exciting."

Derek gestured her toward the elevator off the main entryway.

"More exciting than a parasite who preys on the fine citizens of Los Angeles being brought to justice?"

"Better. I've got paperwork. Reams and reams of paperwork."

"A dream come true."

The forlorn passenger who'd ridden in her car had vanished, replaced with a man fully in his element. Derek had tossed a black sport jacket over his T-shirt, and the pressed material only emphasized the width of his shoulders. Which she really wouldn't have noticed—at all— if he hadn't stopped and turned toward her the moment they paused at the elevators, a broad grin on his face.

"I'm sure it is."

They stepped through the sliding doors, his gaze growing speculative. "So detective shows, huh? I'd have pegged you as a reality junkie."

Landry fought a hard snort and simply batted her eyelashes. "You're lucky we're in a place crawling with law enforcement professionals. I'm tempted to hurt you for a comment like that."

"Note to self." Derek mimed flipping open a detective's notebook and jotting down a few lines. "No mention of singers, ladies who lunch or pregnant teenagers."

"Thank you."

"No. Thank *you*." He gestured her toward a large room marked Archives. "I can keep my knowledge of a certain wealthy, home-based executive's wife with extracurricular activities to myself, guilt free."

"The FBI follows them?"

"The FBI follows a lot of people."

Landry maintained a light, breezy air, even as his words struck a discordant note.

The FBI *did* follow a lot of people. And her aunt had thought her current family situation was bad enough to warrant that sort of scrutiny. She knew Aunt Kate was acting in what she believed was the Adair family's best interests, but Landry also knew there was more to it.

An outsider—and a highly trained one at that—could see things others would miss, and Kate was canny enough to recognize that distinct benefit.

If she were smart—if they were all smart—they'd do well to remember that simple fact.

Derek laid a hand on her arm, the warmth penetrating the thin sleeve of her sweater. "You all right? You disappeared there for a minute."

"Don't be silly. I'm right here."

His dark gaze sought hers and held it for a moment before he gestured toward the archive room. "After you, then."

The subfloor hallway was as ruthlessly clean as the lobby, the scents of industrial cleaner and old paper mixing in the thick air. She knew it was silly, but Landry could swear she felt the weight of history pressing in on them as they entered the archive room.

Anxious to will away the oppressive feeling, she sought for humor to diffuse the moment. "You take all your fake girlfriends down here?"

"That all depends."

"On what?"

"If an old FBI subbasement seems sexy or creepy."

She couldn't hold back the light giggle at his words, but before she could answer him, he pulled her farther into the room. "Come on. There's a workstation down here that's not used very much. It'll give us a chance to sit and hunt around for a while."

In moments Derek had them logged into a computer

terminal, the screen awaiting his search query inputs. He'd shed the jacket for comfort, and her gaze was once again drawn to the powerful body beneath the thin veneer of black cotton. Corded muscles roped his forearms, tapering down to firm, capable hands.

Hands that had held her, caressed her and pulled her against his warm frame.

"Noah's thirty-seven?"

The question pulled her from her musings before she nodded, her voice tight when she finally spoke. "Yes."

If Derek heard the distress he ignored it, instead typing in Noah's name, year of birth and parentage into the query field. Even with all their efforts to lighten the mood, Landry couldn't quite vanquish the well of sadness as she watched him type her cousin's name into the search bar.

While their failed kiss had been more the cause of her cool attitude back at the house, she hadn't lied about Noah. The thought of what they were doing—and the consequences for her cousin—was tough to swallow.

Two months before, her father had been ripped from her life, the cruel hand of death dealt by another. If she and Derek discovered proof that Noah was the missing Adair heir, wouldn't they be doing the same in reverse?

Ripping him from the only life he'd ever known? And the comfort of an identity he'd lived with since he was an infant.

On a resigned sigh, she admitted to herself that wishing the truth away—or worse, attempting to hide it—wasn't the answer, either. "You need to add Ruby to your next search string."

"Your father's first wife?"

"Yes. Ruby Townsend Mason."

"Her daughter, Georgia, is Carson's fiancée, right?"

"Georgia's her stepdaughter, but they might as well be related by blood. The two of them are incredibly close."

Again, the pressure of the past few months weighed on her as she thought about the woman who'd come into her brother's life, brightening his entire world and helping to ease the pain of wartime that had scarred him, both physically and emotionally. Georgia was an incredible person, and she'd been raised with an abundance of love and caring. Ruby Mason might not be her biological mother, but she was Georgia's mother in all the ways that mattered.

It was humbling to contrast the relationship to the one she shared with her own mother. As they always did, thoughts of Patsy Adair managed to make her feel sad and stifled, all at the same time.

"I'll include Ruby's information next." Derek's voice broke into her thoughts as he set up another query while the first was running in the background. "It's interesting that it was Georgia who made the connection about Noah."

"She saw an old picture of Ruby's father and was shocked by how much the man resembled Noah."

"Connections." He muttered the word as his fingers flew over the keyboard. Strong. Efficient. Competent.

An entirely unexpected flutter settled beneath her skin and Landry tried to shake off the strange well of attraction. Seriously? When did a man sitting at a computer terminal become sexy?

When he wore a black T-shirt and low-slung jeans like Derek Winchester, that's when.

Ignoring the sexual buzz—especially in light of the fact that Derek seemed to be oblivious to one, his gaze focused on the computer screen—Landry's thoughts returned to Georgia. She knew the suspicions about Noah had been weighing heavily on Georgia's mind.

Was Noah really Jackson?

And could it even be possible he'd been a part of their family this entire time?

Georgia hadn't wanted to get Ruby's hopes up, so instead of reveling in the celebration of her engagement to Carson, the woman was busy keeping secrets from her stepmother.

Landry fought back a small sigh at the realization that yet another layer of deception and mystery permeated her life and the lives of those she loved.

It was further proof that the grounds of Adair Acres held as many old secrets as new ones.

Chapter 5

Derek retrieved the results of their search queries from the printer and briefly toyed with hunting down Mark for an update on the Frederickson case. He'd managed to put some of his seething frustration aside since taking on Kate's request to help the Adairs, but the case wasn't ever that far from his thoughts.

The Bureau-imposed leave of absence hadn't helped.

The case had captured his attention from the start, but the addition of too much time on his hands and a young girl still missing had been agony.

No matter how he worked through it in his head, he always came up with the same answer. He'd had no choice but to discharge his weapon, especially when their suspect—a low-level drug runner who thought he'd increase his income by kidnapping young girls—intimated he had Rena and then moved as if he were pulling a gun of his own.

It had been a race to see who pulled their weapon first, but Derek had beat Mark to the punch and fired. And it was only when he ran to the struggling, bleeding man on the floor that he realized he was unarmed.

In moments, it had also become clear the man didn't have Rena.

One moment Derek was milliseconds from bringing a low-life scum to justice and saving the life of a young girl, and the next he was defending his job to the brass over a botched warehouse raid. He fought the roiling, seething anger that still rose up and grabbed his throat at odd moments. They'd worked so hard. And he knew they were close to finding the girl if he'd only had more time to keep pushing.

Instead, he now cooled his heels while the Bureau worked through its reams of paperwork and protocols. His section chief had been decent about it—and had practically pushed him toward the Adair case when it came up—but he'd still forced Derek to play by the rules and take some time off.

Wounding the main suspect in the kidnapping of a teenage girl was a Bureau no-no, no matter how badly the bastard deserved it.

The rip of paper pulled him back from his thoughts, and he glanced down at the printouts in his hands. The thick stack was crinkled in his fist, several edges torn. Easing up, he forced a sense of calm back into his thoughts. The situation was monumentally unfair, but he was working through it.

And he'd get through it.

"Derek?"

Landry stood over him, an even larger stack of papers in her hand, curiosity riding high in her gaze. "I made a few copies of the files you called up. I'm not sure there's much there but I erred on the side of pulling more so we could sift through it later."

"Good."

She hesitated, that vivid blue gaze roaming over his face as if searching for answers. "Did you find something?"

"No. Nothing yet."

"Well, that's good, then. No evidence points to the fact that Noah's not exactly who he thinks he is. Who he's always been."

"We'll see what leads turn up after we spend some time with the material."

"Of course." Her lush mouth settled into a thin line, and the urge to apologize hit him square in the chest. When the impulse faded, one more powerful rose up in its place.

The desperate need to uncover the truth.

It was the hallmark of his personality, and it had been the driving force of his life, calling him to a career in law enforcement.

Landry settled into the cubby next to him and made herself busy with the stack of printouts. The stiff set of her shoulders hadn't faded, but her focus on the material took some of the edge off. He watched as she typed notes into a small tablet on her lap, and he took the quiet moment to observe her.

She was prickly, yes. And she could turn on the haughty-rich-girl attitude at a moment's notice. But he'd also seen glimpses of another woman beneath those shields.

She was loyal to her family, even though several of them didn't seem to deserve the allegiance. And her thorny demeanor hid a deeply compassionate person.

First her devotion to her children's charity and then her obvious concern over digging into Noah's background.

Landry Adair cared far more deeply than she was likely comfortable admitting.

A sweep of hair framed her face where she'd pushed it behind her ear, and Derek followed the firm line of her jaw. She was a beautiful woman, there was no doubt about it, but there was something else there.

Something rather fierce, if he wasn't mistaken.

Landry Adair had the soul of a warrior. And after spending a few days with her he was more and more sure the people she surrounded herself with were completely unaware of that fact.

Her parents were more concerned with their own lives than the lives of their children. Her oldest brother, by all reports, had been maniacally focused on his career before settling down a few months ago. And her next oldest brother had spent his life in military service. Fair choices for both Whit and Carson, but it would have been all too easy to dismiss their little sister as they went about, focused on their own lives.

With that thought came another—an unbidden memory of Sarah.

She'd been the youngest of several children and had used her role as the baby of the family all too often to get her way. One of their last fights before they broke up had been about what she wanted.

She'd resented his job. She'd hidden it well during their courtship, the subtle disapproval rearing its head only on rare occasions. After they got engaged, though, her attitude had changed.

Resentment over his devotion to his work.

Anger over his long hours.

And bitterness for the victims—missing persons with no one to stand for them—that he worked so hard to find.

The day she left he'd been surprised, blindsided by her abrupt decision. But it was only later, when he tabled his hurt male pride, that he remembered all the signs that had littered the journey of their failed relationship.

While he couldn't let go of his need to see the Frederickson kidnapping through to completion, his memories of Sarah had faded to near nothingness. The wounds still flared up at ill-remembered moments, but the pain of ending his engagement had lost the twin edges of regret and disappointment.

Now there was simply indifference.

"I heard you were down here in the boiler room. And with a beautiful woman, no less."

Mark's voice interrupted his musings and Derek glanced up to see his partner's jovial face. The harsh glare of the fluorescent lights hit his features at odd angles and Derek stood, taking his friend's outstretched hand. "There hasn't been a boiler down here for ages."

"Once a boiler room, always a boiler room."

Derek didn't miss Mark's pointed stare at Landry—or the scrape of her chair as she stood—and he made quick work of introducing the two of them.

"I guess I know why Derek picked the darkest place in the building instead of his desk upstairs." Mark's smile grew even broader, his eyes flashing amusement.

"Why's that?" Landry's polite smile never wavered in return, but Derek heard the notes of steel that lay beneath the polish.

"He clearly wants to keep you all to himself."

"Then Derek and I are on the same page."

Landry settled a hand on Derek's shoulder, the warmth of her fingers at odds with the chilly tone of her voice.

Mark had never been the most suave fellow—and beautiful women made him nervous on the best of days—but his wide eyes and even wider smile had Derek reconsidering the wisdom of bringing Landry here.

Although their office was well integrated, with several female field agents on the team, it was no place for someone he was pretending to romance.

Landry's touch—and the not-so-subtle implication they were a couple—only added to his conviction they should have stayed away.

Mark's eyes widened a bit further before he visibly backed down in the face of Landry's cool reception. "I just wanted to come down and say hi. Give Derek an update on the latest with some of our cases."

"Don't let me stop you."

If the notes of dismissal weren't clear in her tone, her return to her seat and obvious fascination with her tablet did the trick. Mark gestured toward the hallway and Derek followed, resigned to the explanations that would inevitably come when he and Landry reached the car.

Landry focused on her notes and tried to ignore the lingering unease Derek's partner had managed to stir up. She had no doubt Derek trusted him—there was no way you could work that closely with someone if you didn't—but she couldn't shake the sense of dissatisfaction that had registered in Mark's eyes.

Cold, flat and envious.

She'd seen the look often enough in the people her parents associated with. Other society families who didn't have properties that matched the lushness of Adair Acres or business owners who hadn't seen quite the same annual profits that AdAir Corp generated.

Humans liked their boundaries. And they liked it

even more when they were the alpha dog. Landry had sensed—no, she'd known—in mere milliseconds that Derek was the alpha in his partnership with Mark.

"You hungry?"

At the mention of food, Landry's stomach growled as she glanced up from her notes. "Where's Mark?"

"That was a quick visit. He's working a field assignment and had to get back to it."

The statement gave her the opening she was looking for. "Is that a big part of the job? Field assignments?"

"It can be. Depends on what your job entails, but yes, it's a significant part of an agent's duties."

"Is my family considered field duty?"

"No."

The finality of his tone brought her up short. "Your time investigating my family isn't sanctioned by the FBI?"

"I've been given leave, but this isn't an FBI matter."

The husky timbre of his voice wavered on the word *leave* and once again, Landry struggled to understand what was going on. While she'd blithely followed Derek down to the archives earlier, the afternoon had given her new perspective.

The FBI subbasement obviously held the tools they'd needed, but Mark's visit had clued her in that it was a little odd that Derek hadn't even tried to take her past his desk.

"If we're not a field assignment then why are you staying at Adair Acres?"

"It's awfully hard to play your boyfriend from Los Angeles."

"Maybe." She cocked her head and evaluated his sexy, trim form.

Probably, her conscience taunted. Besides, would she really want him a hundred miles away?

"And I'm sure you know best of all, but no one argues with a favor for the former vice president of the United States."

Derek's smile was broad, bordering on cocky, and she gave him credit for the quick save. As answers went, it was effective yet evasive. But as a woman used to digging for the answers that lay underneath what people said, it was the fact that his grin didn't quite reach his shuttered gaze that had her antennae on high alert.

"I would imagine it's a challenge living like that. Always in the field."

"How so?"

"Part of the fun of a job that's always changing is that things are always different."

"Sure." Derek nodded. "I can see that."

"In your case, the scenery changes but the lowlifes never do."

Where she expected that stoic reserve to remain, instead something in the dark depths of his eyes seemed to open. "No. They never do."

Landry wanted to dig further but sensed he'd opened as wide as he was going to. Instead of her normal bullish rush to have things her way, the realization that she might get better information if she bided her time had her nodding. "Why don't we go get that late lunch, then? I know a mean little stall at Farmers Market that makes the most amazing hummus."

"The one by the nut place?"

"Yep."

"Let's go."

She navigated the normal midday traffic as they left

FBI headquarters, excited for a stop at one of her favorite LA spots.

"I have to admit I'm a bit surprised."

Landry turned toward him as she waited for the turn onto West Third. "Surprised about what?"

"I wouldn't have taken you for a Farmers Market girl. The Grove, I can see. High-end shopping and eateries. But its sweet, old-fashioned neighbor is a surprise."

Derek's words struck like swift arrows and she swallowed hard, fighting off the initial urge to offer up a smart-ass remark. Instead, she took her turn at the light and used the moment to marshal her thoughts.

How did they keep coming back to the same place?

No. Correction. How did *she* keep coming back to the same place? *Landry Adair, society girl.*

Although she knew herself well enough to know she'd fastened on her cool, rich-girl attitude from the first moment with Derek, she also knew she'd let it slip more than once.

Was it possible that sense of connection she'd felt hadn't been there at all?

With an indifferent shrug, she answered his question in simple, perfunctory tones. "I like being outside. I like food prepared by hand. This place has it all."

"I always imagined the Farmers Market would be a great first-date place."

Since she'd put on the shield of disinterest, she couldn't exactly pull it right back off, so she kept her voice cool as she maneuvered through the parking lot. "A date?"

"Absolutely. It's casual here but the market has the sophistication of being a part of old Hollywood. Definitely good first-date vibes."

"So how many women have you brought here?" She

put the SUV in Park and turned toward him, intrigued regardless of the shield of disinterest.

"Well, despite the brilliance of my plan, I am forced to admit I've never actually brought a first date here. But Sarah and I used to—" He hesitated before moving on quickly. "I used to come here often."

Sarah?

Landry fought the subtle squeeze of jealousy that he'd spent considerable time here with another woman, firmly pushing the green monster away. Derek wasn't a date, he wasn't her boyfriend and he wasn't a man she wanted to get to know better. They were playing parts, and his background was none of her business.

And if she said it often enough maybe she'd start believing it.

The scents of the market surrounded them as they walked past the vibrant stalls. As usual, Landry nearly changed her mind ten times before she reached the small stand that served the best hummus outside Greece.

Derek put in his order, then gave her his full attention. "You're a determined woman. I'd have stopped several stalls ago and begun working my way here."

"If I tried all those places I wouldn't have room for the hummus."

"Isn't that part of the fun?"

"You might be able to consume mass quantities of sugar- and butter-based deliciousness, but I'm not quite so lucky."

"Oh, I don't know." Derek's gaze turned heated as it flickered below her line of sight. "You work out often enough. Live a little."

Her gaze traveled over his fit physique in return, the

image of a male in his prime stamped in every inch of the large arms that crossed over a broad chest. "Maybe."

"I'm serious. Have a doughnut. Eat a scoop of ice cream. Oooh." He pointed toward an area several counters down. "Or those really awesome crepes at that stall down there are incredible."

"I don't eat those things. And when I do I certainly don't eat them all at once."

"Iron-willed control."

Years of her mother's sharp censure rang in her head. Patsy Adair believed a woman needed to look a certain way: slender to the point of waifishness. Landry had never quite lived up, her tall physique more athletic than her mother deemed fashionable, but she made up for it with ruthless attention to everything that went into her mouth.

"For the record, your first-date skills suck."

Derek shrugged. "So noted."

Their teenage waitress shot him a look across the counter while she finished filling a takeaway tray with their lunch. Landry took the tray the moment the girl set it on top of the counter. Her hands shook with subtle anger as she walked toward an empty table with her food.

She had spent her life since hitting puberty having this argument several times a day. First with her mother, then later with herself.

An Adair had to live up to expectations.

An Adair had to set an example.

An Adair had to be perfect.

And where had it gotten her? Or any of them? With a dead father, a mother who'd run off and a mysterious kidnapping that was still unsolved nearly four decades later.

Perfect? Hell. She'd settle for normal.

* * *

"I can't seem to help myself." Derek set his tray down but stayed standing, willing Landry to look up at him. When she finally did, he saw the misery stamped clearly in her gaze and cursed that damn streak inside him that had to tug line after line.

Landry Adair was a grown woman. She could eat whatever the hell she wanted and it wasn't any of his business. So why had he pushed?

"Can't help yourself with what?"

"Acting like a jerk."

"No, you can't." She tore off a piece of pita and dipped it in her hummus before looking back up at him, her voice softer. "You're an observer by nature."

At the evidence of a softened beachhead, Derek took his seat. "So are you. You watch and notice things. You're always thinking, and your innate intelligence has you processing the world around you very quickly."

Surprise registered itself in the flawless beauty of her face, followed by something he could only call delight. "Since that's one of the nicest things anyone has ever said to me, I'll consider tossing you a bone. If you answer me one question."

"Shoot."

"I can't believe you care that much about what I eat. So what's your question really about?"

On some level his question *was* about the food, but not entirely. "I've noticed your inhuman ability to turn down sugar and it's made me curious."

"Like I said. A lot is expected of me and I don't need to eat bad food anyway." She swirled a piece of pita in her hummus before glancing up. "So what else has you curious?"

"I asked the question because it's tied to a bigger issue in my mind."

When she said nothing, he pushed on. "Why do you care what anyone else thinks?"

"My mother cares, and that's all that matters."

"But she's not here."

"Oh, that's right. She's a killer on the run you're determined to catch."

He laid a hand over hers. "That's not my wish. Not by a long shot."

A sharp sigh whistled through her lips before she laid her food back on the plate. It didn't escape Derek's notice that she kept her other hand beneath his.

"She didn't do it." Again, that sense of something fierce lay beneath her tones, quivering in the hard set of her slim shoulders. "She didn't kill my father."

"Okay." He nodded. "Walk me through why."

Landry had proved herself to be an outstanding partner while they were at the FBI office, providing him with names and dates, various family connections and a history of the Adair lineage, all the way back to her great-grandparents.

She'd even added in a few anecdotes about Kate that had him laughing and seeing his former boss and mentor in an entirely different light.

Maybe she did know something about her mother. Or could at least offer up a few strings to tug that made more sense than what he had right now, which was the simple fact that a wealthy woman had managed to vanish into thin air.

"My mother's complicated on a lot of levels, but very simple in others."

The comment was a surprise—not to mention an interesting place to start—and Derek felt himself pulled into the story. "She's got a reputation for flawless beauty and high expectations of others."

"She does. And there's no one she had higher expectations for than my father."

For the second time in as many hours, images of Sarah filled his mind's eye. Their terse words that led to fight after fight. The seemingly endless tears. And the abject frustration that perpetually marred her features when he was working on a big case.

Rena Frederickson's kidnapping had been the final straw...

"She loved him once. I've always believed that."

Landry's words pulled him from the abyss of memories, an odd punctuation to his thoughts of Sarah. "Sometimes a person is simply unable to be what someone else wants them to be."

"Or sometimes they're trifled with until their love changes into something else entirely."

She slipped her hand from beneath his and reached for her bottled water. "Of course, it's observation only. My mother would never speak of anything as delicate as her pain or her feelings."

"Back to that public image again?"

"But of course."

Derek had spent many years in the FBI observing some of humanity's worst behavior. He'd thought himself well educated on how many ways humans could hurt each other. But sitting here with Landry, a light breeze whipping through the open-air market, he saw yet another facet of pain and loss.

"Do you think she loved your father?"

"With her whole heart. It's the only reason I have

for believing her innocent. Her love for him never truly went away, despite my father's very best efforts to kill all trace of it."

Chapter 6

Landry curled up on the couch in her sitting room. She'd made her excuses when she and Derek had arrived home and hadn't left her room since. A bottle of Cabernet sat, open but untouched, on her small coffee table.

She'd thought to go straight to bed, the shock of the day mixing with the bone-deep weariness she hadn't been able to shake for weeks. When sleep proved elusive, she'd roamed the room on restless feet before sending down for the wine.

Then the wine had arrived and she hadn't wanted that, either. So here she was. Unable to sleep or relax with a drink to think through her problems. Or the endless questions those problems churned up.

What did she come from?

The question had sneaked beneath her defenses after the initial shock of her father's murder had worn off and had gotten louder—like a drumbeat—in the months since.

She'd been honest with Derek. She believed to her core her mother was innocent of killing Reginald Adair. But Patsy had a long line of sins since that fateful night in her father's office, and Landry couldn't explain them away no matter how hard she tried.

And at the top of the list was Patsy's attempts to kill Whit's wife, Elizabeth.

"Who did that?" The words were out before she could stop them, a harsh cross between a mutter and a moan.

Was she really the child of a woman who thought so little of another's life she'd seek to take it? Her mother had claimed it was because she thought Elizabeth was Reginald's pregnant paramour, but even that betrayal didn't excuse her behavior. It only added to the possible body count had Patsy been successful in her attempts.

The knock on her door brought her up short, and Landry briefly toyed with ignoring it before crossing the room. After the wine, she'd left specific instructions not to be disturbed, but maybe her brothers didn't get the message.

Or maybe Derek was back to question her.

Although she'd struggled with his questions earlier, it did matter to her what he thought. Of her family. And more important, of her. With the investigation into her family and their morass of secrets, Landry was fast coming to assume he thought very little.

The knock came again and she resigned herself to the inevitable questions. And promptly burst into tears at the sight of Rachel Blackstone on the other side of the door.

"Hey now." Rachel entered, her arms wide before they wrapped around her in a tight squeeze. "What's wrong?"

Landry hung on for another moment before she pulled back. "How'd you know I needed a friend?"

"I came for the gossip." Rachel closed the door behind them, then pulled Landry in for another tight, side-armed hug. "But clearly I was needed for other reasons."

Landry looked down into vivid green eyes that normally danced with amusement but were now filled to the brim with concern. "What gossip?"

Rachel couched her obvious concern underneath a bright smile and animated voice as she beelined for the wine and poured them both glasses of the rich red. "Hell yes, gossip. Do you really think it would take me very long to find out you spent the day in Los Angeles with a hot hunk of a man who Marcie Willoughby swears— and I quote—'is so movie-star sexy he should be on billboards in his underwear'?"

"I'm… Well… We—"

"Yes?" Rachel smiled, clearly enjoying herself.

"He's not a movie star." Landry managed to get that out, her only coherent thought as her imagination stubbornly stuck a picture of Derek in his underwear in the forefront of her thoughts.

And it was a really good picture. Amazing, really.

"So who is he?" At what had to be a blank stare, Rachel pressed on. "The non-movie-star underwear model."

"You wouldn't believe me if I told you."

Those green eyes softened once more, the humor fading in the reflection of true and lasting friendship. "Try me."

Long minutes later, after Landry had outlined all the reasons Derek had arrived at Adair Acres, she was left with one last, lingering piece of the story.

Rachel refilled both their glasses. "So he's here to investigate your mother?"

"Among other things."

Rachel's eyebrows rose over her glass of wine. "There

are other things? Besides your mother freaking out and fleeing the country?"

Landry took a deep breath and leaped.

"There's suspicion that Noah is really my older brother, kidnapped as a baby."

"Noah?" Color drained from Rachel's normally bright, vivid features. "Kidnapped?"

"I don't want to believe it. And I've told Derek there's no way it could even be possible. Who steals a baby from one woman to give it to another? Which is what it amounts to if he's really my father's son raised by my father's sister as her own."

"But kidnapped?" Rachel set her glass on the coffee table, and Landry didn't miss the subtle shake of her best friend's hands. "News like that will devastate him."

"Rach? You okay?"

Landry watched as her friend visibly pulled herself together. Like a phoenix rising from the ashes, Rachel's initial shock faded as if it never was, morphing into a stoic mask of concern and friendly support.

"Have you told Noah what you suspect?"

"We can't." Again, that heavy weight of suspicion pulled at her with thick, clanking chains of guilt.

"Why ever not? You can't really think Noah's a part of what happened to your father?"

"Of course not. But if it's remotely possible Noah is Jackson Adair, then his mother becomes chief suspect number one."

"Your aunt Emmaline? A kidnapper?"

Landry swirled her wine, the reality of Rachel's question not lost on her. Her aunt had never seemed like a very strong person. She wore her wealth and privilege like a shawl, rarely taking it off. It hardly seemed possible the woman would have had the means or the wherewithal to kidnap any baby, let alone her own brother's child.

"I know it does sound crazy. Which is why we have to be absolutely sure."

"So how is Derek getting around the property and asking questions?"

Landry braced herself for the fireworks. "He's pretending to be my boyfriend."

Rachel's eyes widened, bright green orbs flashing with surprise and—if Landry wasn't mistaken—ribald good humor. "You can't be serious. Are you sure he's not really a movie star and this isn't some zany fifties sex comedy?"

The heavy weight of the day—heck, of the past two months—lightened at the humor she saw in her best friend's eyes. "It does smack of elaborate drama, doesn't it?"

"In spades." Rachel reached for the wine once more, filling them each up and finishing off the bottle. "I guess that means you're going to need to play this whole relationship up."

"Where?"

"Everywhere."

"What's that supposed to mean?" Landry nearly bobbled her glass as Rachel's words sank in.

"It means you need to get sassed up, get that gorgeous man on your arm and get yourselves out on the town."

"Town isn't the problem. Whatever we're dealing with is here at Adair Acres."

"Very practical." Rachel nodded, but Landry didn't miss the twinkle in her eyes. "Let me ask you another question."

"What?"

"Do fake boyfriends come with fake kisses, too?"

* * *

Light breezes blew in from the coast, cooling the valley with that unique blend of sea air and moisture that was so specific to California. Mark punched in the stable code he'd secured from that washed-up track master in LA and stepped into the barn. The stink of animals filled his nose and he held back the urge to gag. He'd be on his way shortly.

The various snorts and whickers of the horses whistled past his ear as he walked the length of the stalls, and he pushed hard against the faint sense of discomfort at their size. He just kept reminding himself they were locked in stalls. Four-legged beasts.

Four-legged *thoroughbred* beasts, of course.

Just like Landry Adair.

He'd known it the moment he'd seen her. Long, coltish legs on a ruthlessly perfect body. Pristine blond highlights she no doubt kept regular appointments for. Cool, assessing blue eyes that could turn a man on or shrivel his parts, depending on what mood she was in.

Oh, yes, Landry Adair was a prize.

He'd kept his ear to the ground and knew Winchester was on the Adair property to work a case as a favor for his old boss. He might be on leave, but the brass would jump for good old Lady Kate, yes siree.

Mark had actually been grateful when he'd realized there was a project afoot. Derek had been up his damn ass, asking about the status of the Frederickson case since he'd been put on leave. Daily updates. Calls at odd times to share a theory on the signs they must have missed, which was why they'd never found Rena. He'd even sent a series of emails with theories he was working on.

Derek and his questions. The bastard was full of them. *Mark, did you file that report?*

Mark, did you do that background check on the runaway's family?

Mark, did you know the perp was unarmed?

A hard shot of fury whipped through him like brushfire, and Mark pushed it back. He'd set the perfect trap, and soon it would all be over.

Derek would get his.

And Mark would have his position at the Bureau and his happy ever after with Sarah.

A win-win, in every way.

In the meantime, the former veep had conveniently given him a bit of breathing room and Mark was sure he wasn't going to squander it. Since Derek's visit to FBI headquarters hit a little too close to home, he figured it was in his best interest to get down here and create a bit of a diversion.

Mark kept his steps light, his gaze taking in the lush stalls and the signs above each. Feeding timetables. Riding schedules. Vet visits. All the responsibilities that went into managing a barn the size of the one at Adair Acres were divided up across various members of the household and staff.

The cloth bag grew heavy and he shifted it to his other hand, another layer of distaste coating his mouth with harsh metal.

He could do this. And he would do this.

It was just one more step in the destruction of Derek Winchester.

His gaze scanned the boards next to each horse's stall, and he'd nearly cleared the length of the stable when he finally came upon the name Pete. The notes for this horse indicated he had an early-morning ride with one Landry Adair.

Perfect.

Mark made his way to a wall of built-in containers a short length down from Pete's stall. Each was marked with a different horse's name, and he lifted the lid for Landry's horse, slipping it aside. A heavy metal bin sat inside the enclosure, about half full of oats and whatever else horses ate.

He was careful as he worked the top of the writhing cloth bag in his hand, settling his bundle gently on top of the mix of oats. The light shake of a snake's rattle broke the hush of the barn, where it echoed off the metal walls of the can and Mark stood back as the sleek body wove its way out of the thick canvas.

The rattle echoed again, louder this time when the snake bumped into the metal edge of the feed can. Despite his fascination, Mark took a quick step back and closed the lid on the mesmerizing display, deliberately leaving the wood frame slightly askew. His thoughts had already drifted to the surprise that awaited the first person who reached into the can for the horse's feed.

He could only hope it was Landry Adair.

Derek fought the sucking gravity of memories as the nightmare pulled him deeper into his subconscious. On some level he knew it wasn't real. Knew the cool stench of the old warehouse in downtown Los Angeles was a mirage in his mind.

But no matter how hard he willed himself to come out of it, he couldn't shake the need to put one foot in front of the other. Step by careful step.

He only had to take the required steps before he'd find Rena and this nightmare would be over.

Rena. The young girl with the haunting eyes. She'd gone missing the month before, a runaway without any protection or anyone to stand up for her. She'd come to the attention of the FBI through one of the vice cops at the LAPD. The man they believed kidnapped her was an international drug runner with a predilection for taking young girls out of the country.

Derek and Mark had picked up the case and were working it as fast as possible to keep that all-too-common outcome from happening yet again.

The light scrape of a shoe pulled Derek up short, and he motioned Mark to take the far wall. An old door hung at a lazy angle, and when the shoe squeaked once more, Derek pointed toward the closed room.

"On three." He mouthed the words, hardly daring to breathe and tip off their quarry.

Mark nodded and they moved through the door in unison, guns drawn.

Thin, drawn cheeks and several days of unkempt beard covered the man's face, but the perp met the description and photos from the vice squad. Albert "Big Al" Winters. A nickname at deliberate odds with his scrawny frame and small stature.

"Hands!" Derek hollered the standard protocol and knew he needed to keep his focus on the man. But damn it, where was Rena?

His gaze flew around the room, desperately seeking some sign of the kidnapped girl, but other than an old cot and a twin mattress covered in dirty blankets against the far wall, there was no one but the scraggly excuse for a human being who stood before them.

Mark added his directive for a show of hands and Derek moved closer, his gaze drifting from the dime bag on the floor back to the shaking frame of the low-level enforcer they'd been hunting for.

"Where's Rena?" The question fell from his lips in

a harsh bark, a strange, desperate panic clogging his breath.

"Rena who?" The man was partially bent at the waist, his hands still out of sight. A creepy giggle rumbled under his question before his voice echoed in a singsongy chorus. "Rena who? Rena who? Rena who?"

Something cold and hollow filled Derek's chest, replacing the lack of air with something else entirely. Disgust and repulsion, but something more. Something far more insidious.

Bone-deep hatred.

Derek struggled to keep himself in check, the anger a living, breathing thing inside his body. He'd worked so hard to bring an innocent home. Had followed every lead and spent hours tracing her possible whereabouts.

And what did they find instead?

An addict on a bender, so blitzed out of his mind he had no idea where he'd even put the girl. Derek hollered the order for hands once more before Mark's scream echoed off the dingy walls. "Gun! Derek!"

His partner's cry was like an accelerant to flame. The cold burn that lived under his skin burst into a raging conflagration as pure instinct took over.

Gun.

Kidnapper.

Danger.

Derek lined up his shot, intending first to hit the perp's shoulder and then his hand if a second round was needed. Neither was meant to be fatal.

The shot echoed, registering even before the gun recoiled in his hand. The scene swam before his eyes as emotion swirled and panic eddied down to his very core. And like a mirage before his eyes, Big Al had already started moving, lunging toward Mark over the man's battle cry about a gun.

Derek rose straight up in bed, his hands trembling as he squeezed off the imaginary shot. No matter how many ways he played it in his mind—or in his subconscious while asleep—the outcome never changed.

The perp shifted and the shot meant for his shoulder landed in the upper right quadrant of the chest, instantly shattering the collarbone.

Pale light colored the slats of the blinds as Derek fought to come out of the nightmare. With slow, aching breaths he became aware of his body again. The hard set of his shoulders. The sweat that poured down his face. The tight clench of his hands that he gently unfisted.

He was okay.

Deep breath. In. Out.

The department shrink had given him some tools to use when the panic came on, and even though it pained him to do so, he focused on the woman's gentle instructions.

Count backward. Focus on the present. Maintain your breathing.

Step by step, he felt the calm return. Felt the tension ebb from his body. Although he couldn't shake it completely, the worst of it was over, the hard wash of memories fading back to the place in his mind where he kept them locked up.

In.

Out.

With swift motions, he scrubbed his hand over his jaw, the scratchy stubble pulling him firmly back to the present.

He was here. Now. A quick glance around had him remembering he was in one of the guest rooms at Adair

Acres, and the rest of his reality slammed back in one great, gulping wave.

Landry Adair.

The image of perfect features, sky-blue eyes and lush lips skyrocketed through his thoughts. Although he'd done his level best to keep his attraction to her in check, the combination of the early morning hour and the visceral image of her alive and well in his mind's eye had his body hardening beneath the sheets.

She was a looker, he'd give her that. But over the past few days, he'd come to realize the exterior was actually a very small part of who she was. A very enticing part, but a small part all the same.

Landry was sharp, her mind rapidly assessing the world around her. He'd observed her the day before at headquarters, her ability to scan the reams of data they were reviewing both swift and nimble. Yes to this document, no to another. Questions about dates that led them to another search query.

He'd seen her concern for Noah. Knew she was upset about what they might find, yet she stayed focused as they searched for the truth.

And then you went and fouled it up at the market.

With another scrub to his cheeks, Derek got up and walked into the en suite bathroom. He made quick work of his morning routine, the echoes of his lunchtime interrogation still ringing in his ears.

"Why do you care what anyone else thinks?"

"My mother cares, and that's all that matters."

"But she's not here."

"Oh, that's right. She's a killer on the run you're determined to catch."

The food was a prickly point, no doubt about it. Yet he'd pushed anyway, anxious to understand the issue beneath the surface. And wasn't surprised when it circled back to Patsy Adair.

The search for Reginald's missing son had ruled their marriage for over thirty-five years.

What did that do to a woman?

To be married to a man who couldn't move on? Couldn't move past the tragedy? Was it possible she murdered her husband?

Landry refused to believe her mother had done it and had made some fairly persuasive arguments to support her point. None of it changed the fact that Patsy had proven herself willing to take a life with her attempts on Whit's new wife, Elizabeth.

But her own husband?

Derek snatched a fresh pair of jeans and a T-shirt out of his duffel and added a windbreaker after considering the cool California air in the morning. The nightmare over the Frederickson case had him up, and now that his mind was whirling he wanted a place to put all that energy to good use. He'd enjoyed his time on a horse the day before.

He'd saddle up and see if he couldn't puzzle out some of the mystery as he flew over the grounds of Adair Acres on Diego.

Landry walked into the barn, the normal, sweet scent of hay masked by a layer of something sour, like rot in a garbage can. She'd thought to get in early and ride Pete, but at the evidence that something wasn't right, she came to a halt inside the barn.

Did one of the horses get sick?

She stood still for another moment, trying to orient her senses and identify the scent, but the exercise proved futile.

Although early-morning light filtered through the high barn windows, Landry flipped on all the overheads to check each stall. The horses were all awake and alert, their breaths quick as they watched her pass. She greeted each one by name, stopping to pat their noses and stare into their eyes.

Damn, but what had them riled up this morning?

There hadn't been any storms the previous night, and when she'd spoken to Noah yesterday before going up to her room he'd said that every horse had been well exercised.

So what had everyone upset?

She moved from stall to stall, checking each horse while her gaze roamed over their bedding and food supply. Everything appeared to be in order, yet their discomfort was real. Tangible. And if anything, it had gotten worse since she'd walked into the barn.

Diego greeted her with a hard shove of his nose on her hand and she took an extra moment to soothe him before heading for Pete. The large thoroughbred shook his head, his agitation more than obvious when she finally reached his stall. "What's wrong, baby?"

With soft tones, she kept her voice level, crooning to him through the open window of his stall. They were nothing but nonsense words, the sort one would use with a colicky baby, but nothing she tried seemed to settle him.

Even with his nose nuzzling her hand and her cheek pressed to his, that sense of agitation never wavered.

"What is it, buddy?"

When Pete only shook his head and stamped his front hooves, she stepped back.

Landry kept contact with Pete, but allowed her gaze to travel the length of the barn and back. Whatever was going on wasn't obvious, but something had the horses spooked.

She turned on her heel and walked into the small office they kept inside the barn. The three-digit code to the main house was answered immediately, despite the early hour.

"June, this is Landry. Is Noah up yet?"

The woman was sweet and efficient and seemed to sense the urgency immediately. "No, but I can go get him for you."

"Please send him straight down to the stables. Something has the horses agitated and I'd like to have him here."

"Can I send someone else down, Miss Landry? Are you there alone?"

Landry forced a sense of calm into her tone. "I think Noah will be enough. Let him know I'm calling Dr. Walters, as well."

"Of course."

The vet's number was tacked on the wall in bold letters, and she called him next. She'd barely heard the first ring when a loud series of whinnies had her slamming down the phone.

"Hey—" Landry stopped midsentence when Derek's broad form filled the walkway.

"What's going on in here? Why are the horses so upset?"

"I don't know." Sly, panicky fingers gripped her stomach and she fought down the sick ball. "They've only gotten more agitated since I got inside."

"Should we let them out into the corral?"

"I'd like to get Noah here first. And I was about to call the vet." Landry hesitated before she spoke. "Pete seems the worst. Maybe you can help me calm him down. Or between the two of us we can get him outside?"

Derek nodded. "Where's his lead?"

"Everything's in the feed room, stored in cubbies for each of them."

A sense of calm punched through that hot ball of lead, Derek's presence more soothing than she could have ever imagined. How did he know she needed help? Now that he was here, she had to admit she felt a little silly.

Goodness, but she'd spent her entire life around horses. She knew how to handle herself and how to handle the animals. So what the heck had her so spooked?

"Which would you like me to use?" Derek pointed to the large cubby and the various pieces of equipment stacked neatly in the efficient space.

"I'll get the one I like."

She passed Pete's stall on her way to Derek, shocked when the animal shoved his large form against the stall door, an agitated cry escaping his lips.

"Pete!"

Derek pulled her close, his arm wrapped tight around her shoulders. "Has he ever done this?"

"No. I can't imagine what it—"

The sharp, swift shake of a snake's rattle had the words dying in her throat.

But it was the sight of a large, coiled brown body on the edge of the feed bin that had a scream crawling up to take their place.

Chapter 7

Derek pulled at Landry's shoulders, pulling her just clear of the snake's striking range as it fell off the feed bin, primed to attack. Her booted foot got tangled with his and they nearly fell into a heap before he righted them, dragging her back several feet.

"Hold still." Landry hissed the words, her voice barely above a whisper.

"Are you out of your mind?"

"It's startled. Give it a minute to settle. We can't lose sight of it and risk it getting into one of the stalls."

Derek eyed the agitated snake, its body coiled to strike as its dark rattle lit up the quiet of the barn. Even the horses had gone still, their heavy breathing the only sign they were there. "You ever dealt with one of these before?"

Her body quivered under his hands, but she held her ground. She maintained that quiet tone and he marveled that she could manage the thread of calm woven underneath the words. "Not like this. No."

"How are we going to take care of it?"

"We're going to give it another minute to calm down and then you're going to back away slowly behind me and grab the metal shovel from the tack room."

"I'm not leaving you here."

"I'm closer. And my boots go up to my knees if it does decide to strike."

Derek knew his city upbringing hadn't prepared him for this sort of scenario, but he also knew enough about threatened animals to know she put herself in danger.

"I'll stay here and you go."

"Go now. Please." She shoved at his arm. "I can't put the horses at risk. They trust me."

The knowledge that she'd protect the horses at such risk to herself was as maddening as it was humbling. Unwilling to argue any longer than necessary, he took a few steps back, stopping once more when the rattle began to click faster.

"Derek. Hurry."

He kept his steps even, one foot behind the other, as he moved toward the tack room. With each deliberate step, the lingering vestiges of his nightmare rose up, tightening his chest and trapping the air in his lungs.

The predator might be different, but the threat was all too similar.

That familiar anger—the one he'd held on to for the last several months—warred with the lack of air and he ran the last few feet to the tack room.

He'd get there in time. He *had* to.

The shovel was right where Landry said it would be and he grabbed it before rushing back to her.

"On my mark, Landry."

"Derek—"

"Move now!"

She was already in motion as the thin edge of the shovel came down, his aim true. The snake's body continued to move, but the severed head lay separate and no longer a threat.

He reached for Landry and dragged her close. A hard tremor started in his arms and he clung to her, willing the shaking to subside.

"You didn't have to yell, you know." Her terse grumble was muffled against his chest as she pressed her face into his shirt, her arms tight around his waist.

"I wasn't yelling. I was ordering. There's a difference." He'd meant the words as a joke, but the guttural exhale of breath messed up any attempt at humor.

He took the moment to simply breathe her in before he pressed his lips to her head. Images of what could have happened rose up along with a sudden shout.

They pulled back as Noah barreled into the barn, an unbuttoned shirt on over his jeans and boots. "What happened?"

Landry stepped back and pointed toward the now-still rattler. "We had a poisonous visitor arrive last night."

"What? Where?" Confusion grooved sharp lines in Noah's face before he crouched down to look at Derek's handiwork. "Clean work. You got him on the first try."

"I didn't plan to miss." Some measure of equilibrium had returned to his voice, but he still wasn't able to quite hit the casual, humorous note he was going for. "Damn thing fell right out of the feed bin."

"What the hell?" Noah was back on his feet, stomping toward the line of individualized bins. "Where?"

"Right there." Landry pointed toward the bin labeled

with Pete's name. "He was coiled on top of Pete's feed bin."

"I closed that last night. Secured it myself after I fed him."

"So someone else must have pushed it aside."

"No." Noah shook his head. "No. I left pretty late and I checked everything myself. I'd already sent Mac and Wendy on their way."

Noah walked the length of the sealed feed bins, his hands running over the edges.

"Be careful." Landry stepped forward, and Derek fought the desperate need that clawed at him to lay a hand on her arm to keep her still. "Where there's one there could be others."

"Not this time." Noah lifted the lid of Pete's feed bin and reached inside. When he came out, he had a thick canvas bag in his hand. "That snake didn't find its way in here on accident. Someone put it here."

Landry let the wild air whip around her face and willed the events of the morning to fade from her mind. She'd never been as scared as the moment she saw the snake coiled on top of Pete's feed container.

But to know someone put it there?

The powerful body beneath her bunched and moved, all sinew and corded muscle, and she leaned into him, willing the animal to take her wherever he wanted to go.

Away.

Far, far away from whatever threat lurked around her home.

She'd believed herself immune to the same danger as the rest of her family, but now she wasn't so sure. The snake was placed in *her* animal's feed bin. And her schedule wasn't exactly a secret to many people. She often rose early to go to the barn. Heck, Noah kept updated schedules throughout the barn at all times so they kept track of which horse needed a workout and who needed rest.

What if the snake had been meant for her?

And what if someone else had found it instead? She didn't make it to the barn early every morning. And in point of fact, Derek had been the one to get to the feed bin first, searching for Pete's lead.

The cool morning air coated her body. Where it normally invigorated, all she felt was a bone-deep chill that had nothing to do with the weather and everything to do with the threat that had suddenly decided to target her family.

The pasture at the far end of Adair Acres beckoned, and she added pressure with her legs to slow Pete down. While she'd love nothing more than to run all morning, her beautiful boy probably needed a rest.

And no matter how badly she wanted to put it off, it was time to talk to Derek.

The whistle of the wind faded. Pete reduced his speed, and she felt his subtle prance as they drew nearer to the field. The thunder of hooves grew louder and she turned to see Derek and Diego headed their direction.

Her breath caught in her throat at the picture he made atop the horse. Even from a distance, she could see the corded muscles in his forearms and how his powerful thighs bunched around in the saddle.

She allowed herself a moment of pure feminine appreciation to watch the view.

And wonder how he always managed to catch her off guard. As though her memory of him never quite competed with the reality of Derek Winchester in the flesh.

Rachel's words from the night before whispered slyly

through her thoughts, and before she knew it, Landry had a very vivid image of Derek in his underwear, splayed across a billboard fourteen feet high.

The man was a vision; there was no doubt about it. But the past few days had ensured that her image of him continued to grow and expand. From his competence at the FBI offices to his pushy lunch conversation at the Farmers Market to his role as protector this morning.

She'd felt his barely leashed strength as he stood behind her in the barn while they dealt with the snake. She'd also recognized his ire when she sent him off to get the shovel. Despite the fear that the snake would strike one of them or the horses, she'd had a moment of pure pleasure, too.

He hadn't wanted to leave her behind.

"That was quite a ride." He pulled Diego into a walk, their pace acclimating to hers and Pete's, and she let the fleeting thought fly off into the breeze.

"After this morning, I'd say it was a well-needed run for all of us."

"No arguments here." As if providing further evidence of his skills, Derek stayed close enough to communicate, but maintained a distance between the two animals. Their morning scare still had the barn's residents skittish, and she appreciated that Derek understood each horse's need for individualized attention.

"You're quite the rider. Where'd you learn?"

"You wouldn't believe me if I told you."

She cocked her head at that, the challenge in his answer too tempting to resist. "Try me."

"College."

"I figured you for a city boy with a criminal justice degree."

"I was both of those things, but I got my degree at a

rural college in Maryland. Equestrian lessons were electives, and I decided to take a class."

"What was her name?"

The question was out before she could stop it. When she was rewarded with an easy grin that suffused his face in carefree lines, Landry was glad she'd asked the question.

"The girl I liked or the horse?"

"Both."

His dark eyes grew reflective, and she saw the years fade away. "Emma was the girl. Harlow was the horse. Both were beauties."

"Harlow?"

"The owner had a thing for old movies. He named all his mares after Hollywood stars. Which, I might add—" his gaze darkened as he glanced at Pete "—is a far more elegant name than Pete."

Landry leaned forward and pressed her lips to the top of Pete's head. "Don't tease my baby."

"Why Pete?"

"Why not?"

"Because he was sired through a Triple Crown winner's lineage."

"All the more reason he should have a normal name."

"Nope. Not buying it."

Although she wouldn't exactly call Derek Winchester an open book, there was an honesty about him she found refreshing. Unlike the society crowd she'd run with her whole life, there was something simple in his direct approach to life.

Add on the fact that he didn't pull any punches—if he had a question, he asked, and if he had an opinion, he stated it—and Landry found herself growing more and more comfortable in his presence.

It was an odd sensation—both the lack of artifice and the fact that she was enjoying it. And it was more than a little unnerving to know she couldn't quite get her footing with him.

What was even more unnerving was realizing that perhaps she didn't want to.

"I never cared about his lineage."

"Didn't you pick him out?"

"In a way. When I showed an interest in riding, my father encouraged it. It was the one thing we could do together, and I loved every minute of it. Being with him, in his orbit, with his full attention focused on me."

"So what changed?"

"When I began to get good at it, my mother stepped in. She felt that riding was an acceptable activity for a young girl of wealthy means and proudly preened to all her friends and acquaintances about my advancing skill. She also felt it would help me keep my weight in check. She pressured my father to get me a spectacular horse."

"So they gave you Pete?"

"My mother went on about it for weeks. How I'd get a fancy horse and show up every family in the county. The more she talked about it, the more I wasn't interested."

"Yet you went along with things anyway?"

"Of course. The good daughter, following her mother's instructions."

While she would defend her mother's innocence until the day she died, Landry had to admit that the last few months since Patsy fled had been freeing. She'd known her mother's ways were oppressive, but it was only with her finally gone that Landry could admit just how bad things had become.

The endless censure and criticism. The prying eyes and leading questions, wondering when Landry's next

date was or why she'd stopped seeing that Asher boy.
Even Carson's arrival home from the military—injury
and all—hadn't shifted her mother's eagle-eyed focus
off Landry's life.

"So what happened?"

"My father scheduled an afternoon with the owner
of Pete's dam for us to take a look. I'd spent the car ride
sullen and irritated and had played 'Let My Love Open
the Door' on repeat the whole way."

"Pete Townshend?"

"Yep."

"And then I got out of the car and walked into the stable and fell in love with my own Pete, and that was the
end of my complaints."

Derek's eyebrows shot up, a wry grin on his face.
"Love opened the door?"

Landry bent down and wrapped her arms around
Pete's neck. "I guess it did."

Derek had never been jealous of anyone or anything
in his life, but in that moment he had to admit he'd finally experienced the emotion.

And how the hell was a grown man jealous of a thousand-
pound horse?

He'd listened to Landry's story, and similar to their
lunch the day before, had taken away yet another facet
of her life. What appeared perfect and pristine on the
surface hid a wealth of anger and frustration.

Who treated their child that way?

While he'd never considered his upbringing much
more than average, the more time he spent with Reginald Adair's family the more he realized just how good
he'd had it. Two parents who'd loved each other. A sister
and brother he still talked to and enjoyed spending time

with. And a pool of memories that weren't filled with experiences based on how he looked or what the neighbors might think.

As that thought hit, another followed, and that sense of jealousy faded to nothingness. "I'm glad you had Pete."

"I am, too."

While he'd admired her persistence earlier and her commitment to the animals in the Adair stables, he hadn't fully understood why she'd put herself at risk for the horses.

With the understanding of what the horse meant to her, he saw her actions in a new light. He couldn't quite assuage his frustration that she'd put herself in danger, but it helped to understand it.

"Who do you think left the snake?"

The proverbial storm cloud that had hovered above them all morning finally opened up. He'd spent the ride turning it over in his mind, but he was no closer to an answer. Nor could he come up with a place to start looking for one.

"The one you insisted on charming?" He hadn't quite hit the point where he could be carefree about the morning's events, but he could add a small bit of levity to what was going to be unpleasant territory.

"I did no such thing. I let it calm down."

"You know, it's funny but I remember our morning a bit differently."

"One thing I think we both remember the same way. The bag it was delivered in."

Derek would have found an excuse to get the bag away from Noah if he felt he could have learned anything off the material, but the canvas drawstring tote was a dead end. Bags like that were easily available and could have been purchased at any number of stores.

Landry continued. "What I don't understand is why whoever did this left the bag behind."

"To send a message."

"It's an awfully cryptic one. If you're sick enough to send a snake and someone at Adair Acres was the target, send it to the house. Or put it in the car. Something."

"And risk having a servant find it instead?"

At her sharp intake of breath, he saw the recognition light in her eyes. "Someone could have been hurt."

"I think that was the general idea. But it's not a targeted way to harm someone, which is why I think this was meant more as a message than an actual attempt at doing real damage."

"I have to talk to Whit and Carson, and we need to talk to the staff. Tell them to be on their guard." A hard laugh escaped her lips. "Won't my mother be pleased to come home to half her staff having resigned."

"No one will do that to you and your brothers."

"How can you be so sure?"

He shrugged, the interactions he'd observed over the past few days more than obvious. "They love you. And they don't stay because of your mother. They stay for you and your brothers."

Her mouth drooped in surprise before she firmly snapped it closed. Although he'd only had a few days, it hadn't been hard to size up the dynamics at Adair Acres. Patsy Adair might rule the roost, but her chicks held the true power.

Since he suspected that depth of knowledge would only make Landry feel more guilty about the danger to her staff, he pushed forward with more questions.

"How accessible is the stable?"

"It's open. I mean, we don't always lock it." She pulled

Pete up as they approached a long stretch of field and rose up in the saddle. "Want to walk for a bit?"

He dismounted from Diego and attached the horse's lead to allow him his grazing reward after their hard run. Landry stood a few feet away, her voice gentle as she thanked Pete for the good ride.

A few strands had come loose from her ponytail and Derek watched, mesmerized, as they blew against the soft curve of her cheek. She was a vision. The long, firm body. The porcelain skin. And the innate care and awareness of others that was easy to overlook when she was pulling the princess-of-the-manor routine.

But he had seen it.

Had seen glimpses of the caring woman underneath.

Her love of the horse was one small example. He'd also seen it in her concern for the staff. Her fierce defense of her mother.

Landry Adair was a woman who, by all accounts, had made herself. Out of a loveless childhood and the rarefied air of wealth and privilege, she'd emerged, like Aphrodite on the half shell. Fully formed and fully lovely.

His stomach tightened on a hard knot of need and he willed it back, refusing to allow it any more control over his thoughts.

This was a case.

A *job*.

And he couldn't afford to lose sight of that.

Voice gruffer than he intended, he returned to the morning's incident. "Who knows the stable's open?"

Landry's eyes widened slightly, but if she sensed a shift in the conversation, she said nothing. "Everyone, I guess. But it's not like the property's open. You can't just stroll through the front gates."

"The ranch is nearly 200 acres. All someone needs is

determination and a bit of patience and I'd wager they don't need to use the front gates. An old line of fence or a thick copse of trees and someone could get through."

"Which is why we keep track of the main perimeter of the house and stables, as well."

"The stables, too?"

"Of course. We have hundreds of thousands of dollars of horseflesh in there, not to mention top-of-the-line equipment."

"Do you have video equipment? Eyes on the stables?"

"Yes. It all feeds into the main security system in the house."

He cursed himself for not thinking of it immediately. His thoughts had been so full of Landry while they were still in the barn that he hadn't even looked at the situation through the eyes of a trained operative.

With a hard, swift slap, the same shame he'd known at his failure to protect Rena rose up to knock him down. He was already on leave for one failed attempt at protection. Would he fail Landry, too? And by default, her aunt Kate?

The calming benefits of the hard ride vanished as reality came crashing back in.

His last case was still a disaster.

Adair Acres still held a wealth of secrets and sins.

And Landry Adair was still in terrible danger.

Chapter 8

Landry fought the urge to ignore her work in favor of pacing the small room she used as an office. But she did give herself a moment to simply sit and stare at the wall. And brood.

The room had been her play area as a child, but she'd traded dolls and stuffed animals for bookshelves and a writing desk years ago. The soft cream-colored walls, dotted with vivid prints to add splashes of color, were her sanctuary. But not today.

Maybe because you're hiding.

Her conscience rose up to taunt her and she resolutely ignored it. She wasn't hiding. She was doing work. Good work if the letter she was drafting to the governor would ever get written. A thank-you note for his support and the confirmation that her children's charity had received his promised funding.

So why was her mind filled with Derek? They'd

worked as partners this morning. First in the stable and then after, helping Noah calm the horses and resettle them into their routine. Even their ride had been full of carefree moments as they flew over the grounds of the ranch.

Easy.

The moments had been easy, even with the danger of the morning hanging over them. Sure, they'd need to consider all the angles around the break-in to the stable and put together a suspect list of who might be interested in doing them harm. It was tension-filled work, especially since she couldn't dismiss those she knew completely out of hand.

But they'd agreed to partner on investigating what was happening at Adair Acres. And they had a comfortable camaraderie that was friendly enough. Pleasant, even. If the sexual tension reached up and grabbed both of them every so often, well, she could live with that.

They were working in close proximity to each other.

And then he'd gone and checked out. She'd seen it happen, too. One moment there was a deep smile reflecting from those midnight-dark eyes of his, and then the next he was shuttered and terse. All business with an edge of annoyance.

Landry searched her memory for something she might have said or done, but knew she wasn't at fault. Whatever was going on was his problem.

So why the hell was she upset about it?

Minimizing the window on her computer, she shifted into her email. A few notes from friends. Some names she recognized from another charity whose board she served on. And a note from David Asher asking if she wanted to accompany him on a date.

She tackled David's note first. The decline was easy—

she didn't want to go, and the wedding was the same date they'd planned Elizabeth's upcoming baby shower, so she had an easy excuse. Besides, it was obvious she was a last-minute choice if he was asking her for the following weekend.

"Jerk," she muttered out loud as she hit Send on her politely worded email that dripped social niceties like a sieve.

"Was that directed at me?"

The moment of self-righteous indignation was short-lived as she glanced up to see Derek in the doorway.

"If I said yes would you know why?"

"I've got a pretty good idea."

His admission of guilt was such a surprise she could only sit there, stunned.

"I suspect it has something to do with my grumpy-ass attitude while the horses were grazing."

"What happened?" The question slipped out, and she cursed herself for giving him any leeway at all.

"It's nothing you did, but it's not something I talk about." He moved into the room, his hands shoved in the pockets of his jeans. "Ever."

So much for leeway.

She was used to being shut out. Her parents had no problem leaving their children to fend for themselves emotionally, and her relationship with her brothers had always held elements of the same. The fact that Carson was four years older and Whit seven had contributed, Landry knew.

In fact, it had been only recently that they'd begun to push back some of the walls that had always kept distance among the three of them. But despite their recent movement in a positive direction, the Adairs weren't inherently close, and they weren't particularly adept at sharing their thoughts with one another.

None of it changed the fact that they *were* a unit.

"Since we were talking about something having to do with me, my family and my home, I find it hard to believe I don't have a right to know what set you off."

"That's not why I was upset."

"Then why are you here? You clearly don't feel the need to apologize, and I, for one, have had enough danger and sleuthing for the day. It's time I got productive and got some work done."

Dismissal rang in the air like a school bell, magnifying her guilt at her terse tone.

"When you do have a moment, please come down to the security room. I'd like to show you the tapes of the stables."

"Fine."

"Damn it, Landry—" He broke off and dragged a hand from his pocket to run it over his short-cropped hair. "I just wanted to say it wasn't you this morning. That's why I came in here."

"I know that." The words spilled forth and she knew them for what they were. A deliberate attempt to pick a fight. "What I don't know is this great, huge, magnificent secret you're determined to keep but which you use as an excuse to act like a sullen bastard the moment you get uncomfortable."

"That's not true."

"Oh, no?" She shoved off her office chair, the movement hard enough to push the rolling piece against the wall. "You arrive here at the ranch and you do nothing but ask me questions. Personal questions that are absolutely none of your business and have nothing to do with investigating my family."

"I'm here to help—"

She shut him down, pressing her point. "Then you toss back some excuse about an issue in your past that you don't 'discuss.'"

She made exaggerated air quotes around the word *discuss*, absurdly pleased when the motion acted like an accelerant to the anger already sparking in those midnight eyes.

"Pain and hurt don't give you a right to act like a jerk with a get-out-of-jail-free card. So the hell with you!"

The air stilled around them, her words hovering like a storm cloud. Oddly, all she could think of was their moment earlier in the barn, as they waited for the snake to make its move.

Strike or retreat.

Stay or leave.

Fight or flight.

Derek reached out, his hands fisting over her shoulders as he dragged her close. His mouth came down on hers and his large frame simply consumed her.

And as she lifted her head, accepting the powerful crush of his lips against hers, Landry knew the sweet victory that Derek Winchester stayed to fight.

Late-afternoon sunlight slanted through the room, highlighting the golden hue of her hair like a halo. It was the last thought Derek had—the last coherent one, at least—before the overwhelming need to consume her gripped him with mad, desperate need.

The barely pent-up anger she'd wielded like a weapon channeled into a different sort of battle as they fought each other for control of the moment. Need shimmered around them in thick, humid waves. He tried to catch his breath, but he couldn't seem to drag his mouth away from hers; the urge to devour—to consume whole—was a living, breathing fire inside him.

Derek knew he needed boundaries—knew pushing this mind-numbing attraction for Landry Adair was a mistake—but he could no more walk away than he could stop breathing.

"I want you." He whispered the words against her lips, his hands roaming over her skin, seeking the heated flesh under her blouse.

She smiled up at him, her eyes filled with a wash of feminine power. "You don't say?"

Before he *could* say, her hands were at his waist, dragging his T-shirt from his waistband and up over his stomach. Her hands splayed over his flesh, a sensual brand that had his skin on fire wherever she touched while she ran a series of nipping kisses over the line of his jaw.

Her hands drove him crazy. Her mouth drove him wild. Hell, the woman drove him out of his ever-loving mind.

"Landry—" A hard knock and a strange voice broke the moment.

A wash of awareness slid over Derek and he dragged himself away from the temptation of the woman before him.

"Oh. I'm so sorry to interrupt."

"Elizabeth." Landry smoothed the hem of his T-shirt back into place. She then kept her hands on his waist an extra moment, as if she were ravished in her office every afternoon, before she turned toward the woman in the doorway. "Come on in."

A light blush colored Elizabeth's cheeks, and Derek suspected if the woman could redo the last few moments, she'd have run for the hills. As it were, she made a quick recovery, her voice brisk and all business.

"Whit wanted to do a family dinner this evening. I was stopping in to make sure you'd both be home."

"Of course."

"Good. I'm going to leave a message for Rachel to join us, too," Elizabeth added.

The thought of a family dinner, him and Landry pretending to be a couple, struck Derek as a strange sort of torture. Despite his misgivings, he was obviously in, prepared to see their charade through.

It would also give him an opportunity to observe how the conversation swirled around their near miss in the stables that morning.

"Noah volunteered to be on grill, but I think he may need to fight Whit off for the spatula." Elizabeth's eyes twinkled as her hand hovered over her rounded belly. "Please don't tell me you're going to fight them for a spot at the grill, as well, Derek."

"My talents around food extend to microwaving water and putting bread in the toaster. Whit and Noah can duke it out."

Elizabeth smiled, her grin going wider as she looked at the two of them. "I'll see you later then. Seven on the back porch."

Whit's wife vanished as quickly as she'd arrived, leaving the two of them.

"Why don't we go down to the security room and look at that footage." Landry wrapped her arms around her waist. "I'm sure the snake incident will be a topic of conversation this evening."

Not for the first time, she surprised him with just how in tune with him she was. "I was thinking the same. Tonight will be a good opportunity to observe."

"Noah's already spread the word, and whomever he missed, the staff has caught up by now."

"I'm not so sure about the staff. I think Noah's playing it a bit closer to the vest than that. He pinged me earlier to see if I'd called the police."

"Hmmm." Her vivid expression grew thoughtful. "He sees more than he lets on. He always has. Maybe he's waiting to see what type of response he's going to get from my brothers."

"He also doesn't know why I'm really here. Or that I've got investigative skills of my own."

A haze of worry dulled those vibrant blue eyes. "That part still feels awkward. We all know why you're here, and he doesn't."

"We could tell him I'm investigating your father's murder. Would that make you feel better?"

"No," she said. "Whit, Carson and I agreed how to approach this, and we're all in. My brothers know because they need to. I'm sure Whit told Elizabeth because he tells her everything and the woman is the equivalent of a human vault anyway."

"She was your father's secretary?"

"Yes." Landry hesitated, her voice faltering. "She found him, too."

"She seems to be doing okay with it."

"Day by day. That's what Whit keeps saying, and it appears to be working. Their focus on the baby is probably helping, too."

"The first Adair grandchild."

"For my father's line. Kate's got grandchildren and so does my father's sister Rosalyn."

"Kate's crazy about that baby. I think it's one of the things that helped her survive the shooting attempt on her life."

Landry's gaze grew thoughtful. "What if they're related?"

"What's related?"

"The attempt on Kate last year. The issue now with my father."

Derek thought back to those dark days. The call from Kate's son, Trey, telling him about the attempt on his mother's life. He'd kept close tabs on her touch-and-go situation in the hospital and had followed the news of the case and the ultimate capture of her shooter through his counterpart in the Raleigh field office.

"Kate's shooter was caught."

"But it is strange, don't you think? The danger she and her family faced last year? The problems we're having here?"

"Landry. I know you want to believe this situation isn't that dire, but I can't promise you that. And I won't placate you to make you feel better and inadvertently put you at risk."

"I know." The light still shone through the oversize windows in the office, small dust motes swimming in the air. Only instead of highlighting her hair in a halo, all he saw were the twin expressions of fear and disappointment that filled her face in the afternoon sun.

He owned putting the disappointment in her gaze—there was nothing to be done about it. But he'd be damned if he'd rest until he caught the bastard who'd marked Landry Adair with fear.

The rich scent of cooking meat wafted toward her, and Landry gave herself mental permission to enjoy dinner that evening. A juicy steak, an oversize baked potato and a piece of Kathleen's cream cheese–frosted carrot cake was in her future, and she couldn't wait.

"Another?" Georgia waved a bottle of wine near her

glass, her sharp green eyes bright with merriment, and Landry nodded for the refill.

Landry took a moment to swirl the pretty Cabernet before taking a sip. Although she usually preferred light, crisp whites in summer, the anticipated steak and the fact that Whit had invested in the vineyard made it an easy decision.

"This is amazing. Whit chose well."

Elizabeth smiled at the compliment before shooting her husband a warm, adoring smile. "He did."

"He chose well with you, too."

Elizabeth's eyes widened on the compliment, a light sheen of moisture coating her warm brown gaze as her hand instinctively rested against her expanding belly. "That's lovely."

"It's true."

"Hear, hear," Georgia added with a lift of her glass.

And it *was* true, Landry realized as she and Georgia clinked glasses with Elizabeth's flute of sparkling water. Elizabeth and Whit's relationship had started under the most extraordinary circumstances, but love had found its way. The bond between them was strong, forged even deeper as they awaited the birth of their first child.

She turned a smile on Georgia. "Carson chose equally with you, my dear. He's never been so happy."

Georgia's smile was warm, her gaze full of the happy secrets of new lovers. "Neither have I."

Even with the pain of the past few months, Landry couldn't help but count her blessings. She had two new sisters—women who had brought a renewed sense of family to both of her brothers—and, by extension, her. They *fit*, she thought as she took in her new sisters-in-law. Elizabeth, with her light blond hair, and Georgia, with her sassy red, fit in as if they'd always been there.

And as they sat next to each other and shared a know-ing gaze, Landry sensed that the familiar was about to become…sisterly.

"So tell us a bit more about Derek."

Landry kept her voice low, unwilling to risk Noah overhearing. "He's here as we've discussed."

"Oh yes, he's definitely here." Georgia shifted to the edge of her chair. "And he definitely notices *you*."

Her gaze drifted toward Derek. He'd stayed true to his earlier promise—he hadn't touched the grill—but he had taken up a very manly pose next to Whit, Car-son and Noah. All four men held beers and had fallen into easy conversation. Their voices drifted across the patio—a rather heated discussion about the Padres' and Dodgers' chances for the season.

Whit and Carson may have known Derek's real rea-son for being at Adair Acres, but they'd fallen as easily into the pretend situation as she had.

It shouldn't be this easy.

When her brothers had told her Derek would be join-ing them, at her aunt Kate's request, she'd been hesitant. Worse, she'd been insulted. Yet Derek had managed to captivate her in a matter of days.

He fit here. And the more time she spent with him, the more she felt that urgent tug that said he fit with her.

As her gaze once more took in the conversation cir-cle around the grill, she couldn't help noticing what an attractive foursome the men made. And she found her-self wondering what it would be like to see all of them huddled together regularly.

"Well, isn't that a charming quartet of testosterone." Rachel's voice interrupted her thoughts, and Landry glanced up to see her best friend smirking down at her, a bottle of wine and a fresh bouquet of flowers in hand.

Landry popped up and firmly tamped down the blush that threatened at being caught staring at Derek. "I didn't think you could make it." She gave Rachel a hard hug. "I'm so glad you're here. I thought you had to go up to San Francisco for the day?"

"I got back early, and when I got Elizabeth's message I thought an evening with friends would cap off a pretty good day."

"What happened? It sounds like a toast is in order." Georgia swapped a fresh glass for the flowers in Rachel's hands before gesturing her toward a chair. "Let's hear all about it."

Landry lost herself in the moment, congenial conversation under the fading light of day. Surrounded by friends and her increasing family, a warm, comfortable hum had settled in her veins. Although the past several months had been the hardest of her life, it was humbling to realize the time had brought good things, as well. Two new sisters and a closer bond with her best friend.

And Derek.

Rachel laid a hand on her knee after Elizabeth and Georgia disappeared into the house. "You doing better after last night?"

She knew the conversation would ultimately swing around to the morning adventure in the stable, but Landry was hesitant to ruin the moment of calm. "Better. Last night's girlfriend time went a long way toward making me feel better."

"And things with the underwear model?" Rachel kept her voice low but her gaze ran high with merriment. "I do hope you've gotten to the kissing part."

When Landry didn't say anything, Rachel's eyes widened. "You *did* get to the kissing part. Oh, please throw the single girl a bone here and tell me all about it."

"There's nothing to tell."

"It's the best friend code of honor to point out that if there wasn't anything to tell, you'd have told me already."

"I don't tell you everything."

"You told me on the phone two days ago you had a chip in your nail polish. If that's not the definition of everything, I'm not sure what is."

Landry laughed in spite of herself. "Maybe I was just savoring it for a while."

"That's a better answer."

She was prevented from saying anything by the arrival of Derek and Noah.

"Did you and Whit fight it out for the grill?" Rachel shifted her attention to Noah, her gaze appreciative. Maybe it was the dying light of day or the poolside tiki torches one of the staff had lit earlier, but something in Rachel's gaze caught her attention.

Was it possible? Rachel and Noah?

Landry let the thought swirl, surprised when she moved so quickly to how she and Derek might use that to their advantage in trying to uncover the truth about Noah's background.

Oblivious to her thoughts, Noah grinned broadly, his gaze fully focused on Rachel. "Nah. I left Whit to the grill. It was his and Elizabeth's idea to have a group dinner tonight and I figured the least I could do was let him do the cooking. Besides, I wanted to get the latest details from Derek on this morning."

"What details?" Rachel went on high alert, her eyes darting to each of them.

Landry lifted her glass in a breezy wave. "We had a snake in the stable. It was no big deal."

"Ignore Landry. She said the same thing this morning, and if it was up to her we'd just brush over this."

Noah patted her on the back before he took the seat next to Rachel. "It was serious."

Noah ran down the events of the morning, and every time Landry tried to brush off the incident, Rachel shushed her until she finally stopped trying. Derek took the seat beside her and linked his fingers with hers. The warmth of his hand enveloped her fingers and she squeezed tightly.

She had an ally in this. A partner. And she was quickly coming to appreciate the fact that she wasn't dealing with this alone.

Was that Derek's real appeal? Or was it something deeper?

Yes, the man was devastatingly handsome. And she had a base attraction to him that she simply couldn't deny. But it *was* something more. Something that went beyond sex or even the appreciation that he was there to help her.

Unlike the majority of the men she'd spent time with, she genuinely enjoyed Derek's company. She'd dated plenty, of course. It wouldn't do for Landry Adair, society queen, to be dateless to any event.

But she'd always felt as if she was going through the motions. Living up to expectations instead of spending time with someone she could come to care about.

"Both of you could have been seriously hurt." Rachel's heated comment and lurch across the small conversation area to pull her into a tight hug had Landry dropping Derek's hand along with her train of thought.

As she held her friend in a tight hug, Landry knew Rachel wasn't far off the truth. They could have been hurt by the threat in the stables.

But if she didn't protect her increasingly vulnerable heart, the possibility of physical danger was the least of her worries.

Chapter 9

Derek settled into the ebb and flow of conversation around the table. Although he and Landry had spent time in the hot seat discussing the morning's danger, the group had sensed when it was time to move on to new ground, as well.

Topics ranged from Elizabeth's pregnancy to Whit's expansion of AdAir Corp to an expected new foal Noah was excited about. It was only now when they sat with coffee and after-dinner drinks that Derek realized he'd actually enjoyed himself.

Until thoughts of Rena Frederickson descended like a black cloud. He owed her better than a night spent in carefree conversation while she still sat in captivity somewhere.

"You okay?" Landry's hand floated over his forearm, gentle as the soft evening breeze that blew around them.

"I'm fine." When his voice came out on a strangled whisper, he took a sip of his coffee. "Fine."

Her smile never wavered, but he saw the confusion in her gaze. Knew another moment of sharp guilt that he'd put it there.

Just like Sarah.

The insult vanished as soon as it arrived, but the moment of surprise lingered on. Landry wasn't like Sarah. Aside from the fact that he and Landry had a pretend relationship while he and Sarah had been engaged and planning a wedding, the women weren't the same.

Landry had proven herself a full partner. Even with her concerns about going behind Noah's back, she'd soldiered on. Sarah, in contrast, had simply sat at a distance and bitched at him for his work ethic.

The guilt that had slithered in, dragging up thoughts of Rena, faded as he considered the past few days. The stress of the Frederickson case had been intense, but it was only with a bit of distance that he'd begun to understand how it had taken over his life.

Sarah hadn't been wrong about that.

He cared about his cases, but something about this one had been different. Maybe it was the clues that pointed to a case of heinous debauchery. Or maybe it was just the last straw in a long line of them that had proven how frustrated he was by his work.

No matter how many missing persons he and his team found, there were always more. More individuals who vanished, their lives and the lives of their loved ones ruined by the evil choices of another.

Coming to Adair had been good for him. Prior to his arrival at the ranch, he'd been on top of Mark constantly. Other than their quick catch-up at headquarters the day before, he hadn't been in touch with his partner. Instead, he'd given himself the gift of distance, even without really realizing it. Much as it pained him to admit it, maybe his team lead was right all along.

Distance from the Frederickson case was essential to solving it.

With that, he laid a hand on top of Landry's and squeezed. He pressed his lips to the shell of her ear, pleased when a light quiver hitched her breath. "I am fine."

She nodded. Her mouth opened, then closed again on whatever it was she wanted to say. His gaze searched hers, but she'd shuttered her emotions along with her lips.

Serves you right, Winchester.

Kathleen bustled out of the kitchen, a large cake held up as she navigated the pathway from the back door through the patio. The men leaped up at once but Noah was closest and took the cake from her hands.

Derek used the moment to once again observe Noah.

The man was comfortable here, that was obvious. His quick grin and wink for Kathleen—and her corresponding blush—as he transferred her masterpiece was easy and comfortable. His conversation earlier around the grill was relaxed and carefree.

The man belonged here.

Whether he really was a cousin to the Adairs or their lost half brother remained to be seen, but he was family. Derek could only hope that bond was strong enough to withstand whatever he and Landry discovered.

Noah whispered something in Kathleen's ear that caused a giggle before she swatted at his shoulder. "You're a tease, young man."

Noah sneaked a finger-full of cream cheese frosting from the base of the cake and popped it into his mouth. "And proud of it."

With the cake cut and distributed, everyone returned

to their chairs. Whit had insisted Kathleen join them, but she'd made several excuses and vanished back to the kitchen.

Patsy Adair's lingering influence, no doubt.

Derek let the other impressions come as they would, the relaxed, semifugue state a good way to see if anything new popped. Sometimes the most important things came into clarity when you stopped looking so hard.

Before they sat down to dinner, Landry had whispered her thoughts about Noah and Rachel. Using her observations as a guide, he focused on the two of them. They'd naturally paired off on their side of the table after everyone else took their seats.

Seating arrangements didn't necessarily mean attraction or a relationship, but it did reinforce how natural the two of them looked together.

Could they use that to their advantage?

Rachel knew why Derek was at Adair Acres and the suspicions about Noah's parentage. She could add her observations to the whole and maybe get additional details from Noah about his background and his formative years with his mother in Europe.

"I thought about something earlier." Landry pushed aside her now-empty dessert plate with a pointed stare before she shot him a wink. "How long was our old stable manager gone before Noah took over?"

"A good year at least. I was spending a lot of time in San Diego but I seem to remember Mom mentioning something about how hard it was to find good help." At the realization of what he said, Whit winced and turned toward Noah. "Sorry."

"No offense." Noah's smile was congenial enough. "Not when considering the source."

"You know—" Carson let the thought hang there as

he swirled his snifter glass. "Mom's ignorance might have had another implication. How many people did flow through the stable after Warren retired?"

Whit shrugged. "At least four or five different people. Probably twice that if you add in the usual turnover in support team."

"That many people with access, codes and keys?" Derek picked up on the conversation and filed away a note to himself to check employment records later on his FBI log-in. "That leaves a lot of people with information on how to get on the property. Do you change security codes every time you have turnover here at the ranch?"

"No." Whit shook his head. "We never had a reason to in the past."

"Clearly we have a reason now." Carson muttered the words before he laid his hand over Georgia's.

Derek knew the Adair children were grown adults, but something in Whit's comment stuck with him. Reginald and Patsy had created a cocoon here at the ranch. An environment ruled by wealth and privilege. Despite its obvious dysfunction, the ranch concealed another problem: isolation.

The pristine paradise had kept everyone who lived there separate. And in its seclusion, it had made them all sitting ducks.

Mark scanned his email, surprised when he saw nothing from Derek. He supposed he should be grateful for a few days' breathing room but the sudden lack of communication was as unsettling as it was welcome.

The ball game blared from the TV behind him as he popped open another beer. He knew Derek cared about the Frederickson case. Hell, the bastard had lived and breathed the case like it was oxygen. And now he just abandons it?

Mark took another large swallow of beer and willed the nausea in his stomach to recede.

Derek had been bothering him for months now, and when things finally get moving the jerk goes radio silent.

He reread the fake letter he'd run through the lab. Just his luck, the inconclusive missive caught the attention of a lab assistant who laddered it up to the big boss. What he'd intended to use to simply keep Derek off balance and engaged in the case had turned on him. Their section chief was even questioning if Derek should be taken off leave and brought back in to finish things up.

He needed to get Derek involved again, and then he needed to end this.

Maybe it was just the natural course of things. He had Rena and her supposed kidnapper. Keeping them both holed up was growing tedious, but he'd come this far. There was no way he was letting it all fall apart now.

It was funny, Mark reflected, how the case of Derek's life would be his ultimate demise.

The bastard's interest in Rena Frederickson had been evident from the jump, his attention fully focused on her photo the moment it hit their desks. The poor little kid who looked like one of those sickly orphans you saw in those commercials that begged for a few cents a day to save them.

Derek had taken one look at the kid and had practically fallen on his sword to help her. Late nights. Weekends. Extra lab work and reports as he dug into her disappearance.

He'd gone along at first. The lost kid had become something of a pet project for the office, and his star could only rise by working on it. The mayor of Los Angeles had held her up as what was wrong with criminals and what needed to be stopped in his fair city.

And the big muckety-mucks at the Bureau had seen saving Rena Frederickson as their chance to cozy up to the mayor so he'd buy into their latest terrorism task force requests.

Politics. Life was all about it. And getting what *you* wanted, which was really what politics was when you stripped away the supposed layers of do-gooding and rhetoric, was his end game.

Derek never understood that. All he wanted was to save the kid. And it was his desire to be a freaking hero that had finally given Mark the in he needed to make Sarah his own.

Sarah.

He thought about her sweet body and lush mouth. She'd be his at the end of it all. She'd already let him know she was interested. Once he proved to the world that Derek was hiding behind a do-gooder attitude and had killed Rena's supposed kidnapper in cold blood, Sarah would be fully his.

No more questions that maybe she'd been too hasty. Or hadn't given Derek enough leeway. Nope. She'd see him for the monster he was.

Or, more to the point, the monster Mark was crafting him to be.

Sarah's sweet face faded from his mind's eye as Landry Adair's sexy lips and high cheekbones took its place. Damn, but she was a looker.

It was a real shame she was likely to get caught in the cross fire, but it couldn't be helped. The little present inside the Adair stables clearly hadn't done its job, but he'd thought of a few other diversions, the first of which was set to go off tonight.

With one last swallow of his beer, he got up to go to the fridge and snag another cool one. It was going to be a late night as he worked through the logistics for his next trip down to Adair Acres.

"You need to play this one straight with me." Carson Adair closed the door to the security room with a light click.

Derek pressed Pause on the computer terminal where he'd toggled back and forth between imagery for the past hour and turned to face Landry's brother. The mild-mannered, jovial dinner companion of earlier was gone. In his place was the former marine lieutenant, straight as an arrow and at full attention.

"I promised you from the start I wouldn't keep you in the dark."

"What happened this morning down in the stables? Landry can gloss over it like it was no big deal, but do me a solid and tell me the truth."

"Someone left your sister a rather nasty message. A rattler inside Pete's feed bin along with the bag he was smuggled inside in."

"What if it was left for you?"

"Me?" Derek bobbled the bottled water he'd lifted to his lips. "No one knows I'm here."

"Don't fool yourself. There are eyes and ears everywhere at this place. People know."

"So take me through it. Who would use the off chance that I might be visiting the stables as a way to harm me? And further, that I'd suddenly engage in managing the animal's feeding schedule?"

Carson took a deep breath before dragging his hand over his military-short hair. His bravado noticeably faded before he crossed to a chair behind one of the room's four computer terminals. "She's my sister. I'm supposed to protect her."

"So am I."

The urge to continue—to define what Landry meant to him—was strong but Derek held back. If he couldn't explain it to himself, he'd be damned if he was going to try to define it to her brother.

"You see anything on the recordings?"

"Shadows, but nothing more concrete. You appear to have a ghost."

Carson leaned forward, the bright blue eyes so like his sister's backlit with curiosity. "Take me through it."

Derek spent the next half hour walking Carson through all he'd found. The various images from around the grounds. The perimeter cameras on the front gates. Even the cameras they had throughout the stables. All appeared undisturbed, yet there were swaths of time he couldn't account for on the time stamps.

"Here and here." Derek hit Pause, then toggled backward frame by frame. "You have a quick jump in time, then that small shadow on the screen like something's been covered over or blacked out."

"Hell." Carson leaned closer, his finger sweeping over the screen. "Right there."

"Yep. Looks like it was around three this morning, best as I can tell."

"Nothing matches on the front cameras?"

"Not at all. I've been through the footage several times and can't see anything that looks unusual or has been tampered with."

"Do you think we're dealing with someone already here on the grounds?"

Derek had wondered the same and had kept a mental list since arriving at the ranch. Despite questions, he'd yet to see anyone who seemed suspicious or even overtly strange. "Everyone appears to love the family. And please don't take this the wrong way, but the staff seems positively giddy with your mother out of sight."

Carson grinned at that—his first since walking into the room. "My mother is a tyrant on the best of days."

"Do you think she killed your father?"

Derek let the question roll, curious to see Carson's reaction. The man had walked in loaded for bear—Derek figured he might as well use the cruddy mood to his advantage. When he got a short laugh and an exaggerated eye roll instead he had to reconsider his tactics.

"You'd get a different answer if you asked Whit. Especially since it's his wife my mother did actually go after. But no, I don't think she killed my father." Carson held up a hand. "Don't get me wrong, she's got the chops for attempted murder as Elizabeth can well tell you, but she didn't have it in her for my father."

"That's an awfully big leap. From a possible scenario of playing the scorned wife, ready to take down the mistress and not the husband, too?"

Carson shrugged. "The best I can tell you, it's not my mother. She and my father had a loveless existence, but it was founded on great love. Hers far more so than his."

"Sounds like you, Landry and Whit have spent your lives paying for it."

"Oh, I don't know." The congenial light fled Carson's eyes, replaced with something more somber and solemn. "I'd like to think we've learned from their mistakes and are bound and determined not to repeat them."

Cycles were tough to break—Derek had seen that proven true in the course of his job more often than not—but he had to admit that if anyone was capable of breaking out, it was the Adair children. Both Whit and

Carson had found strong women to share their lives with. And Landry—

He stopped short, his thoughts drifting to the memory of her hand in his, their fingers linked.

She would definitely break the cycle, of that he had no doubt. She was a bright, vibrant woman, beautiful inside and out. Any man would be lucky to have her. To make a life and build a family with her.

"Why don't I let you get back to it, then." Carson stood and extended his hand. Derek appreciated the gesture and took the proverbial olive branch, satisfied he and Carson Adair had crossed some sort of unspoken chasm.

After Carson left, Derek allowed his gaze to drift back to the computer screen. A dark shadow still smudged the center of the image, proof someone had been in the stables and then erased the evidence. A nameless, faceless threat, determined to bring irreparable harm to Landry and all she held dear.

He'd protect her. He knew that with a bone-deep conviction that he didn't question. But recognizing that he'd need to walk away from her when this was all over?

His phone buzzed in his pocket, shattering the morass of thoughts. With a glance at the readout, his responsibilities came crashing back. Responsibilities he'd taken on before Landry Adair came into his life and responsibilities that would be there long after he left her.

He slid his finger along the glass. "Mark? What's going on?"

Landry paced her bedroom, the roller coaster of the day weighing heavy on her mind. Although the danger that started the day was vastly different from the danger that ended it, she had no illusions of just how much trouble she was in.

Death threats were one thing, but a man who managed to get under a woman's defenses and strip her bare was something else entirely.

Damn it, how had he managed to do it?

Derek Winchester was hell on a woman's good sense.

He'd said he was going to spend another couple of hours in the security center before heading to bed. It had been a couple of hours and she hadn't stopped thinking of him since.

Should she go?

Should she stay?

She glanced at the clock, the readout ensuring it was too late to suddenly arrive in the security room as a curious observer. No, a woman who went hunting for a man this late at night had one thing on her mind.

When her body responded in a wave of tingles that centered at her core, she knew the late-night jaunt through the ranch had better be something she was prepared to see all the way through. Not because Derek would expect it, but because she did.

No, she mused. He wouldn't expect anything at all. Derek Winchester was 100 percent gentleman.

The light knock on her door broke into her thoughts, but it was the whispered "Landry" that had her heart beating double time.

"Derek." She opened the door, delight quickly turning to concern as she ushered him in. "What's wrong?"

Lines carved hard grooves into his lean cheeks and she wrapped an arm around his as she walked him toward her small sitting room. "What happened?"

"Rena."

A hard chill gripped her at that single word. A woman's name. How could she have been so stupid?

They hadn't discussed their pasts or their relationships. He'd mentioned someone named Sarah at the Farmers Market and spoke of her as though she was a part of his past, but that didn't mean there wasn't someone else.

Someone who even now waited for him to come home to her.

A hard metallic taste swam in her mouth, nausea threatening the contents of her stomach. She'd allowed her imagination to make something out of nothing.

Forcing a calm she didn't feel, she gestured him toward her sitting area. "What's happened?"

"Rena's—" He scrubbed at his face, his dark eyes going even darker with the tinted circles beneath them. "She's my case. Or was my case. My last one before I had to take a leave of absence."

Unease whipped through her like a summer storm. Here he was, genuinely in pain, and she was too busy working up a good old-fashioned date with the green-eyed monster. Settling them both on the couch, she worked on coaxing the story out of him. "Tell me about her."

"She's young. Just fourteen."

Derek's words struck like freezing rain, and her guilt only grew deeper. Fourteen years old? And part of an FBI case?

She still remembered fourteen. The carefree days, even with an often-unsettled home life. Time split between the mansion in San Diego and Adair Acres, pulled back and forth like a pawn in the demise of a marriage. Despite the frustration of living under the rule of Reginald and Patsy Adair, she'd been safe. Protected. She'd known it then and understood it now.

"After I left the Secret Service, your aunt helped me find my way into the Bureau. Missing persons."

"That must be difficult work." They had spoken briefly about his job on their ride to the fund-raiser in San Diego, but he'd limited his comments and she hadn't probed. "Rewarding, but difficult."

"Mark. The guy you met yesterday. He's my partner, and he and I were working this case of a girl who went missing after she ran away from the projects, likely kidnapped."

As Derek wove the details—a young girl, snatched from her impoverished existence by an international crime lord—she began to get a picture in her mind of exactly what he dealt with day to day in his job. How did anyone handle that? And certainly not for a number of years. How would a person bear up under that sort of strain? And the hopeless reminder of how depraved human beings could be?

"How'd you get her case? Isn't that the jurisdiction of the LAPD?"

"The case fell into our jurisdiction because all signs pointed toward him taking her across international borders."

"Human trafficking."

He nodded. "Unfortunately, yes."

"So why aren't you on the case now?"

The wall she'd observed repeatedly began its descent, and rather than take it personally, Landry used the opportunity to push back. "Oh no. You did that too many times already. I ask for details and you poker up. Why won't you realize I can help you?"

As he'd spoken, their hands had entwined without her even realizing it until he stared down where they were joined. "I can't taint you with this. Or with my failure."

"Excuse me?"

Of all the things he might have said, the idea that he

saw himself as a failure was the very last thing she expected. "How did you possibly fail?"

"I was pulled off the case for shooting the suspected kidnapper."

"So?"

His gaze never wavered, but she didn't miss the hard bob of his Adam's apple as he swallowed. "I was put on a leave of absence. I'm not allowed to work the case any longer. That's a pretty big failure in my book."

"So how do you know about what happened today?"

"Mark's been feeding me details on the sly, and I keep sending him things to look into or different insights I've gleaned from other cases. I can't give this up. I won't give it up. I owe it to Rena to see it through."

While she admired his focus and desire to bring the child home, she struggled with his partner's role in things. "Can't Mark work this on his own?"

"He's been working—"

When Derek stopped midcomment, Landry saw some of her questions reflected in his gaze.

"Of course he can work it on his own. And he does. Is."

"But?"

"He's a good agent, but not the strongest agent we have."

"And if he stays partnered with you he looks better?"

Landry let the question hang there, curious to see what conclusions he might draw.

She'd observed his partner the day they were at headquarters and hadn't been impressed. Thinking back on it, it wasn't simply his strange gaze or slightly odd comments. There had been something more.

"We were assigned together a few years ago. He'd had a big case come in and was riding high on that. My old partner had just transferred to another office. The window of opportunity was open and we clicked well enough."

"Well enough?"

"Well, sure. He's a bit hotheaded and I don't always agree with his leaps in logic, but Mark's a good man. He cares about his cases and goes the extra mile."

The man she'd met didn't strike her as the extra mile sort, but Landry held her tongue. She figured she'd planted enough seeds and would give Derek some time to work things through in his mind. "Do you need to go back to LA?"

"Not tonight. I'll head in tomorrow and meet Mark for lunch. He said they got another note from the kidnapper, this time with more concrete details on where he's keeping her."

Landry knew she was out of her depth, but the pieces didn't fit for her. "I thought you shot him?"

"Wounded him."

"So now he's out and sending notes on his victim's whereabouts?" Something struck her as off about that sort of behavior, but she reminded herself that she wasn't a criminal. She'd heard internet jokes for years that they weren't all that smart, and this latest run of evidence pointed once more to that very fact.

"The lab results are somewhat inconclusive, but they match the MO on the previous notes. And the bastard skipped out on his bail two weeks ago, completely in the wind."

The depth of his knowledge on the latest details in the case only reinforced the fact that he'd been working it on the side. "Is this what had you so upset earlier?"

"Landry...I—"

"Because I'd like to know."

"I couldn't talk about it with you."

"Why?"

He dropped her hands. "I failed at this. You think I want to broadcast that?"

"From where I'm sitting, you failed at nothing. You have a criminal who's eluded you despite what is obviously all your time, effort and energy. How is that failure?"

"You don't understand."

"Then explain it to me."

The same bleak expression she'd seen that morning after their ride once again covered his face in harsh lines. Pain so raw and so deep she wondered if it had a bottom seemed to well up and spill over. "I am my job. I live these cases, determined to bring justice to those who aren't capable of getting it for themselves."

"No doubt one of the many reasons my aunt thinks so well of you."

"I let this girl down. I missed something in the clues and I failed her when I had the chance to take down her kidnapper."

"But you just walked me through it. The man lured you and Mark to that old warehouse and Rena wasn't there."

"She had to be close."

Landry stood, unable to sit still while he paced like a caged animal. "You've lost perspective on this."

Derek stopped at that, all the leashed fury she'd seen in his large frame suddenly provided with a target. "You know nothing about it."

"Oh, no?" Like staring into a mirror, Landry saw her own pain and anger and swirling fury reflected right back at her.

Like hell she didn't know.

"You think I don't know what it's like to live, day in and day out, determined to make the world better and never seeing it happen?"

"I—"

"Let me finish." She kept her hands at her sides, fisted tight for fear she might walk up and slap him if she didn't. "You think somehow because you acted quickly and made the only freaking decision you possibly could under the circumstances that somehow you've failed?

"I live with that every day. If I'd only followed my parents' wishes. If I'd only tried harder to have a relationship with my dad. If I'd only read the signs and understood what was happening around me instead of burying my head in the sand like some clueless society girl, I might have been able to step in and save my father!"

Chapter 10

Sometimes the most important things came into clarity when you stopped looking so hard.

Derek could only stare at the volcano erupting before him, his earlier thought at dinner coalescing into reality. He thought he knew grief—and he thought he'd sensed the depths of Landry's pain—but he obviously knew nothing. She'd hidden it so well and so deep, now that it was out, there was no putting it back where it had lain hidden.

"You can't possibly think you're responsible for your father's death."

"Me. My brothers. My mother. We all are. There was a threat lurking here beneath our noses and we all missed it."

"You can't know that."

"How can't I know that? There was no struggle in his office, he was shot at point-blank range and the security cameras were off for a maintenance upgrade. My father knew his killer."

"Yes, he did." There was no way you could add up that series of facts and believe anything else. "But it still doesn't mean you were responsible."

"Funny you can assume that logic about me yet can't apply it to yourself."

Derek saw how neatly she'd boxed him in. "Rena's my job."

"And Reginald was my father. It's not about logic or reason, Derek. It's about emotion and that's why it's so hard to let go."

She moved closer, and the light scent of honeysuckle he'd noticed during dinner tickled his senses with its sweet overtones. He'd believed the scent had carried from the gardens, but with Landry so near he now knew the sweet scent was her. Fresh and airy, it suited her to a T.

And when she moved closer still, he took another deep breath, filling his lungs with the rich, clean bouquet.

"If I let go, there won't be anything left."

"Or if you let go, you can finally reach for something new."

Her lips pressed to his jaw, and she trailed a line of tender kisses over hard bone. The moment was both tender and erotic, especially when she flicked her tongue over the edge of his chin before continuing a path toward the other side of his face. "Tell me you want me."

"You know I do."

"Tell me there's no one else."

"There's no one—" He broke off, her words like a pinball in his mind. "No one else? Of course there's no one else."

A light blush worked its way up her cheeks, but her gaze stayed level. Determined. "I just wanted to make sure. You...you mentioned someone named Sarah the other day. At lunch."

"Ah."

He stilled, the urge to brush it off warring with the need to be honest. She'd had the guts to ask, and he at least owed it to her to tell her the truth. "Sarah was my fiancée. We've been broken up for a few months now. Another casualty, along with my day job, of Rena's case."

"Oh."

Derek hesitated, then went with instinct. He traced the line of her jaw, his fingers mimicking the same play of her lips mere moments before. "Turns out in the end Sarah didn't want to be a glorified cop's wife."

"That's what she said?"

"In pretty much those words. And, as it turns out, I'm happy being a glorified cop. Or I at least want to be with someone who will support me for as long as I want to be one."

"Why do people want to change the ones they're with?"

Head bent, he pressed his lips to hers, murmuring against their sweet softness. "I have no idea."

"I think—" She broke off, her breath mingling with his before she kissed him fully.

"You think what?"

He felt her smile as it spread against his lips. "I think you talk too much."

Her hands settled at the back of his neck, pulling him closer and deepening the kiss. He allowed himself to be dragged along, into the sweet abyss of need and desire and something incredibly soft and warm that he'd never felt before.

The swirling vortex was all-consuming, and in moments, the sexy banter and lingering kisses had turned urgent. Greedy. And oh, so enticing.

With careful steps, he walked them backward toward the love seat in her sitting room, pulling her on top of him when he felt the plump cushions at the backs of his legs. He fell into the pillows, rewarded with even more softness when her breasts crushed against his chest.

The careful dance they'd maintained between them vanished as the rush of the moment overtook them both. A rich, carnal craving settled into his veins, and Derek felt himself going under, a drowning man without breath who needed only the woman in his arms to sustain him.

An abstract image of a siren on a rock floated through his mind. If the siren was anything like Landry, no wonder sailors crashed to their doom. He'd follow this woman anywhere. And he was fast coming to believe he'd do anything to possess her.

Just as earlier, her hands were like a brand against his skin. Fires flared high everywhere she touched, and he felt the world melting away as Landry Adair became his entire focus.

She had the material of his shirt up and over his head before moving into a seated position on his lap, her hands on his shoulders. "Those are some awfully impressive muscles."

The thin blouse she wore was in his hands and up over her head before she could blink. He took in the strong lines of her body and the shape of her full breasts where they spilled over the silky cups of her bra. "Likewise, Ms. Adair."

A sexy, bewitching smile spread across her lips. "I do believe we've got a mutual admiration society going on here."

He leaned forward and pressed a light kiss to her

chest, flicking his tongue over the generous flesh of her breast. "What I feel is considerably deeper than admiration."

At her sharp intake of breath, he continued his exploration, tracing a path down the silky edge of her bra with his tongue. Her hands stayed firmly positioned on his shoulders. Every time he hit a particularly sweet spot, her palm flexed against muscle like a telegraph of her pleasure.

And when he finally slipped one silky cup beneath her breast and took a nipple into his mouth, he was rewarded with a hard cry of pleasure that filled the air between them.

"Derek." His name floated on the air before her head fell back, her eyes closed as she took pleasure in the moment. The soft light of the lamp beside the bed sheened her skin in a golden glow, and Derek let the moment spin out, the sweetest taste of her on his lips.

His hands stayed firm across her back, holding her in place as he worked the sensitive flesh between his lips. His fingers drifted to the clasp of her bra, anxious to have no barrier between them.

The silky material fell between them and Landry was bared, naked to his gaze. "You're so beautiful."

The words exhaled on a reverent hush as he gave himself a moment to simply look at her.

"Who's complaining about my willpower around doughnuts now?"

A light tease suffused her husky words and he found himself captivated by her sultry gaze. The bright blue of her eyes had turned a vivid indigo, the darkness of her pupils wide with desire.

But it was something else—something that hovered beneath the desire—where he saw the question.

Am I enough?

Anger, honed to a fine point, lit him up inside. What had her family done to her? While her brothers had suffered through the obvious expectations of their father, she was left to her mother's endless criticism.

How could a woman so vibrant—so caring and aware of others—believe she was somehow lacking?

"You're gorgeous, Landry. Inside and out. Nothing will change that. Ever."

He bent his head and took her lips with his, slipping his tongue into her warm mouth. Her tongue tangled with his, drawing him in with the warmest welcome.

It might take time, but he was going to convince this woman of her worth. He believed she knew it—somewhere deep inside her there was a light Patsy and Reginald Adair hadn't been able to snuff out—but he also knew it would take time.

And he was more than up to the task.

Long, lush moments spun out between them, growing more urgent with each passing second. Their touches grew more frantic and their breathing more urgent as they pushed each other onward.

He shifted beneath her, the hot heat of her core driving him wild with the need to make her fully his. And when she reached between them, her hands slipping beneath the waistband of his jeans, Derek knew the deepest satisfaction as her hand brushed against his hard body.

"Well, what have we here, Mr. Winchester?" That teasing note was back, and he fought the groan as her fingers closed around him.

He pressed his forehead to hers and closed his eyes, the wash of pleasure so immense he needed a moment to get himself in check. But when the hints of laughter faded, replaced with a quiet urgency, he knew he was lost.

"Please, Derek. Let me."

He took her mouth once more, his only answer to the warm, willing, generous woman in his arms. His body was already strung out, pushed to the limit with the desperate need for release, but still she urged him on.

"Landry—" He broke off, unsure of himself. He wanted her. With madness that ran so deep he didn't know if he'd ever recover. But he'd also just shared the realities of his life.

Rena.

His forced leave of absence.

His ruined engagement.

All were realities that weren't going to go away if they made love.

"Landry—" He held her still, one hand on her shoulders while the other covered her hand. "Wait."

"Hmmm?" Confusion lit her features as she slowly recognized he had stopped her. "Derek?"

An apology was already springing to his lips when the room plunged into inky blackness.

Landry willed herself to surface from the sexual haze that consumed her. Derek had been so willing—so into the moment—before he halted it.

And now the lights were out?

Despite the fact that her brain was still trying to assimilate all the facts, the irony wasn't lost on her.

Abstractly, she realized the position they were still in and removed her hand from beneath his. His sharp intake of breath as her fingers slid along his length gave her a grim sort of satisfaction.

Why had he stopped her?

She lifted off his lap, her movements stiff as her body still struggled with abandoned desire. Her slacks were unbuttoned and her blouse had disappeared somewhere. She kept one hand on the cushions, reaching for the drawer in the small end table at the edge of the couch.

Her hand closed around a lighter and she pulled out the cool metal, flicking the starter. She focused on the flash of warm light and ignored the heavy cadence of both their breaths. Within moments, the small, fragrant candle she kept on the end table flared to life, illuminating them both in the glow.

She ignored Derek and went to work righting herself. Her blouse was in a heap beside the couch and she slipped it on, regretting the lack of bra but unwilling to spend any more time naked before his gaze.

"I'm going to go down and see what this is about."

"I'm going with you."

"Suit yourself."

"Landry—" His hand closed over her forearm and he pulled her close.

"Yes?"

"I want you. I might be a clumsy ass with equally clumsy timing, but know that as sure as we're both standing here. I want you."

She nodded around the hard lump that welled in her throat, but didn't trust herself to speak.

And then there were no words because Derek had her in his arms, his mouth fused to hers, those same sparks flaring to life as if they'd never been dulled.

When he finally lifted his head long moments later, his voice was husky, stamped with need. "I want you."

He dropped her hand and made quick work of finding his T-shirt and zipping up his jeans. She moved equally quickly, sliding her blouse over her head and fluffing her hair into some semblance of order. She could only hope whoever they ran into in the hallway saw her messy hair and blamed it on bed head instead of passionate kisses on her love seat.

Derek grabbed the squat candle from the end table. "Let's go see what this is about."

They wove their way through her wing, toward the large staircase to the first floor. Landry heard a sharp cry from the direction of the kitchen and picked up her pace. She called out so as not to surprise anyone. "Kathleen?"

"Miss Landry?" Another sharp cry added to the question and Landry raced for the swinging door into the oversize kitchen that was Kathleen's domain.

She gasped and dropped to her knees. "Kathleen! What happened?" Several plates lay shattered a few feet away from their cook's supine figure, her leg trapped underneath her at a funny angle.

"I tripped." The older woman tried to move and another heavy cry fell from her lips.

"Shhh. Shhh now." Landry took her hand, grateful when Derek dropped to his haunches on Kathleen's other side.

"You're going to be okay." His voice was calm and quiet as he set the candle down next to her. "I'm going to leave this here and I'm going to call for help."

He already had his cell phone out of his back pocket and was dialing as he crossed to the far side of the kitchen.

"I was just putting some things away. That's all. Just a few last-minute things before bed."

Landry sat down and wrapped her arms around the woman as she let her talk. She crooned nonsense words, trying to calm Kathleen's obvious shock as she babbled about putting away dishes from the night's dinner.

"I know. I know. You like a clean kitchen before you go to bed."

Voices echoed outside the kitchen door as Carson and Georgia came in, followed closely by Whit and Elizabeth. "What?"

Landry shot her brother a dark look and waved them in. "The blackout scared Kathleen and she tripped."

Her sisters-in-law went to work immediately, Georgia picking up the shattered plates while Elizabeth crossed to the pantry to grab a broom. Whit followed his wife, beating her to the broom and dustpan. "I don't think so, babe."

"I'm pregnant, not disabled," Elizabeth said, obviously disgruntled.

"Let him spoil you, sweetheart." Kathleen waved a hand from the floor before trying to move again.

Landry held her still but figured her ability to key into what was happening in the room was a good sign.

Carson stood on the far side of the kitchen with Derek, their heads bent now that an ambulance had been called. Landry knew without being told that their little pow-wow was because neither thought the blackout was an accident.

There was no bad weather, and the house had a backup generator that kicked in when they did lose power. The pitch black that had descended over Adair Acres was immediate and absolute.

And it put them in jeopardy.

With no backup generator, the house alarm and every bit of security was turned off.

Carson swung the beam of his flashlight across the wall of the security center. The panel that was perpetually lit with blinking lights was dark, snuffed out by their latest power problem.

"There's no way this is a fluke. Someone did this."

"The security center *and* the generator." Derek swung his own beam of light, searching for the circuit breaker he'd seen earlier. "Yeah. Someone's behind this."

"But who? I know we've not been as on top of the employees coming and going, but the security here's good. Top-of-the-line. My father would expect nothing less."

"You and Whit have both dealt with problems in the last few months." Derek found the panel on the far wall and unhooked the thin metal door. "Is it possible they've come back to roost?"

"I find that hard to believe. My mother was behind the danger to Elizabeth, and I took care of the bastard who was after Georgia."

Derek digested Carson's words as he examined the circuit breaker. Even though he wanted to find some other answer for what was happening, Carson wasn't off the mark. The recent threats felt new—and different—from what the Adairs had been living with since Reginald's murder.

It was possible Patsy Adair could have hired someone again, but he had a hard time believing she'd threaten her own daughter. And while obviously scary when they were happening, the threats on Elizabeth and Georgia had been dealt with.

Which left Landry as the current target.

"Only a few people know the reason why you're here," Carson said. "Whit and Elizabeth, Landry, our aunt Kate, and me and Georgia."

"Yet none of this started happening until I got here. Why?"

"I have no idea. You've done a convincing job of making everyone think you're my sister's new boyfriend."

Derek didn't miss the slightly disgruntled tones in Carson's voice but ignored them. Instead, the heated moments in Landry's room came flooding back, filling his thoughts with vivid, erotic images of them together. His already-heated body responded and Derek was grateful for the dark.

He went back to work on the breaker panel, willing his body to calm. But the woman had him in knots.

"I want to go out and look at the generator." Carson disappeared and Derek let out a raw breath. It was only when he turned back toward the unit that he saw a set of lights flash on the server panel connected to the security center. Light illuminated the hallway, and Derek reached for the room switch they hadn't bothered to turn on when they arrived.

Overhead light flooded the darkness, and several beeps echoed from the computer monitors as they rebooted.

Although he'd taken all the requisite training in cybercrime and basic technology courses, he was still out of his depth when it came to all the ins and outs of computer forensics. Mark was a whiz, and he'd depended on him for the heavy lifting when necessary.

Even with his limited knowledge, he knew enough to know the wavy lines growing brighter on the screens were a bad sign. The whirling of sirens dragged his attention from the immediate problem and he vowed to return after they got Kathleen safely to the hospital. He'd give Mark a call and ask him to walk them through correcting it if need be.

He'd nearly left when Noah came barreling through the door, his breathing heavy. "What the hell is going on around here? I heard the ambulance and just saw the sirens. Who's hurt?"

"Kathleen. She tripped when the lights went off. It looks like she broke her leg."

"When did the lights go off?" A puzzled frown crossed Noah's face, his hands on his hips. "I've been down in the stable for the last two hours doing some paperwork and had power the whole time."

"Nothing went out?"

"Nope. I'd still be down there if I hadn't heard the sirens."

Derek's knowledge of electricity was even less developed than his computer skills, but even he knew that was odd. "The power went off up here, along with the backup generator. Doesn't that power the stables, too?"

"Nope. We have a separate generator down there." Noah shook his head but a heightened sense of awareness sparked in his eyes as he let out a sharp expletive. "This isn't an act of Mother Nature. Someone did this."

"On that we're in agreement."

"Just like a snake doesn't magically get into a sealed feed bin."

"No. But like leaving the snake's canvas bag behind, whoever did this left us a clue."

"I don't think I follow."

"The bastard wasn't aware of a backup generator in the stables. Which means we should be able to backtrack through the security feeds from the barn and find out what he did."

"You can do that?"

"I can't. But I think I know someone who can."

Chapter 11

Landry fought the urge to lay her head on Derek's shoulder and instead watched the strange ballet that was a hospital waiting room. Doctors or nurses came in frequently to provide updates to loved ones. She'd watched through the night—had seen the look of hope cross each face, followed by sobering relief or the heartbreaking reality of grief—and had wondered how those kindly souls could keep doing it.

Day after day, caring for those who'd been hurt, sometimes beyond repair.

They'd been fortunate to receive good news of their own—Kathleen was in surgery now to repair her broken leg—but even knowing she'd recover, things had irrevocably changed for their cook.

"She'll be okay. It's a bad break, that's all. They'll fix her up."

Derek had tried repeatedly to reassure her, but Landry

couldn't stop worrying. Kathleen was seventy-one. A break like this would be hard for anyone to recover from, but a woman of her age wasn't going to simply bounce back.

Whit had taken Elizabeth home earlier to rest, and Carson and Georgia had gone off to fetch bad coffee from the vending machine. There had been one other couple in the waiting room who finally left, and she and Derek had the room to themselves.

Tabling her worries about Kathleen, Landry focused on the bigger picture. "The house power and the generator? There's no way both went out at the same time. It smacks of sabotage."

She appreciated when Derek only nodded his agreement with her assessment. Maybe they really had become partners.

In name only, her still-bruised ego bandied back at her.

But partners all the same.

"Noah was down at the stables when it happened. The generator there was untouched."

A renewed wave of panic swamped her as she thought about Pete, Diego and the other occupants of the barn. "What is wrong with me? I didn't even think about the horses."

"There's nothing wrong with you and there was nothing to think about. Noah was with them the entire time and they're safe. And possibly sitting on the clues we need."

"What clues?"

He walked her through his theory—how the fact that the security wasn't breached in the stable meant they might be able to electronically backtrack to the person trying to do them harm. "You know how to do that? Work your way through reams of computer code?"

"No, but Mark does. I'll call him in the morning."

A wholly unreasonable shot of alarm clenched her stomach in a hard knot. Unable to stem the rising panic, she fought to keep her voice calm. "Are you sure about that?"

"Of course. He's good at it, too. It's how he ended up in missing persons."

"Computers?"

"He cracked a major drug ring in the Pacific Northwest, tracking it back to a series of cyberattacks they'd perpetrated."

"That group a few years back? The Rainier Cartel?"

That sting had made the evening news, and Landry recalled the importance of the bust and the positive effect it would have on crime as far south as San Diego.

"Mark did that? The man I met the other day?"

"That was his case. Or he was part of the team on that case. It's how he ended up getting his transfer to Los Angeles."

Landry tried to assimilate an agent capable of cracking down on a problem that large and the man she'd met at the FBI offices the other day and found herself unable to reconcile the two.

The man she'd met had seemed soft and deeply lazy. And not because of hours spent behind a computer, working through layer upon layer of code. No, it was something else.

She respected Derek's opinion, but no matter how hard she'd tried to reframe her image of Mark, her first impression had been of a man who was jealous of those around him.

Perpetually overlooked by the brass and forever angry, convinced it was someone else's fault.

"You don't think all that well of him, do you?"

"I didn't get a good vibe off of him. So. Well. No, I don't."

She saw Derek nod, his gaze considering. "Would you feel better if I called someone else at the Bureau to help?"

"You'd do that?"

"Of course. I trust Mark but I trust you, too. And I've got a few other team members I can call. I'll get one of them to look into this for me."

"Thank you."

The sexual disappointment she'd felt earlier came back in full force, tinged with a layer of sadness.

The two of them were good together.

Their chemistry was explosive, yes, but it was something more. Something that went far deeper than simple attraction. And she'd sensed it from their very first morning ride on the horses.

She and Derek Winchester clicked.

Over the past few months, she'd observed the same sort of chemistry when she watched her brothers and their new wives. She'd been unable to put the sense into words, but it was fascinating to now realize she understood it on a personal level.

"Miss Adair?" Landry was pulled from her musings by the nurse who'd been giving them updates all evening. "Kathleen's out of recovery and in her room. You can go in and see her now."

"Thank you."

"Go ahead in. I'll wait for Carson and Georgia to get back and then we'll join you."

Landry nodded and followed the nurse. The private room they'd requested for Kathleen was only a short way down the hall, and in moments the nurse had ushered her through.

Their sturdy cook, a fixture at Adair Acres since

Landry and her brothers had been small, smiled back at her from the bed. "All this trouble."

"Nonsense. It's no trouble at all." Landry picked up the older woman's hand and squeezed it tight. "All we need to focus on now is getting you well."

Kathleen's tremulous smile fell, tears welling in her eyes. "There's so much to do. So much to be done. Miss Elizabeth's baby shower and keeping everyone in line for when your mother returns."

"Shhh, now." Landry pulled a chair toward the bed, then settled Kathleen's blankets more firmly around her. "You're not to worry about any of this. Georgia and I can finish up the details for the shower, and I know Rachel will be happy to help, too. You're going to focus on getting well and enjoy being a guest. The doctor said you only need to stay for a day and then you should be ready to go home."

Kathleen greeted her with sleepy protests, and Landry could only be grateful the woman would likely remember nothing of the conversation. They'd focus on pampering her for the next few days and getting her settled at home. Whit had already sent her a text saying that he was looking into home health care, and they'd make sure she was taken care of to the best of their abilities.

"How's she doing?" Derek stepped into the room, Carson and Georgia in his wake.

"As well as can be expected. And very upset she hasn't finished all the details for Elizabeth's shower."

"That's the least of her worries." Georgia moved to the other side of the bed and patted a now-sleeping Kathleen's shoulder. "She needs to focus on getting well."

Landry couldn't quite hold back the rueful smile. "I think that will be easier said than done."

"Unless…" Carson moved around to stand next to his wife.

When they all only stared at him, Carson gestured them back toward the lobby. "I've got an idea."

"You're up early." Derek reached for an empty coffee mug off the sideboard in the dining room. Landry sat, pert and perky as a daisy at the table. That delicious honeysuckle scent of hers drifted his way and went a long way toward clearing the early-morning cobwebs from his mind.

They'd finally arrived home at four and said goodbye at the entrance to her room. He'd wanted nothing more than to come in and finish what they'd started earlier, but had gone on to his room after saying good-night, well aware he had no right to finish anything.

Another hour of tossing and turning in bed, thinking about Landry, hadn't gotten him any closer to deciphering his sudden attack of nerves about the shoddy state of his life. Instead, he'd cursed himself for walking away from the woman he was fast coming to believe was the best thing that had ever walked into his life.

"What are you working on?" He pointed toward the tablet at her elbow.

"I'm reviewing the notes I've taken so far from our trip to LA. I want to get your take on them."

"I've got my own notes, but I think I can remember most of them. Let's compare."

She shifted her chair closer to his and another wave of honeysuckle washed over him. Without giving himself time to check the impulse, he leaned forward and pressed his lips to her ear, inhaling deeply.

"You're beautiful."

She stilled, her blue eyes going as soft as a field of bluebonnets. "Thank you."

"I meant what I said last night. I want you. And I spent what was left of last night cursing myself and my damned conscience."

"Would it make you feel better if I told you I lay awake cursing your damned conscience, too?"

A heavy laugh hit him and he couldn't hold it back, the sheer joy of being with her replacing whatever lingering frustration he might have had. Her laughter joined his, quickly capturing both of them in the moment.

Still grinning, he couldn't resist placing another kiss against her ear as their laughter quieted. "Maybe you'll give me another chance."

"Maybe I just will." She pressed a lingering kiss against his lips, the light coffee-flavored taste of her going to his head like the most potent whiskey.

In spite of all that was going on, nothing mattered but being in her orbit. Power outages and snakes and kidnapped babies simply faded away in the reality of her.

"Derek." Her voice pulled him back to the present.

"Hmmm?"

She laid a hand on his shoulder, holding him still. "We need to go through this."

"Maybe you can sit on my lap when we do."

He was rewarded with another giggle before she tossed her napkin at him. "As I was saying."

And then she had the tablet, her tone all business, even if she did keep a hand over his as she spoke. "The first place I started was the immigration records you pulled. My aunt Emmaline was in Europe when my father's son was born. She was pregnant with Noah at the time and on bed rest."

Although he wanted nothing more than to find someplace secluded and finish what they'd started, Derek had to admit she had him at the details. Years of training and natural curiosity had his gaze drifting off her lush mouth and toward the screen of her tablet. "Your aunt never traveled at all?"

"No." Landry tapped on the screen, then pointed toward a section of notes. "Right there. Between the death of her husband and her difficult pregnancy, she didn't travel at all for almost a two-year period, both before and after Noah was born. And even for years after that, her travel was sporadic."

"She was widowed? That long ago? That never made it into Kate's briefing."

"About six months into her pregnancy."

Derek considered that tidbit. On one hand, he could understand leaving it out. The notes had said Emmaline was widowed young. But something in the fact that it happened while pregnant struck Derek as important. Poignant, somehow. "What does that do to a person?"

Landry's eyes narrowed as she considered his question. "Grief is a horrible thing, and it's not logical when it comes."

"No, but to lose your spouse—your support system—at the very moment you need it most?" Derek took a sip of his coffee. "That must have been horrible for her."

"I'd say so." Landry scrolled a bit further in her notes. "It's also another reason why the idea that Noah is Jackson seems so off. Emmaline couldn't have taken Jackson. She was nowhere near him."

"True." Derek reached for her tablet again and scanned the meticulous accounting of dates and had to concede her point. They could have as many suspicions as they wanted, but none of it changed the fact that by all accounts, Emmaline Adair Scott was living a life in Europe, content to stay there and raise her own family. "What else?"

"I also scanned the investigation records quickly. It was almost four decades ago and I didn't spend much time with them, but I'm surprised the police records from North Carolina are so spotty."

"I noticed that, too." Derek had thought the records inconclusive, as well, but he'd taken it a step further and questioned the overall investigative skills of those assigned. It might have been nearly forty years ago, but good investigative technique wasn't only in the purview of those who had computers and smartphones at their disposal.

The cops on the Adair kidnapping had done a terrible job. In one report they have neighbors claiming a car had circled the block several times the day the baby was taken, but no one had followed up on the make or model.

And yet another report had said there was a statewide search, yet Derek hadn't found any proof of much beyond a few door-to-door checks of known offenders out on parole.

None of it made much sense. A child goes missing and the cops do everything they can to bring the child home. The child of a wealthy family goes missing and no one in law enforcement sleeps until they have answers.

Yet Jackson Adair vanished from almost right beneath his mother's nose, never to be seen again, and the case seemed flubbed or misguided every step of the way.

Curious, he waited to see Landry's take.

"I know this isn't my expertise, but the police records seem awfully incomplete."

"Because they are."

Landry was prevented from replying when Noah walked into the room. She recovered quickly, leaning forward and giggling against his cheek, looking for all the world like a woman in a heated flirtation with her boyfriend.

The quick thinking had obviously worked when Noah wiggled his eyebrows in Derek's direction from the spread set out on the sideboard. "I'd ask what you two are up to but I think I can guess."

Landry stood to refresh her coffee and pressed a kiss to her cousin's cheek. "Mind, gutter, Noah. Disengage the two."

He pulled her close in a side-armed hug and dropped a big smacking kiss on her cheek. "You know no one's good enough for my little baby cousin."

Derek fought the wince at Noah's loaded words, especially since the man was oblivious to the conversation he'd interrupted. While Noah fixed his breakfast, Landry flitted around the dining room like a queen bee, keeping things light and easy.

Heck, if Derek hadn't just gone over the data with her, he'd never have believed the two of them were just questioning Noah's parentage.

"The shower's later today. Is your mother coming down from Palm Springs?" Landry asked.

"She wouldn't miss it. The woman's crazy about babies. It's all she can talk about. Especially when it comes to my getting in gear and giving her a grandchild." Noah tucked into a large bagel he'd smothered with cream cheese, the move doing nothing to erase a quick and irritated frown.

"A woman's prerogative."

"As is a man's right to choose when he procreates."

"Touché."

Landry picked at her own breakfast, tearing off a

small piece of toast. "Your mom's picking up Aunt Rosalyn and Uncle Sheldon, isn't she?"

Derek sat, fascinated to see how she manipulated the dialogue.

"Better her than me." Noah visibly shuddered. "Sheldon's getting more and more crochety by the day. It only rivals his all-around general craziness."

"I wish they'd get him to a doctor and have his memory checked." Landry made a small *tsk*ing sound. "Maybe get him some meds. That nasty disposition of his only gets worse with age."

"Well, I for one can't wait to meet your family, babe." Derek laid it on thick, draping his hand over hers and leaning forward to press a quick kiss to her lips. "I think I might have something to do this afternoon."

He shot a pleading look at Noah. "You sure you don't need help down at the stables today? I can exercise the horses. Feed them. Muck stalls."

"You'd take stall mucking over a baby shower?" Landry pretended offense, but he saw the humor lighting the depths of her eyes.

Derek shot Noah a wink before pressing another kiss to Landry's cheek. "Any day, babe. Any day."

Georgia handed her one end of a blue streamer and pointed toward the far side of the living room. "Let's tack it on the end of the fireplace."

Landry unrolled as she walked, twisting the streamer to create an arc of baby blue. "I'm going to be an aunt. Every time I think I have a handle on it, I have a moment when I realize in a few short months there will be a baby here."

"I know. Things have happened so fast, but I can't wait to meet him." Georgia pulled a tab of tape off some contraption she wore on her wrist. "Do you think we're doing the right thing?"

"Elizabeth wanted something quiet at home."

"I mean about Noah."

The quavering voice reached her a moment before a quick, hard sob. Landry dropped her end of the streamer roll and pulled Georgia into her arms for a tight hug. "Come on. What's the matter?"

"I feel like Pandora. I'm the one who made the connection about the picture of Ruby's father and Noah, and now I can't take it back."

"You shared an observation, Georgia. You didn't do anything wrong."

"I know, but that was before I knew him well. And now that I've spent more time with him—" She broke off, another sob spilling from her throat as tears rolled down her cheeks. "I feel like I've set in motion the steps to ruin his life."

"No, no, no. You can't think that way." Landry kept her arm around Georgia's shoulders and tried to comfort her, but even her attempts at soft, soothing words felt flat to her own ears.

Hadn't she felt the same?

Hell, just that morning she and Derek had worked through their notes from the FBI almost beneath Noah's nose.

"I'm not sure what I hate more," Georgia said. "The questions, or the fact that we all think this huge, enormous secret and haven't shared it with him."

"I understand and feel the same way. I know we need answers, but we don't have to like it."

Georgia dashed at the tears that covered her cheeks. "What if we're right?"

"We love him. And if we find out that your suspicions

are correct, then we'll continue to give him all the love and support we have."

As they finished with the decorating, Landry couldn't help wondering if she was being too optimistic. Yes, they would all support Noah no matter what the outcome, but would he want their help once he knew the truth?

Landry slipped on a thin pair of sandals to match the light wrap dress she wore and closed her bedroom door behind her. She felt better after sharing the time with Georgia earlier, even if the guilt over what they were doing increasingly weighed like an anchor.

At least their conversation had reinforced that the others felt as bad as she did.

She loved Noah; she always had. And until recently, with the reading of her father's will and the revelation that he'd had a child from a first marriage, she'd had no reason to view Noah under any light except that of favored cousin.

None of it changed the fact that Reginald and Ruby had spent their lives bereft of their son. Was it possible her father died never knowing his son had actually been nearby his entire life?

The two had always gotten along. Her father had kept his distance—she'd always believed he knew no other way—but it hadn't stopped a bond from forming between them anyway. Their mutual love of horses had shaped much of it, but Reginald had always been a father figure, especially with Emmaline's husband having already passed away.

The doorbell rang, pulling Landry from her thoughts, and she opened the door to see Emmaline, Rosalyn and Sheldon at the door. "Hello! Come in."

Landry braced herself for the onslaught of familial

hugs and the usual banter that accompanied a visit from her father's sisters. Sheldon grumbled about keeping his hat and she deftly ignored him, swooping in for hugs from her aunt Rosalyn and her aunt Emmaline.

As Landry pulled Emmaline close, she wondered who she held in her arms. A sweet, loving aunt who still grieved the loss of her brother so soon after his passing? Or a cold, brittle woman who'd betrayed that brother by taking and raising his only son?

If she had done it, how did she live with herself?

Whit was about to have a baby boy, and Landry held nothing but excitement for the arrival of her new nephew and happiness for her brother and his wife. She couldn't even imagine touching a hair on the new baby's head, let alone taking him away from his parents.

Was she actually related to this woman who possibly felt neither of those things?

Stepping back, Landry let her gaze travel over her aunt. Slender and petite, Emmaline's features were small and birdlike. Her thick brown hair was shot through with gray and she had it pulled into a severe bun.

She hardly looked like a kidnapper.

But what did that really mean?

Afraid to get caught staring, Landry quickly ushered them into the dining room for some refreshments. "Kathleen's been cooking for a week to get ready for this. Please, help yourselves."

Sheldon's eyes lit up when he saw some small pastry-wrapped hot dogs, and he beelined toward them with a speed that belied his age.

"Not too many, Sheldon."

Sheldon waved a hand in Rosalyn's direction. "Don't fuss at me, woman. I'm fit as a fiddle."

"It's a baby shower, not a five-course meal. Make sure you leave some for everyone else."

"We have plenty, Aunt Rosalyn." Landry gave her aunt a good-natured eye roll before leaning in and whispering, "The kitchen knows those are his favorites. Kathleen made sure they cooked extras."

Rosalyn patted Landry's arm. "Such a good girl you are. Reginald had good children."

Landry waved her aunts off toward the living room and the conversation that already hummed with Elizabeth, Georgia and several of Elizabeth's friends. While she wanted to continue her observations, she figured she'd better keep an eye on Sheldon until he'd made a plate or Rosalyn's admonition of vanished appetizers might come true.

So as not to appear as if she was watching him, Landry made a fuss over the table settings and decorations. "How have you been, Uncle Sheldon?"

"Fine. Fine. Fit like I told you."

"Of course you are. I'm so glad you and Aunt Rosalyn could make it to Elizabeth's baby shower."

"Baby?" His head snapped up as he stared at her, his dark brown eyes rheumy with age. "What baby?"

"Whit and Elizabeth's baby. The baby boy they're having in a few months."

He continued to putter his way around the table, muttering to himself the whole time. Although she'd been joking with Noah that morning, her uncle really was worse off than she'd realized.

"Babies. Always talking about babies. Live ones. Dead ones."

The hair on the back of her neck stood on edge and Landry stilled her movements. The stack of napkins in her hands flopped and she dropped several on the table.

Bending down to retrieve them, she forced a calm she didn't feel into her voice. "What dead babies, Uncle Sheldon?"

"The one that died. Right?" He shook his head. "Or maybe it didn't die."

She moved around the table to settle a hand on his shoulder. "What baby didn't die, Uncle Sheldon?"

"Emmaline's baby. He was born sick and we thought he died but then he didn't. Right?"

"Of course. Noah's fine and well, Uncle Sheldon. In fact, he's here. He'll come into the party later and say hi to everyone."

"Right as rain."

"Yes, Noah's fine." She steered him toward the living room, adding a few extra puff pastries on his way through the door to keep him occupied and his mouth busy.

Shock raced through her, slamming her heart against her ribs as Landry fell back against the wall and closed her eyes. Had her senile old uncle just confirmed the truth behind their questions?

And if Emmaline had a baby who died, then who was Noah Scott?

Chapter 12

Derek stayed true to his promise. In exchange for skipping out on spending the afternoon with Landry's family, he helped out wherever he was needed in the stables. The work was sweaty and tiring, but he took pride in the finished product—a stable that positively sparkled.

"We've got an opening if you want it." Noah's grin was infectious when he handed over a cold bottle of water. "You're a natural in here."

"It was time well spent. I can feel my muscles."

"There's something to that, isn't there?" Noah took a seat opposite him in the small stable office, his skin as covered in dirt as Derek's.

Noah's gaze traveled the office walls. "It's something my mother's struggled with." When Derek said nothing, Noah added, "My interest in working here. Taking care of the horses and the grounds. She has some idea that it's beneath me."

"Parents don't understand everything."

"Do yours?"

"I got pretty lucky." Again, he was reminded that his own upbringing was fairly idyllic. But even amid the seeming perfection, there had been holes. "But parents don't always know how to express their feelings. My mother didn't like a woman I used to be engaged to."

He'd deliberately pushed those early days with Sarah out of his mind, but his mother hadn't been crazy about his choice and had made sure he knew about it, too.

"What happened?"

"Let's just say I figured out before it was too late that you can't share your life with someone who wishes you were a different person."

"That's for damn sure." Noah waved his water bottle. "You introduce your mother to Landry yet?"

"Not yet. But soon."

Derek knew he was only playing a part, but suddenly he had a vision of bringing Landry home to meet his parents. The two of them, seated at his mother's dining room table, sharing a meal as his mother trod that delicate balance between being nosy and interested, and his father kept a sweet, supportive smile pasted on his face.

"What about you? You ever get close enough to getting married?"

"Not yet. That's my mother's other bone of contention with me. She hates my job and is upset she doesn't have any grandchildren. She's accused me of being a rolling stone." Noah took a last long swig of his water, a hard laugh bouncing off the stable doors. "I just tell her she's obsessed."

Noah snagged two more waters out of a cooler by his side and tossed Derek one. "So we've mucked stalls all day, groomed horses and even shared nagging mother stories. You going to finally give in and tell me what you really do? Because I find it hard to believe you're a simple, carefree, jet-setting playboy."

"Will I ruin your image of me if I say no?"

"Nah. I figured you from the first. But watching you the last few days and how much Landry digs you have only confirmed it."

"That was your clue?"

"Hell, yeah. The woman's dated far too many jet-setting playboys. They bore her to tears. And you don't."

The door was open—all Derek had to do was step through it. But he liked Noah and respected the life the man had carved out for himself. He didn't like lying to him, but years of FBI training kept him from giving up the charade before he had something concrete to prove or disprove his theory.

"I used to work on Kate's Secret Service detail. When news of what was going on out here reached her in North Carolina, she asked me to come here and keep an eye on things."

"It's a good thing you're here. They need looking out for. I know Carson and Whit would balk at that, but it's true. It's a big part of why I came here after Reginald's murder."

"And now? Why do you stay?"

"The work." Noah's gaze took on a faraway look. "And maybe I'm enjoying getting to know a certain socialite who does far too much work and far too little jet-setting herself."

Rachel.

Landry had sensed something was going on the night before, and he'd gone along with it because in his experience women loved pairing up unattached people. But now, looking for himself...yeah, he could see that extra shot of heat fill Noah's gaze.

Noah crushed the empty water bottle in his hand.

"We should probably get inside and get cleaned up, then. Go visit those socialites who've captured our attention."

"What? We're not dressed for a party."

Derek slapped Noah on the back. "I'm not sure we're dressed to set foot in the house."

Landry was still struggling with Uncle Sheldon's weird comments about dead babies, even though she'd spent the past two hours trying to convince herself otherwise. Maybe she hadn't heard him right. And maybe there was a time-bending space portal to Paris in her backyard, too.

The man might be senile, but he had no reason to make that up. Especially something so specific.

No. He had a memory of something, and she needed to find out what.

The shower was winding down, and the dining room showed the evidence that people had enjoyed themselves. She busied herself combining some of the trays of food, condensing some and emptying others for the kitchen.

"Why are you in here cleaning up?" Emmaline bustled in, her face awash in horror. "That's what the help's for, dear."

"It doesn't hurt to make things a little neater."

Emmaline shooed her hands from the table, gesturing her back toward the living room. "Nonsense. Leave those things."

With her irritation spiking at the end of a long afternoon, Landry nearly snapped out that she was fine, until she thought better of the reaction. "You're right. We've barely had a chance to visit at all. What with Daddy dying I feel like I've been so wrapped up in my grief I haven't even tried to reach out."

Not that her aunt had made an attempt in return, but Landry decided to push it and see where it got her.

"Grief affects us all, darling." Emmaline perched next to her on the sofa. "Speaking of which, I didn't want to say anything in front of the company but how are things with your mother?"

"None of us has heard from her."

Emmaline's eyebrows rose, her lips pursing in distaste. "To think she might have killed your father, then left all of you here to fend for yourselves."

She knew her mother wasn't anyone's favorite. Heck, taking potshots at Patsy was a sport around Adair Acres, the result of long years of personal torture and abuse of all she knew and loved. But something in her aunt's tone had Landry's spine straightening up.

"She didn't kill my father."

Emmaline blinked, her bright blue trademark Adair eyes blank with confusion. "But she tried to kill Elizabeth. I simply assumed she was responsible for your father."

"That's an awfully big leap, Aunt Emmaline."

"Hardly."

She was prevented from saying anything by Rachel's arrival in the living room. Her best friend carried two glasses of wine, and she shoved one off on Landry with a wink before taking a plush chair opposite the couch. "We got all of Elizabeth's amazing gifts situated in her and Whit's wing. The room's nearly done and all these gifts will finish the nursery off."

"They've finished the nursery already?" Emmaline teetered on the edge of the couch. The tart, gossipy woman who'd sat next to her seemed to shrink before Landry's eyes. "Isn't it a bit early to do that?"

"The baby's arrival is only a few months away. I think they want to be prepared."

"Yes, but it seems a bit early to finish everything. What if—" Emmaline broke off as if catching herself. "Well, you kids nowadays. You like to be so prepared."

"Everyone's so excited. A baby on the way." Rachel sighed. "I can't believe how fast it's happened. It's all Noah's been able to talk about."

"My son's been talking about the baby?"

"Oh, yes." Rachel nodded and Landry could only sit there, amazed as her best friend worked her magic. "He's so happy here. And he seems really excited for Whit and Elizabeth."

"You'd never know it when I talk to him. I've been after him for simply years to settle down and give me grandchildren."

"And if he hasn't found the right woman yet?" Landry asked, curious as to the answer. She knew love hadn't been a huge priority in her father's generation, as evidenced by her parents' marriage as well as her aunt's. Although Emmaline's husband had died early in their marriage, she had to wonder if it was a love match.

"Love has its place, but so does moving on with your life. Growing up and having a family. Carrying on your family name." Emmaline's gaze narrowed on Rachel. "You say you've been spending time with Noah?"

"Yes." She nodded, her green eyes sparkling. "He's been helping me with my riding technique. And we've picked up a few rounds of golf at my club. You know how horrible I am, Landry, and if I don't get any better at it I just know they're going to kick me off my position on the hospital board."

Landry picked up on the charade, ready to keep it going when Emmaline interjected. "Do you care for my son, Rachel?"

"Of course. He's a great guy."

"Yes. But are you interested in him?"

"Well, I…" Rachel dropped her gaze, a small, shy smile edging her lips. "I do a bit. I mean, I would like to see it through if he were interested."

Noah's deep voice carried down the hall and Emmaline was prevented from saying anything else. For her part, Landry was near ready to hand Rachel a gold statue, her performance had been so incredible.

Noah stepped into the room, his head still damp from a shower, giving away how he spent his afternoon with Derek.

"Did you just get back from the stables?" Landry asked.

"After putting in a full and honest day's labor with your boyfriend." Noah winked before crossing the room to his mother. "I'm glad you're still here. I wanted to say hi before you headed back with Aunt Rosalyn and Uncle Sheldon."

"Where did they get off to?"

"Sheldon's terrorizing another round of dessert out of the kitchen and Rosalyn's still upstairs oohing and aahing over the nursery. I said hi before I started down."

"What's she going on about? She's got grandchildren. You'd think she knew what a nursery looked like."

"Mother." Noah took her hand in his, his voice gentle. "She's excited for Whit and Elizabeth."

Noah seemed to have a calming effect on his mother, and her acerbic tone faded as they spoke. "Of course she is."

Landry searched her memories for images of Noah

and Emmaline through the years. She had vivid memories of having Noah at the ranch, but her aunt, not so much. Although she had been much younger then, Landry recalled that her aunt had accompanied him on every trip to Adair Acres until he was of age. So why was it so hard to remember them all spending time together as a family?

"I'm going to go up and check on Kathleen. She's still recovering and today took a lot out of her." Landry made her excuses and used the opportunity to escape. She shot Rachel an apologetic smile but her friend's subtle nod assured her she could handle herself just fine.

The walk to the servants' wing took her through the security center, and she was surprised to find Derek in there, his head as damp as Noah's. "What are you doing in here? With the door open, no less?"

She closed it behind her. "What if someone finds you in here?"

"I told Noah I was here at your aunt's request."

Landry pushed herself off the door and took the seat next to him at the line of computer terminals. "Why'd you do that?"

"Because he asked. And I didn't tell him what we suspected about his mother, but I did tell him I was here to keep an eye on you. Kate's orders. He seemed relieved.

"He also figured out I wasn't a playboy globe-trotter."

"What was his first clue?"

Derek pulled her chair closer and closed his hands over the arms, effectively caging her in. "He said it was because you were actually interested in me. And if I was some wastrel globe-trotter you'd have kicked me to the curb by now."

She was as delighted by the observation as she was surprised. Noah obviously saw more than he let on, and the idea that he understood her ennui around the majority of men she'd dated was a bit of a wake-up call.

Perhaps she wasn't quite as hard to read as she thought. Or hoped. "What if he's right?"

"Then I think maybe I should press my advantage."

Derek pulled the chair closer until their knees touched. He closed the remaining distance and pressed his lips to hers, the warmth and security welcome after a day full of unsettling questions.

She sank into the kiss, open and ready for him, and marveled at how quickly she could lose herself in the amazing attraction that lived and breathed between them.

The moments spun out, as tender and sweet as cotton candy, and Landry gave herself the permission to simply sink into the pleasure that flowed so naturally.

A loud *ping* resonated from the desk, and Derek pulled back. "I'm sorry. Really sorry."

"What is it?"

"I'm waiting for some feedback from my contact at the field office. He's been looking into the power outage for me, running a bunch of diagnostics."

"Go ahead. Check it. It's important."

He pressed a quick kiss to her lips. "So are you."

Something warm and gooey settled itself in her chest, pushing out the ice that had settled there earlier while she observed her family.

Derek scanned the text message, then turned toward the computer. "He sent me a file to run on the machines. Are you okay if I do that?"

"Of course."

He grew quiet as he worked, his full focus on his task. Landry watched him, fascinated by the efficient way he moved through each step. Methodical and deliberate, he kept toggling back to his email as he completed each phase of the instructions.

"Two more steps and we should be good. Then John will have a full diagnostic of the machines here."

She let him work, content to simply sit by his side and breathe the same air. Which was as strange as it was wonderful.

"Can you call up your work files from here? Like the databases we looked at in LA?"

"Sure. They run a bit slower since the files are so large, but I have remote access. Why?"

"I'd like you to pull something up for me."

In moments, Derek had a familiar-looking visual coming up on screen. He shifted the image to the large viewing station above them and put in the various queries she requested.

"My uncle made a very strange reference to a baby they thought had died."

Fingers still, Derek shifted his focus from the screen. "A dead baby? Have you ever heard anyone say that before?"

"No, and that's what's strange. I've lived in my family home my entire life and never once have I heard any mention of a family member who lost a child or who almost lost a child." Landry hesitated. "He's also suffering from senility. It's gotten worse over the last few years, but it was fairly obvious today he's not all there."

"They say that more recent memories vanish first. If he's referring to Noah it would have happened when he was in the prime of his life, making very solid memories."

"True."

"What else did he say?"

Landry walked him through all the details of her conversation with Sheldon, curious to see how he used the questions to then shape the search queries he put into the system.

"Is Rosalyn the oldest?"

"Bucannon was actually the oldest. He's Kate's first husband. Then Rosalyn and Emmaline, in that order. My father was a bit of a surprise after they thought they were done having children."

"How many years' difference between him and his sisters?"

"Four or five, I think. I can nose around and find out."

"That's okay. We'll start there and then expand if we need to."

Derek worked through several search strings, the depth of information at his fingertips mind-boggling. "That's a lot of information."

"No one really lives off the grid anymore. They might think they do—or wish they did—but they don't."

"You'd think that would make your job easier. But from all you've said, it doesn't sound like it."

"It's a dimension that's gotten easier. We can learn a lot more about a suspect or a victim. Get a better picture of who they are and how they've lived their lives. But even with the technology, if someone doesn't want to be found, they can often find a way."

"Like my mother."

Mark kicked the dirty pallet at his feet, the bag of bones who lay there snoring like a lumberjack. "Wake up!"

"Wha?" Al grumbled before turning over again.

Mark thought about kicking him again, this time against his ribs instead of against the old mattress he slept on, but held back. The guy was doing a halfway decent job of keeping the kid occupied, and he'd have a hard time doing that with broken ribs.

Rena stared up at him from her spot against the wall. Her dark eyes bored into him with hatred that ran so deep it actually warmed his heart.

He'd done that. Had generated a reaction so hard and so deep she'd never be free of it.

Just like him.

Now all he needed to do was find a way to use it to his advantage.

"You didn't eat again."

"I don't like slop."

"It's fast food. What kid doesn't like fast food?"

"Me, that's who." Her little chin quivered, but the steady hate in her tone never wavered. "I want something fresh from the store. Fruit. Vegetables. Not fake meat."

Mark shrugged and pulled out the burger he'd bought for himself. She could suit herself and pretend she didn't want to eat. He'd leave behind what he bought for her and wouldn't be surprised if she worked her way around to it eventually.

"What do you want with me?"

Rena asked the same question every time he showed up to feed and water her and the dirtbag. He had to admire her persistence, even though there was no way he was risking telling her she was a pawn in a much bigger game.

"It's not about what I want with you. It's about what you can do for me."

"I ain't doing anything for you."

"Sure you are." He wadded up the empty wrapper from his burger and tossed it at her. "Just by being here you're doing something for me."

She stared at the ball of paper where it landed in her lap but didn't make a move to toss it back.

"Why don't you just kill me?"

He had to hand it to her, the kid had ice in her veins. "What fun would that be?"

"You think this is fun?"

"Baseball's fun. Se—messing around's fun. This is necessary. There's a difference."

"Does that mean you'll let me go?"

"I haven't decided yet."

Sure he had, but he wasn't letting her know. The kid could still be useful, and he needed her thinking she still had something to lose. It was basic Victim Psychology 101.

Tired of the chat, he got down to business. "I need you to write something for me."

"What if I don't want to?"

"Then I go over there and kick Big Al a few times until you do."

Her focus drifted to Al, then back to him. The softness he'd seen in her eyes for the older man faded when she met his gaze head-on. "Give me the paper."

"I've been looking into your mother. Nothing's popped yet. We know she used her passport to leave the country, but then the trail goes cold." Derek grimaced at the screen as he typed a few more commands.

"She vanished? Just like that?" Every time she thought she had a handle on the way Patsy betrayed the family, something rose up to slap at her again.

If her mother had vanished, it was because she'd meant to.

And if she'd meant to then that also meant she'd had an escape plan all along.

"Landry?"

"Hmm?"

"You okay?"

She waved a hand. "Sure. Nothing like realizing the woman who gave birth to you is a soulless monster who plotted for some length of time to leave you, never to speak to you again."

With a tight leash on her anger and disappointment, Landry continued. "Emmaline asked about her. Made a big show of acting concerned, but the censure underneath suggested my mother had killed my father."

"Have you prepared yourself for that?" Derek laid a hand against her cheek, tracing the bone with his thumb. "Others are going to think it, too. People with an interest in gossip and innuendo."

"They're already doing it. Why do you think I pared back my charity commitments as far as I have?" She leaned into his hand, the show of support so welcome.

And more needed than she ever could have imagined.

On a sigh, she closed her eyes, the pain of the past few months bubbling up in a witches' brew of frustration, anger and bone-deep weariness. "The thought of being whispered about like that? No, thank you."

"You aren't responsible for your parents' actions. And it would be a shame for those who benefit from the incredibly good work you do to lose out on that gift. Don't let anyone take that away from you."

He was right. She knew he was right. Funny how much it helped to hear it.

A pop-up window appeared on the screen, catching her attention. "Looks like the query's done running."

Derek called up the data, scrolling through key dates and names until he stopped and toggled backward. "There. Look right there."

The tip of his finger rested on the screen and she followed the paragraph he pointed to. "Adair invests in airstrip? What's that about?"

"It's from the late sixties. Your grandfather apparently decided to put some of his vast wealth into an upgrade for the greater Raleigh regional airstrip."

"I was small when he died, but I know he had a plane. Several, as a matter of fact. My father, too. At the risk of getting my snob on, it's sort of table stakes at a certain level. Besides, at the time my grandfather did this, there were few others who could have made such an investment."

Derek continued to scan the article, picking up on key elements. "It says here he wanted a small regional airport that could accommodate larger jets, capable of sustaining intercontinental flights."

"Which makes sense for his business."

"But it also means he had the private means to quickly get to Europe."

"He never made a secret of how much he loved London, Paris, Rome. He and my grandmother were jet-setters in the truest sense of the word, and they spent a lot of time away from home."

"His jets provide opportunity."

"Opportunity for what?"

"Opportunity to kidnap Jackson and whisk him out of the country."

Chapter 13

"Oh, come on. My grandparents kidnapping their own grandchild?"

Landry stood to pace, the momentary quiet vanished in the wave of what they'd discovered. "I know we put standard dysfunction to shame, but what you're talking about is just not possible."

"You've already taken the leap that Emmaline raised Reginald's son as her own. And we know she never left Europe during the time of his birth. How else did she get the baby?"

"I don't—"

He saw it the moment the truth registered. The pacing stopped as a connection painted her face in thoughtful lines. "That's why she was never around."

"Around where?"

"Earlier. I had a thought about when I was a kid. I

always remember Noah being around the ranch during the summer, but memories are fuzzier about my aunt."

"Did she send him here and go off on her own?"

"That's what's so odd. She came for every visit, but after thinking about it, I realized that she was always like this ghost in the background. Present, but sort of hazy and faded. She must have wanted to avoid all of us, especially my father, as much as she could, but she didn't want to let Noah out of her sight."

"She was probably scared your father might figure it out at some point and wanted to be able to run at a moment's notice."

"So why bring him at all? They spent much of Noah's formative years in Europe. They didn't need to be here."

Derek had spent his professional life dealing with the minds of criminals. While their choices often made no sense, there was an underlying sense of logic and order that made perfect sense to them. "Maybe it was guilt? Or a desire to give him some exposure to his father, even if Noah only ever understood his relationship to Reginald as uncle to nephew?"

"That still assumes we're right about this whole thing."

"I want to look into flight plans. The Adair family might have bought off the airstrip but there was no way they'd have been able to hide flight plans, especially internationally. If your grandparents did take the baby, there would be a record of them delivering him to Emmaline."

"Can you pull the plans now?"

"Maybe. The airport's small and I might have to call directly if I can't find it here in our files. Either way, we'll get our hands on the records from the window when Jackson was kidnapped."

Landry leaned back in her chair and swirled gently on the casters. "It's real, isn't it?"

"It appears that way."

"I've hoped. All along I've hoped we were somehow wrong about the whole thing. But if we're not…" She stopped swiveling. "If we're right we're going to ruin everything Noah's ever known. His whole life will not only be a lie, but it will be a lie perpetrated by his mother. Who does that?"

"A desperate woman."

She dropped her head in her hands, her voice muffled through her fingers. "You must think we're monsters. Crazy, insane, evil monsters."

"I don't think that."

Her head popped up, her normally cultured voice ragged, like she spoke around shards of glass. "How can't you think that? *I* think that and it's my family."

"You're not defined by your family, Landry. And neither are your brothers."

If she noticed that he lumped Noah into that category, she said nothing. She just shook her head, the tears that filled her eyes spilling over onto her cheeks.

"Do you know what I thought about today?"

The need to comfort was a living thing inside him, but when he reached for her, she shifted back, rolling away. He ignored the hurt that speared through his chest and focused on giving her what she needed instead. "What?"

"I'm hanging decorations and putting out food for my brother's wife's baby shower and I actually thought about what it would be like if I stole the baby." She waved a hand and rushed on. "Not because I actually want to steal the baby, but because I simply couldn't imagine any scenario where I'd consider that even remotely acceptable behavior."

"Desperate people do desperate things. And you're not desperate."

"But don't you see? This was what I spent my time thinking about at my nephew's baby shower. Not how much he was going to weigh or how many inches or even what day he might make his arrival. I thought about someone taking him. About Elizabeth and Whit spending their lives trying to find him."

She tried to hide her face from him, but Derek wouldn't be stopped this time. With one hand he kept a solid grip on the chair handle and pulled her close. "Landry. Look at me."

Tears had turned her vivid blue eyes into watery pools. The bright vivacity normally found there was nowhere in evidence, replaced by a horrified awareness she couldn't undo.

He knew that look. Had lived with it his entire professional career. It was the haunted look in the eyes of the people he worked so hard to save. That look drove him on, even when he had to pull from the very reserves of his soul to continue a case.

Before he'd felt compassion and an overwhelming sense of duty to restore order and justice to a life. But with Landry it was different.

With her, he wanted to share the burden.

She leaned forward and pressed her lips to his cheek, a kiss of thanks. Of understanding. And of something more…

"Stay with me." Her words whispered, featherlight, where she pressed her lips to his ear.

The secrets that swirled around Adair Acres nearly held him back. He cared for her, and he didn't want to take advantage of her situation. A situation that *would* have a resolution.

Her lips moved once more against his ear. "Make love with me because it's what we both want."

When he hesitated, torn between what he wanted and what he believed was right, she pushed on. "This is what *I* want, Derek. I want you. Forget all the reasons we shouldn't. Be with me. Just because."

He'd felt himself capitulating, but it was only when she said the last words that he knew he was lost.

"Yes."

Just because.

Landry heard the song lyric years ago, and it had always stuck with her. Do something for no reason other than because you wanted to.

She knew making love with Derek would add further layers to an already complicated situation. And sex always complicated things on the best of days.

But oh, how she wanted him.

And in the moment he pulled her close, his lips firm against hers, she knew the sweetest victory. "Yes."

The hands on either side of her chair shifted to her legs as he ran long, lazy strokes over her thighs. She kept her hands on his shoulders, reassured by the ready strength she found there. No matter what happened—and she knew there was so much they still had to navigate—this was absolutely right.

"Let's go upstairs."

He nodded before pressing his forehead to hers. "Let's go."

Their footsteps echoed on the Spanish tiles that made up the broad hallways of the ranch as they navigated the walk from the security center up to her bedroom. She expected that the path would be quiet and solemn, both of them well aware of the step they were about to take, when Derek tickled her ribs on the stairs. She turned into him on a muffled scream. "I'm ticklish!"

"I was hoping so."

He reached for her again, his hands grabbing at her waist to pull her close while he pressed a heavy line of kisses along her neck. The giggle in her throat faded to a hard moan when his fingers shifted up over her stomach before they feathered over one breast.

The thought abstractly crossed her mind that they might get caught, but the house that had been active all day was blessedly quiet and they made it to her room in a tumble of arms and legs as the door slammed behind them.

"Locking this, too."

She could only smile at his proprietary tone. "No one comes in without knocking."

"Let's just say I'm hedging my bets."

"Hedge away." She flicked a hand toward the tie that held her wrap dress together, but he rushed forward, gently removing her hand.

"Let me."

"Hedging your bets again?" The light tease drifted out on sultry tones, and she marveled that she was the one saying the words.

In the past she'd use that tone to manipulate a situation or to get what she wanted. How humbling and awesome at the same time to realize that teasing tone was only an additive to the giving and receiving of pleasure.

"No. Just reveling in the moment."

Then his large hands were on her, his dark, enigmatic gaze engaging hers, and Landry let herself fall. Golden light flooded the room, the tail end of a glorious spring day. The naturally bronze tones of Derek's skin grew darker, a captivating contrast to her own paler skin.

She ran a hand along the thick stretch of muscle that made up his biceps, trailing her finger down over the firm strength of his forearm. "I never did ask about your heritage. Gorgeous tanned skin like this looks natural."

"Cherokee. Amazingly enough, from both my parents. Quite by accident, they each decided to research their heritage and found each other in the stacks at a library in DC."

She smiled at that, the randomness of his parents' meeting juxtaposed with the clear evidence they were meant to be. "Life is funny that way."

"So it is."

"But it also explains a lot. The first morning I saw you riding on Diego, I could see you in my mind, galloping across the plains, the wind whipping your hair as you protected what was yours."

The image had only grown more pronounced as she'd spent time with him. He was a protector. A righter of wrongs. And for tonight, he was hers.

"It's a far cry from law enforcement."

"Oh, I don't know." She ran her fingers over his shoulders, unwilling to break even that simple contact. "Keeping the world safe smacks awfully hard of protecting what's yours. You're just painting on a much broader canvas."

"Thank you." His fingers slipped over the tie at her waist, tugging on the thin string.

She would have responded—would have found something sexy or flirty to say—but her breath caught once more at the reverent expression that suffused his face and turned his gaze dark with desire.

"I want you, Landry. I know your life's been a roller coaster, but I won't hurt you. I *will* protect you. And I promise, I will never hurt you."

"I know." She reached for his hands and glided them down to her breasts. "I trust you. With my body." She pressed a kiss to his lips, the tension in him still as strong as ever.

She sensed his hesitation, knew he struggled with what he perceived as his duty to her and her family. And knew that the only way she could finally convince him tonight was for both of them was to show him.

With a slight wiggle of her arms, she shed the wrap dress and felt the cool material slide down her back. When he shifted his hands to her waist, she reached back and unhooked her bra, slipping from the straps before the material floated on top of the dress.

With one last shift, she ducked from beneath his hands and shed her panties, one last piece of silk following the others.

"With my life, Derek. I trust you."

Whether it was her words or her actions—likely a combination of both—she saw the moment he acquiesced. When he finally acknowledged that what was between them could no longer be ignored.

His hands came around her, urgent and fiercely demanding. Landry allowed herself to be swept up—in the moment, in the man—and gloried when the dam on his self-control burst wide open. He crushed his lips to hers, their tongues dueling a battle for control.

"You're wearing too much." She already had her hands at his waist, material fisted, when he smiled and shifted away.

"I can do it faster."

"A challenge?"

"A fact. And—" The word hung there as he flipped his shirt off, then followed with his jeans and briefs all in one clean sweep. "I'm done."

Laughter, deep and rich, welled up in her throat. She'd expected power and strength when they finally made love, but she hadn't anticipated the laughter. It bubbled in her chest, spilling over in great, glorious bursts.

Derek moved up and pulled her into his arms. The strength of his body wrapped around her, while the proof of his desire pressed to her stomach and indicated how much he wanted her. "Don't you know it's bad form to laugh at a naked man?"

"I'll have to make it up to you." The laughter faded, but her smile stayed firmly in place. She reached between them and her hand closed over the thick length of him. She was rewarded with a sharp intake of breath as he pressed himself into her palm.

She worked his thick flesh in her hands, thrilled when his eyelids dimmed to half mast, pleasure rapidly taking over his self-control. The line of his jaw hardened as she put him through his paces, unwilling to let up.

Unwilling to give him any further opportunity to think.

Only to feel.

Murmured words floated between them. Echoes of need. Of want. And of a powerful desire neither could deny.

Derek gave her a few moments more before he reached down and stilled her movements, his breath exhaling on a hard rush. "You're driving me crazy."

"That's the whole idea." She nipped a quick kiss at his collarbone before drifting her lips along the sensitive line of his neck.

"Actually, you're killing me. Decimating me so I can barely stand."

She smiled against that sensitive skin. "I'll consider that the highest compliment."

Without answering, he twirled her in his arms, then lifted her in one swift move. "There's no way you get to have all the fun."

Landry felt the world tilt, the arms beneath her back and buttocks strong and sure as he carried her toward the bed. He laid her down with gentle movements, the sensation that she was precious quickly overpowering the aura of fun that had gripped both of them.

He treated her as though she was cherished, as though she mattered.

How had she never understood how important that was? Or how desperately she missed mattering to someone?

In their own way, her family loved her. Her brothers were fierce protectors who would do anything for her. But during this past week with Derek, he'd given her a gift beyond measure. He'd shown her what it meant to feel loved.

"What's the matter?"

Unaware of the tears until they spilled over, hot against her cheeks, Landry shook her head. "It's silly."

"Landry?" The haze of passion rapidly faded from his gaze, replaced by a very real concern in those dark depths. "What's wrong?"

"It's nothing. Nothing." She shook her head and tried to dash away the stubborn tears that continued to fall. "I think too much, that's all."

He kept his arm around her but laid them both back on the bed, face to face. "Please tell me what's wrong."

"Nothing. That's the problem. Absolutely nothing is wrong." A hard sob welled up and she tried to swallow it back. "And now I'm ruining this between us."

"You're not ruining anything."

"I'm certainly not helping."

Despite her rising embarrassment, he said nothing, just continued to hold her. She willed the tears back, swallowing around the hard knot in her throat before she spoke. "I'm crying because you look at me like I'm precious."

His arms flexed and tightened before he brought a hand to her chin, lifting her gaze to his. "Because you are. Precious and rare and incredibly special."

"Yes. But—" She broke off, well aware she'd ruined the mood between them and any chance of returning to the sexy, lighthearted passion that had carried them upstairs.

"But what?"

"Until a few moments ago, I'd never realized how rare that was. Or how rare it's been in my life."

"I know this can't make up for it, but you do realize that's their problem? That the inability to show love and affection rests solely on your family? Your mother and father. Your aunt. Your grandparents."

Landry knew he was right. And still the pull of a lifetime of inertia held her back. "I'm a part of that. Descended from that."

"Yet you've made yourself. And you make choices every day that prove you're not like them. From your charity work to your love of animals, you have chosen a different life. A different path."

The lure of what he promised pulled at her, more tempting than she ever could have imagined. "You make it sound so simple."

"Because it is." His gaze never wavered. Where in the past she might have thought that sort of intensity was too much, Landry found herself unable to look away.

"You make me feel things, and I'm not entirely sure what to do about it."

The smile filled his dark eyes first, before it spread to his lips. "If it makes you feel any better, I'm not sure myself."

Whether it was the smile, the words of support or the gentle honesty, she wasn't sure. But as she reveled in the glow of simple understanding, her sadness faded, replaced with a life-affirming need to be with him.

His arms were still locked around her, the two of them curled against each other on the bed. She used their proximity to reach out and run her index finger over his broad chest. His skin tensed wherever she touched, a live wire sparking under her explorations. When she reached a nipple, she ran the tip of her fingernail gently around the flattened edge, gratified by his sharp intake of breath.

"You really do kill me."

"I really do need you alive for this." Feminine anticipation filled her with a buoyant spirit. "Perhaps you could find a way to hold on?"

His hand came up and covered hers, flattening it against his chest. "I'll do my best."

Derek pulled her close, his lips finding hers once more, eager to pillage and plunder the rich depths of her mouth.

Had he ever seen such deep-rooted pain?

The thought drifted through Derek's mind, along with a healthy dose of anger, before he pushed them both away. There'd be plenty of time to analyze later. For now, it was enough to simply be with her. To make love with her and push the demons they both carried to the furthest reaches of their minds. What came before and what would come after had no place in this moment.

No place at all.

Hungry for her, Derek pulled Landry against him,

shifting their positions so he covered her body. She responded immediately, a small mewl of pleasure rumbling from the back of her throat as her long legs came up to wrap around his waist.

Heat assailed him, scorching his skin from the top of his head to the tips of his toes in every place they touched, and it took every ounce of willpower he possessed to remember the small packet in his jeans.

"Damn it." The curse came out on a hard moan and he reluctantly dragged himself from her.

"What's wrong?"

"I need to get something."

Awareness flashed, along with a broad smile. "End table. Top drawer."

He snaked out one long hand, gratified to find the condoms right where she promised. "You're amazing."

"I did a bit of advance planning when I was out running errands for Elizabeth's shower. I thought—" She broke off. "No. I hoped."

The emotions that had threatened earlier swamped him with a heavy sucker punch to the gut, and when he finally spoke, the words were a low whisper. "I hoped, too."

The packet disappeared between her fingers and he lifted up on his elbows to give her room to maneuver. She finished in moments, then guided him into her body, welcoming him home.

Derek stilled and took the moment to watch her as her body adjusted to his. And when he sensed she was ready—when he simply couldn't wait another moment for her—he began to move.

The emotional moments between them gave way to something raw and needy, both of them hungry for completion. He filled her and with each thrust, felt himself slipping further and further away.

Here there was no danger. No lurking threats. No unfinished assignments. In this moment, there was only Landry and the mind-numbing passion that had a grip on them both.

Her breathing quickened and her cries grew more urgent. He increased his pace, willing himself to hold on until he sensed she was near peak. And as a hard cry escaped her, her fingers flexed along his back. She pressed herself to him; he allowed himself to let go.

Chapter 14

Landry listened to the quiet sounds of Derek's breathing and let her mind float in long, lazy circles. She thought about the first morning she met him, his large form staring down at her as she finished her pool laps. Their horseback rides and their day in Los Angeles.

She even thought about the tense moments in the stables as they worked in tandem to eliminate the snake.

Had it really been less than a week? Less than seven days for him to walk into her life and make such an irrevocable place for himself it was hard to imagine life without him?

Her racing heartbeat had begun to slow, but at that thought—spending her life with Derek Winchester—it sped right back up. They'd had sex. Amazing, awesome, incredible sex. And if she had anything to say about it, they'd have quite a bit more.

But sex was different from permanence. He was here

to do a job and when that was over, he'd go back to his life, as would she. The two of them didn't have a relationship. They had a fake arrangement that was in place to expediently deal with whatever wasteland her family had managed to scorch over the past four decades.

Thinking otherwise would open up a world of emotions she would prefer stayed closed.

What she would take away was how he'd made her see herself. The encouragement and support inherent in who he was and how he saw others had given her a boost she didn't even realize she needed. If nothing else came out of their time together, she was grateful for that.

"You do realize your thoughts are louder than a marching band on the Fourth of July."

"Hmm?"

"I can hear you thinking." Derek pulled her close, wrapping his arms around her waist and drawing her back to his front. "And sex that amazing shouldn't include any thinking afterward."

"You're talking, which means you're thinking."

He pressed a kiss to her neck. "My brains have already leached out all over the pillow. I'm simply babbling incoherently until I manage to drum up a thought or two from whatever's still left."

"A woman's mind is never still."

"Pity." He kissed her neck again before snuggling into the crook between her head and shoulder, his hands traveling on a lazy exploration over her stomach before reaching up to cup one of her breasts.

Her earlier thought—to simply enjoy the time together—skipped its way through her mind as his hands worked magic over her skin. But when his thumb pressed over her nipple, shooting sparks to her core, she gave up her resistance.

There'd be time for thinking later.

Right now, there was Derek.

She turned in his arms, giving him better access to her body. He took full advantage, changing the direction of his kisses from her neck to shoulder to chest. When she thought he might drive her mad with the teasing flicks of his fingers in counterpoint to the erotic play of his tongue over her skin, his mouth closed over one nipple and she pressed into him on a hard cry.

Hot, wet suction dragged another cry from the very depths of her as an elemental sort of electricity began to swirl beneath her skin.

That wet heat continued to torment her as his hand drifted lower, back over her stomach before settling between her thighs. His clever fingers pressed against her core, igniting sparks she was helpless to resist. Ruthless, he drove her up, pushing her toward another release so soon after she'd come apart in his arms.

Shocked by her body's readiness, she clung to his shoulders and rode the current. Hard, churning waves buffeted her through the storm of pleasure, but he was her true north throughout. His big, strong body and the safety to be found with him, even as he pushed her toward the most vulnerable moment of her life.

And then she was tumbling, screaming his name, falling into the swirling storm.

Darkness had fallen while they slept and Derek awoke to the disorienting sensation of his phone's muffled ring. He normally slept with it near his head, so it took him a moment to realize it was across the room, tucked in the pocket of his jeans.

He disentangled himself from Landry's warm body,

her small sigh tugging at something deep inside him when she sprawled into his place on the bed.

The muffled phone rang once more before it went to voicemail, and he was tempted to leave it. Ignore whoever lay on the other end and wake Landry back up with an inventive series of kisses...

Heated images faded from his mind as duty stole in like a thief in the night. It might be Mark. Or a lead from his buddy at the office who was looking into the security breach at Adair Acres.

He was here on a job, damn it. How had he forgotten that?

Another glance at Landry, her naked back golden in the moonlit room, and he had his answer.

Landry Adair was the reason he'd forgotten.

She'd gotten into his system like an addictive drug, and now that he'd had a taste of her, there was no going back. No unremembering the moments in her arms. Or the taste of her skin. Or the generous way she shared herself fully in the act of giving and receiving pleasure.

His hand closed around the flat, rectangular shape of his phone and he fought to keep his mind on whatever issue had generated a call at almost eleven at night. He swiped through the screens and hit Voicemail.

Mark's frantic voice barked out words on the message.

He needed to come. Now. To the warehouse they'd staked out early on but thought was empty. The one down past LAX.

A vision of the abandoned space came to mind. The building had been between tenants when they caught wind it might have been a temporary home base for Rena's kidnappers before they moved her out of the country. He and Mark had spent a long week staring at the building's exit points, waiting for proof that their lead was sound.

All they'd gotten for it had been several days of stale coffee and a ten-point spike in their cholesterol levels from too many take-out burgers.

"I think we've found Rena!" The message disconnected on Mark's parting words and Derek moved into action. He knew he owed Landry and her family his attention, but he needed to be there in LA.

Needed to see this through and bring that young girl home.

"What's the matter?" Landry's voice drifted toward him and he turned from where he pulled his pants on. She sat up in bed, the sleep fading from her tone. "Where are you going?"

"I got a call. Well, a message." Images jumbled in his mind and he tried to find the right words to reassure, even as the need to leave as fast as possible gripped him. "Mark. He thinks he's found Rena."

"That's incredible." Landry was up and out of the bed, rushing toward him. She seemed oblivious to her nudity, instead crossing with speed and purpose. "Let's get down there."

"You can't go."

She stilled where she was, on her way to her closet. "Why not?"

"This is an FBI investigation."

"You can't go by yourself."

"Like hell I can't."

"Derek." She grabbed a robe off a hook on the door and slipped into it. "You haven't even talked to Mark. Where are you supposed to go?"

"I'll find it. She's at a warehouse we'd staked out early on."

"And you're just going to go barreling in there? With no backup?"

"Mark will be there."

"Then you're both fools."

Frustration punched holes in his patience and he lashed out. "Let me do my job, Landry."

"I'm not standing in your way. But even I know you can't go there unprotected. And where's your boss in all this? Shouldn't you talk to him first?"

"Mark's been keeping me informed on the side. My boss doesn't know I'm up to speed."

She stood before him, her hand on his arm. "Which makes this seem even worse. Why aren't you following protocol?"

"A young girl's life is at stake."

"So is yours." The gentle, soothing calm faded, replaced by a veritable taskmaster.

"And your coming with me is going to make that better."

"Let me at least drive you to headquarters. You're too close to this. I can get you there and you can call for information along the way."

"And risk having my boss get involved, pissed as hell I've been keeping tabs on this investigation?"

She stilled at that. "So getting the brass involved is less preferable to getting that girl home safely?"

"Yes." He dragged at his shirt, pulling it over his head as he tried to calm his thoughts. "No. No, of course not."

"It's over an hour to the office. Let me drive and you can make plans as we go. I promise I'll stay out of the way. But you can't go alone."

"I can and will."

"You don't have to do this alone. I'm offering help. Not to stop you from doing what's right but to make sure you can do what's right. Why won't you let me?"

Determination lined her features, firmly setting her

jaw. She wasn't going to be swayed, and the more time he spent allowing sparks of rational thought to leach into the urgent need to act, the more he knew she was right.

"You're a civilian, Landry. I can't take you into this."

"For the last time, I'm not suggesting you take me on an op. I'm suggesting you let me get you there so you can prepare for it properly."

He thought to argue—and wanted to—but she'd already walked off and disappeared into a closet so large it looked like another room.

It looked as if he had a ride-along partner, whether he wanted one or not.

Landry kept the pace steady as they drove ever closer to Los Angeles. She knew Derek was still mad—she had a good mad on herself—but she was also pleased she'd worked her way around it.

And she'd done it with honesty and direct action.

She'd spent years watching her parents. Their destructive relationship tactics designed to go behind each other's backs to constantly prove some sort of one-upmanship. It was only now, faced with the moment of actually disagreeing with Derek on something, that she realized just how poor an example had been set for her and her brothers.

There you go again, Landry-girl. Acting like this is some sort of real relationship.

But real or not, the man walked a dangerous path, and if left to his own devices, he'd have gone charging off mindlessly.

The very idea he'd go walking into something completely unprepared bothered her more than she wanted to admit. She knew the situation with this young kidnapped girl had wreaked havoc with his career and, she was increasingly coming to learn, his self-worth.

She had no idea it had damaged his judgment, as well.

"Why is this child so important to you?"

The question slipped out and she risked a glance at his profile as she drove, the oncoming headlights painting his face in a wash of harsh fluorescence.

Derek said nothing and she was almost convinced he wasn't going to say anything when he finally spoke. "I don't know."

"You're willing to risk your life for her. You must feel something."

"It's Rena, yes. I want to bring that child home and give her some quality of life. But it's also the idea of her."

Landry nodded, the underlying meaning of his words a strange echo for her thoughts earlier about Whit and Elizabeth's baby. She knew she'd love her nephew, but with all that was going on, that innocent baby had begun to represent something more.

The restoration of her family.

A new life for them all to nurture and help grow into the next generation of Adairs. A stronger generation, if she had anything to say about it.

"That child stands for all that's not right with the world around us. She's the reason I do what I do and she's the reason I hate that my very job even exists."

"Humans can do terrible things to each other."

"Terrible, horrible things. And as long as they do, it's my job to make sure I can save as many as possible."

His comments matched the very same strains he'd mentioned earlier when he finally told her about Rena. But still, she sensed that wasn't the entire story.

"Isn't there something else?"

"Maybe she's—"

Derek was an action-oriented man—she'd witnessed it several times over the past week—so it was odd to see him hesitate.

"Rena's kidnapping forced me to look at my life differently. Where I was going. What I wanted. Who I wanted to share it with. People talk about cases that are turning points in their life, and this case has been one for me."

"Sarah?"

"Among other things."

"What happened?"

"Hell, Landry!" His voice bounced off the confines of her SUV, even the high-end leather not thick enough to absorb his upset and pain.

She wanted to lash out. Might have even a week ago. But she was a different person now. The woman who had stripped away every defense—every pretense—in this man's presence had changed. And she'd grown into someone who expected the same in return.

A wash of oncoming headlights lit the interior in harsh detail while highlighting a sign indicating they were about thirty miles outside Los Angeles.

Thirty miles until he headed straight into danger.

"Damn it." He shifted in his seat, his large shoulders rocking the back of it as he maneuvered.

"Damn. It." He muttered the words once more before he turned to face her, twisting against the confines of his seat belt. "How can you ask me questions about Sarah when we were in bed an hour ago?"

"It's a simple question."

"No, actually, it's not."

Now it was her turn to shrug. Yes, she wanted to know more about the mysterious Sarah, but she also wanted him to know he had a safe space to share. Whatever had come before they met, Derek had made it more than clear he wasn't in love with his ex-fiancée any longer. Landry knew most women would still find the circumstances a threat, but strangely, she didn't.

"She's a good part of the reason this situation with Rena is so upsetting to you. Whatever else might have come between us this past week, I hope you consider me a friend."

"Of course I do." And then, "I consider you more than a friend."

"So talk to me."

"You are persistent."

"I'm an Adair. It comes with the territory."

"You don't say."

When she made no move to say anything further, he let out a small sigh. "I never saw the signs. Not once until it was too late. I think that's the part I can't quite get past."

She caught the tense set of his body from the corner of his eye. How he shifted against the seat once more, hands clenched into hard fists on his knees.

"Relationships come and go, and while I was planning on making a life with her, it's not the relationship itself I'm upset about." A hard laugh rumbled from his chest. "Which is part of the problem, I'm sure."

"What signs didn't you see?"

"How unhappy she was. How she resented my job. How she quietly and deliberately tried to manipulate me day after day. I was oblivious to it all."

"Relationships are hard. And we all check out from time to time. Sometimes it's easier that way. To let the things you don't like swirl around you while you focus on the other things in your life you can control." She reached out and laid a hand on his arm. "I've dubbed it the Landry Adair Relationship Method. It's been rather effective up to now."

"Don't sell yourself short. I think you've done an incredible job with what you've had to work with." His hand crossed his body to cover hers, the gesture warm and intimate in the darkened car. "Besides. I'm a cop. I should have seen the signs and known how to deal with the situation."

"Ah, yes." She nodded sagely, and purposely pushed bite into her tone. "The Derek Winchester Relationship Method. My profession makes me bulletproof and nothing can hurt me."

"Landry—"

The traffic was light, not a car nearby for hundreds of yards, so she risked a glance his way. "Am I wrong?"

"It's not the same."

"Oh, hell, Derek. It's all the same. Life. Relationships. Human interaction. It doesn't suddenly get easy because you have a certain job or a given amount of cash in your bank account. Life's hard and we all deal with our own fair share of crap."

She slid her hand from his arm, tired of trying to make him see reason. Whatever pain he carried, he was obviously more content to hold it close and allow it to continue eating away at his soul than to get help or share the load.

A dull wash of gray reflected back at them through the windshield as Landry pulled up to a warehouse several blocks down from the one he and Mark had targeted. The dynamics of the area changed block by block, and he knew this corner to be one that was well maintained by the building owner, who also believed in a strong security system. He'd made peace with Landry coming along, but there was no way he was putting her in the line of fire.

An unmarked car sat down the street and Derek knew it to be one issued by the department for sting operations. Even with the seventy-five yards that separated them, the car's inhabitants could be there in a moment if needed.

His gaze drifted over the woman next to him. Strong. Sure of herself. And altogether too determined to have her own way. She'd refused to be shaken off, and he'd already exacted a promise that she'd go straight to a hotel room that had been prearranged and wait for him there.

Anxiety aside, if he were honest with himself, he had to admit her cool head and reasonable logic back at Adair Acres had rung true. The car ride up had given him time to call Mark and work through the details of the operation.

The end of the ride, however, had been a different story.

Was the woman mad?

How could she ask him questions about another woman when he could still feel the heat between the two of them branding his skin? They'd made love for hours and she wanted to know about his ex-fiancée?

Worse, she wanted him to talk about where he'd gone wrong with his relationship. How he'd ignored the signs, or worse, didn't even bother to look at how unhappy Sarah was. Instead, he'd been content to live his life and drag another person along the path of his life choices.

Sarah had hated his life as an FBI agent. Oh, she enjoyed telling her friends what he did, but beyond that, she resented his time in the field. His time away from her.

How had he missed that?

He knew plenty of people who juggled a life in the

Bureau with marriages and families. At one time, he thought himself capable of the same, but now...

Now he wasn't quite so sure.

The Rena Frederickson case had put more into focus than just his career. Maybe that was why, on a visceral level even he couldn't describe, he needed to save this child. For her own life and future, yes.

But somehow she'd become the redemption for his.

"Do you have what you need?"

Landry's voice pulled him from his thoughts. That Zen place he always went to before an op where the things around him faded away, replaced by a focus on what he needed to accomplish. "I've got it all."

His sidearm was in its holster against his ribs, and he knew Mark had an arsenal of backup already with him. With the added men Mark had worked to line up, Derek knew they were set.

"I'm good."

"Then I'll let you get to it."

The limited lighting in this part of town kept the SUV fairly dark, but there was a sliver of moonlight that filtered through her driver's-side door, reflecting off the blond strands of her hair.

Since they'd already agreed she'd wait at one of the luxury hotels downtown, he focused on that simple bit of reassurance. She'd be safe as soon as she drove away. Away from the wash of darkness that had clouded his life for far too long.

"I'll have Mark bring me back to the Bureau when we finish the op and then we'll come to the hotel after we get everything filed. Try to get some sleep as it'll probably be around ten or eleven tomorrow morning before we've got everything wrapped up."

"I'll see you then." She closed the gap between them

and pressed her lips to his. The quiet of the car closed around them like a cocoon, and for the briefest moment, Derek allowed himself to sink into her.

He'd been unable to resist her, but in that moment he needed her with a raw hunger that sent a shiver of fear through his midsection.

When had he gotten so vulnerable?

Landry lifted her head and pressed a hand to his cheek. "Be careful."

Although it was dim, a small swath of light reflected from a street lamp at the end of the block. The angle of the beam framed her gaze and he took the moment to stare into those bright blue depths.

Derek braced for the thinly veiled censure that he was leaving, but all he saw was support.

He slipped from the car, unable to spend another moment waiting. He needed to focus on the op. On the need to protect and defend and finally—*finally*—bring Rena Frederickson home.

Landry drove off as they'd planned and Derek waited, watching the back of the car until her taillights faded fully from view. He'd deliberately selected their stopping point because it put her two simple right turns back to the freeway. She was a competent woman who knew where she was going, and he had to trust she'd find her way.

He'd also reassured himself by punching the hotel address into her GPS, reviewing every prescribed turn on the navigation system in advance.

Landry would be fine. And when he picked her up tomorrow they'd figure out what to do with the rest of their lives.

A hard breath caught in his throat as that image took root.

The rest of their lives.

When had he started thinking about her in terms of something permanent?

And with another dose of reality crashing in, he had to admit it was about ninety seconds after he met her, her blond hair slicked back as she stared up at him from the pool. Even now, he could picture it as vividly as if he were standing there. Sun backlit her features, framing her like a goddess rising from the pool as rivulets of water ran over her face and chest and down her impossibly long legs.

She was beautiful. And in all the moments since, he'd seen how her external beauty was dwarfed by the woman she was inside.

Her care for her family and friends. The focus, attention and devotion she lavished on the charities she was involved with. Even her fierce protection of her mother's name, despite her very real acknowledgment that Patsy didn't deserve it.

Landry Adair was amazing.

And he loved her for all of it.

That sense of vulnerability slapped at him once more but Derek pushed it back. He'd thought himself in love before, only to discover it was a mirage of poor expectations and veiled frustration.

What he had with Landry was different. Her willingness to bring him here was only one example that set her apart. And set apart what they felt for each other.

With one last glance in the direction she'd driven away, Derek shifted his focus inward. He might have just had the revelation of his life, but it was time to do what he'd come for.

There'd be time soon enough to tell Landry how he felt.

The target location was about a hundred yards away

and he kept to the shadows, walking against the outer walls of each building between his drop-off point and the warehouse entrance. He patted the tools in his pockets and sensed the reassuring weight of his gun under his arm and another piece strapped to his leg.

Satisfied with his preparations, he moved on to the next phase. An image of the building's layout filled his mind's eye. Mark said their intel pinpointed Rena on the first floor behind a row of old office cubicles.

Derek kept that image firmly in place and slipped into one of the building's required fire exits. The door had already been identified as a weak spot on their first reconnaissance, and it only took him a few minutes to work his pick tools before a hard snap on the frame finished the job.

A light breeze wafted over his neck, chilling him.

They were almost done.

An eerie stillness descended over him as he moved through the back side of the warehouse, gun in hand. Large, dirty windows filtered what little light was outside, but it was enough to give him a dim picture while his eyes further adjusted to the interior of the building.

The layout was much as he remembered, and he passed several rows of abandoned cubicles. The fabric that lined each cubicle showed its wear, the evidence of rodents chewing through the cloth visible in the frayed fabric and small holes at the base of the various frames he passed as he moved.

When he reached the end of a row, he stilled, doing his level best to orient himself to wherever Rena might be. While he knew there wouldn't be a parade in his honor, he expected some sort of noise, even if it were just the muffled noises of her sleeping.

But no matter how hard he strained, his body still,

he couldn't detect a bit of sound that indicated another human was anywhere in the vicinity.

Another frisson of unease skittered over his skin and he glanced back the way he came. The door had been awfully easy to get through, and the lack of noise persisted. More than the lack of noise, the overarching stillness of the space felt unnatural.

He slipped a small, high-powered flashlight from his pocket and swung it low, illuminating layers of dirt and animal droppings on the floor. The evidence of such filth added a layer of anger over the anxiety and he fought to keep his calm. He'd do Rena no good to get upset now.

There would be plenty of time for anger later.

He kept tight to the cubicle wall and knew he'd pass one more row before he hit the wall of physical offices. Rena would be there.

She had to be there.

On the signal he and Mark had practiced, he tossed a beam up toward an exterior wall of windows, flashing three times. The tomblike stillness wrapped around him as he waited for Mark's response.

Nothing.

He waited, counting off his breaths, then flashed the signal once more.

After several beats, again. Nothing.

An image of Landry wavered before his eyes. She was waiting for him. She expected him to come back. To meet her at the hotel tomorrow morning so they could drive together back to Adair Acres.

Even with the image of her pulling him like a lodestone back the way he came, he pushed himself forward. Toward the wall of offices and the child he knew was there. In life or in death, he needed to go to her. Needed to see for himself.

He stepped forward, his only focus on the office door that sat ajar halfway down the hallway. It was the only reason he stepped into the pool of blood that lay around the scrawny figure of Big Al Winters.

Chapter 15

Time passed in a blur of action and image. Derek dropped to his knees to check for Al's pulse, knowing full well he was too late. The body was still warm, but all evidence of life had drained along with the man's blood.

Derek screamed for help, the remembered protocols flashing through his mind as he hollered out the commands for all clear and victim down, before he searched for the gunshot.

He found two neat, clean holes at the chest and throat.

The shots were precise—and lined up in a familiar pattern—and he stilled a moment to simply catalog the wounds for himself before moving on to the rest of the body.

Al was obviously unarmed and by the look of him, hadn't washed in days. Derek shifted away from the body, determined to investigate the rest of the warehouse. It was only when he glanced down to find himself covered in blood that he stilled.

There was no way they'd recover any additional evidence if he layered the place in bloody footprints.

So he waited.

And watched as Mark came through the door first, gun drawn.

"All clear!" Derek hollered the words, his hands up so Mark would connect the words with the body language. He waited and saw the moment his partner shifted from on guard to aware.

A pained expression filled Mark's face, his eyes dark with worry. "Why the hell didn't you wait for me?"

Derek lowered his arms, his movements slow as the others began spilling in the doors. "Why did you miss my signal? I flashed it several times, just like we arranged."

"Signal? I've been waiting outside for you for the last hour. There was no signal."

Mark was waiting?

Derek ran through the moments when he flashed his light at the exterior windows. He'd made the signal, then waited. Then he'd made it again.

He *knew* he had.

Their team lead, Leo Manchester, came in and took his place behind Mark, interrupting Derek's mental backtrack through the past several minutes. "Winchester. You okay?"

"Fine, sir."

Lines carved deep into the man's face as he held up his free hand in a gesture to stay. His other still held a firm grip on his pistol. "Don't move. Techs are coming right behind."

As several of his Bureau mates flooded in behind Mark and Leo, Derek willed himself to stand still.

And hoped like hell he hadn't just become a sitting duck.

* * *

Landry flipped through the file she'd stowed in her purse, ever hopeful something new would reach out and grab her from the papers. Not that it had so far.

She shook her head, trying to remove the lethargy and cross-eyed exhaustion reams of paperwork could cause in a person. The hours had ticked off the clock with aching slowness, matched only by the tedium of working her way through page after page of government documentation.

She and Derek had reviewed the files they'd printed at the FBI as they'd been able, but always in bunches, stack by stack. When the idea hit her the night before— to lay the papers out in hope of finding a pattern—she'd believed it worth a try.

Now?

She'd finally accepted the fact that she'd spent the better portion of eight hours engaged in a vain attempt to find patterns that simply didn't exist. Add on a vat of black coffee and all she had to show for her time was a case of the jitters and considerably more familiarity with her family tree.

Life events. News clippings. Flight plans.

Each report was yet another piece of evidence defining her family over the past century like a mini film rolling before her eyes.

She reviewed the photo of her grandmother in her Irish lace wedding gown and could picture the same gown where it was preserved behind glass on a dressmaker's dummy in the family house in North Carolina.

A news report announcing the initial public offering of AdAir Corp, her father's proud smile reflecting up at her from the page. The same photo still sat, framed in his old office, a lone hundred-dollar bill set off beneath the image signifying AdAir Corp's first earnings as a public company.

And then there was Jackson's birth announcement, memorialized in a Raleigh newspaper. The notation of his parentage—Reginald and Ruby—and a photo of the two of them leaving the hospital in Raleigh. Some enterprising photographer had expected that the couple might be worth something someday and had camped out to grab the shot. He'd had no idea his photo would become one of the centerpieces of a kidnapping investigation a mere three months later.

Landry rubbed at her arms and dragged the comforter around her shoulders.

Her family records. But were they really the key to uncovering family secrets?

Although her grandmother had died when she was small, she tried to conjure up some memories in her mind. A sleek woman, Eleanor Adair had prized her standing as one of the leading socialites in Raleigh. She'd married into the Adair family to cement that position and ensure she birthed the next generation of Raleigh society.

On the rare occasions they had spent time together, Eleanor had kept them all at a distance. Landry remembered a summer visit when the head cook had sneaked her, Whit and Carson Popsicles and her grandmother nearly fired the woman on the spot for allowing the children on the "good sofa."

Could that vain, vapid woman really be behind it all? Had she stolen from one child to give to another? And to what end?

Landry's gaze fell on the clock and she registered the time. It was ten already?

She'd expected to hear from Derek by now.

The urge to shoot him a quick text was strong but she

had no idea if even the vibration of his phone might alert someone to his presence, so she held back. She vowed to call the FBI in another fifteen minutes if she didn't hear from him.

She sifted through the pile on the bed, digging once more for the articles about her grandmother. The memories of Eleanor had left a funny aftertaste, and she was curious if the woman was as brittle and emotionless as she remembered.

The stack of newspaper announcements she'd placed together earlier—weddings, births, deaths—were in easy reach and Landry flipped through them.

Eleanor's engagement to Baxter Adair. The requisite wedding photos that took up what had to be the entire section of a newspaper at that time. The announcement of Bucannon's birth, followed by Rosalyn's and Emmaline's and then her father's.

She flipped to the last page and found the photos of Emmaline's wedding. Her late husband, Nicholas Scott, stared back from the photo, his hands entwined with Emmaline's.

At the image staring back at her, Landry stilled, Georgia's words coming back to her.

Georgia had believed Noah bore a shocking resemblance to Ruby's late father. A resemblance that was more than evident in photos, which had tipped Georgia off to the possible connection.

And the photo she held in her hand showed nothing similar between Noah and the man everyone believed to be his father. Noah had the Adair blue eyes but he had dark blond hair. No one in the Adair family was blond unless it came out of the bottle, and Emmaline's late husband had dark hair that looked almost black in the photo.

On a frustrated sigh she crossed to the dresser and gave herself a good once-over in the mirror.

It could be a coincidence.

Hair color changed as people aged. Heck, she knew that as well as anyone, since she paid good money for the blond that highlighted her hair. But still…

She twirled a lock of her own hair—dark with blond highlights—and considered the photo on the bed. Noah had a fresh-faced, all-American look about him that didn't mesh with Nicholas Scott's darker European looks.

The connection was skimpy, but it was valid.

Her gaze alighted on one of the other stacks she'd piled up and she dug through, suddenly curious about the birth certificate she'd flipped past earlier.

"Noah, Noah, Noah," she muttered as she worked her way through the stack. "There!"

The birth certificate was in French, the dates reversed in the custom Europeans used. Date first, followed by month and then year.

"Oh, no." Landry scanned the papers once more, her gaze skimming over the dates. "Aunt Emmaline. What did you do?"

Derek sat in the interrogation room, his earlier expectations ringing like a haunting reminder in his mind. He'd been in here for hours, various members of the department taking shots at him with endless questions.

"Walk me through it again, Winchester."

"Damn it, Leo, I've walked you through it. Several freaking times already. Big Al was dead when I got there."

"So how did you end up with all his blood covering you?"

"I came upon him by surprise. You were in there.

You saw how narrow the cubicles were and the position of the body."

Leo shook his head. "You walked into a dead guy? Come on, Derek. You haven't been on leave that long. You know protocol. Procedure."

"And I also know my partner was supposed to have my back and he didn't."

"Yet you went in anyway."

Derek saw the corner he'd painted himself into and focused on his rationale. "Rena's been missing for months now. We owe it to the kid to find her."

"And you owe it to your teammates and yourself to follow the correct procedures designed to keep your ass safe!" Leo slammed his fist onto the table. "Why the hell didn't you wait? Now I've got one of my best agents at the scene of a crime, with a man he's already shot once, gun in hand and blood all over him, and a pattern of bullet holes you're known for."

The adrenaline that had sustained him throughout the long hours of questioning kicked in, drawing on a reserve Derek didn't even know he had. "Excuse me?"

"The bullet holes. The throat and chest. On the vic."

"Yes?"

"It's signature Derek Winchester. All the way back to your days with the Secret Service. Your shots are meticulous."

A terrible cold began to spread through his body, numbing him to his core, and the strange sense of familiarity he had while examining the vic came back to him in full force. "I didn't shoot Al, Leo."

"You had every reason to. You didn't follow procedure. No one was there with you. And the vic bore your signature shot pattern."

"He died at the hands of someone else. All I did was find the guy. And where were you all, anyway?"

"Us?" Derek saw the spark leap into Leo's eyes and knew he needed to tread carefully. When had this gone so far south?

"All of you. Mark wasn't where he was supposed to be. And hell, no one else was where they were supposed to be, either. You guys were parked across from the warehouse and never even showed up until you followed behind Mark."

"We weren't across from the warehouse."

"Of course you were. I saw the department issue when I pulled up."

"What department issue?" Leo pushed forward, his body vibrating with sudden interest. "We weren't there, Winchester."

The cold in his veins receded, replaced by the sudden kindling of anger and betrayal.

Where was Mark in all this?

Mark had given him the intel. Mark had worked through all the logistics with him on the drive up from Adair Acres. And Mark had arranged tonight's drop.

Derek glanced toward the two-way mirrored glass, then caught Leo's eyes. He reached for the notepad at his elbow and scribbled a quick note.

So who was at the warehouse?

Derek was still shaking a half hour later as he sat in Leo's office. He'd finally been given leave to call Landry. A vague sense of shame tugged at him as she was ushered into Leo's office and he tried to push it away.

He hadn't done anything. Yet here he was, stuck in his boss's office waiting for her, unable to leave on his own.

"Derek!" She launched herself at him, her arms wrapping tight around his midsection. She'd asked minimal questions on the phone but he could see that the lack of information had shaken her. Her face was pale and he heard a distinct quaver beneath her words. "What happened? Are you okay?"

"Fine. I'm fine." He leaned in and pressed his lips to her ear. "I'm sorry to do this to you and I'll explain it later, but you need to follow my lead. Nod if you understand."

She pulled back, her eyes wide with concern, but she nodded, the move nearly imperceptible.

"Landry. Let me introduce you to my commanding officer, Leo Manchester."

The two of them worked their way through introductions and it was only when Leo sat behind his desk, his hands folded, that Derek saw the realization kick in as it covered Landry's face in subtle surprise.

She wasn't here for a polite series of introductions.

"Miss Adair. Do you mind if I ask you a few questions about last night?" When she only nodded, Leo pressed on. "I understand you accompanied Derek into the city last night."

"Yes. He's been a guest in my home and when he got the call to come into the city, I told him I'd drive him while he worked on his preparations in the car."

"That was awfully generous of you."

She shrugged, but she never broke eye contact. "I care for Derek. I wanted him to be safe."

"And you thought you could keep him safe?"

"I hardly think a trained FBI agent needs my protection. But I did think he could use the help I was capable of offering, namely a ride."

The two bantered back and forth and, to her credit, she never wavered from her story.

Nor did she back down.

Whatever questions Leo threw her way, she answered back in kind. But it was the last that had Leo stilling in a mixture of surprise and shock.

"Look, Agent Manchester. Perhaps I've been a bit too delicate. Derek and I are in a relationship. We spent last evening together and were, in fact, together when he got the call. I care for him and I refused to see him go alone. Nagged him about it until he gave in, as a matter of fact."

"Were you aware Derek was heading into a confrontation with a man he shot not too long ago? A shooting that was responsible for his current leave of absence from the Bureau."

"Yes, I was."

"Yet you were willing to help him?"

"It was my understanding that Derek's been focused on saving a young girl's life. That's what I was helping him to see through to fruition."

"I think Miss Adair has been rather accommodating, Leo. Are you done with her?" Derek said.

"Actually, I think I can resolve this misunderstanding." Landry laid a hand on his arm. "I don't know why I didn't think of it sooner. My car has the latest in GPS technology. Derek punched in the coordinates for me to the hotel and hit Start on the navigation instructions. There's a time stamp there that should be easy enough to verify."

The slightest smile played about Leo's lips before he nodded. "If we can get your permission on that, I can have a tech check it out and get you on your way." Leo's gaze was pointed. "Both of you on your way."

Derek hadn't managed to shake the vague sense of embarrassed shame that had dogged him since Landry arrived at headquarters, but he'd added frustration and anger to the mix.

What had Mark been thinking?

If Derek were honest with himself, he knew Mark didn't live and breathe the job like he did. Hell, few people lived and breathed the job like he did, and Derek had accepted long ago that wasn't a shortcoming in others.

"You haven't said much." Landry took a sip from a diet soda she'd picked up when they stopped for fast food for the drive back. Her half-eaten burger still sat in the console between them, neatly wrapped.

"I've got a lot on my mind."

"That seems to be going around."

The dry notes of her voice faded into the space between them like dust. "Want to talk about it?"

"Yes, but I want to hear what happened first. I played along with your boss but I want to hear it from you."

"Would you believe me if I said I don't know?"

"Yes."

That one word—sincere and absolute—did more to assuage the roiling storm inside than anything else could have.

She believed in him.

The same clarity that had assailed him as she drove away from the drop site came back once again and he reached for her hand. She linked their fingers, and the physical show of support was as welcome as her simple words.

Words. Actions.

The thought stuck—took root—and Derek turned it over in his mind. Mark's words didn't match his actions. And as he sifted through the past few months in his mind, he realized that Mark's actions had been off for a while.

"Come on, Derek. Walk me through it. Explain it and maybe it will make more sense to you, as well."

The retelling of the previous evening took nearly the entire drive to Adair Acres. Landry had stayed quiet throughout, stopping him only a few times to ask questions. And as they drove through the gates that bore the double *A*s, Derek was surprised to realize how therapeutic it was to talk through the events with someone else.

"Thank you."

"For what?" The afternoon sun was high and she shielded her eyes as she drove down the long, winding driveway.

"You made me walk through it, step by step. Leo was so busy pressing for details it made it impossible to think through the small impressions that mean as much as the large ones."

"There's something else." Landry nodded before pulling into a space near the garages. She turned toward him and took his hands in hers. "Rena wasn't there. I think you need to accept that she might be gone."

The swift sucker punch to the gut had him dragging his hands away as her words stole into his mind like a thief. "We just haven't found her yet."

"Derek. Look at the circumstances. That child's been used as bait, but have you really seen her?"

"Mark's got intel that has put her in each of the locations we've monitored."

"Mark. There you go with Mark again. Why the hell can't you see he's the problem? Did you gather the damn intel yourself?"

"He's my partner. I trust him to gather as much of the information as I do."

"But you haven't gathered anything since you've been on leave. It's been all him."

Derek slammed out of the car, his frustration mounting to the point he needed out of the SUV.

He knew Landry wasn't responsible for the situation he found himself in. He was still figuring out exactly how *he* himself was responsible for all the strange twists and turns that had sent the Frederickson case off the rails. But he also knew he didn't need her poking holes in the things he was sure of.

"I'm on a leave I didn't ask for, playing babysitter, so I've used the resources at my disposal. Namely my partner."

The babysitter arrow was out of the quiver before he could pull it back, and now he had to watch it pierce Landry's chest. Something cold and dark settled in her vivid blue eyes, turning them to ice. "I wasn't aware I was such an imposition."

"Damn it, Landry—" He broke off, well aware he had no excuse for the remark.

Or the bad behavior.

"The remark wasn't directed at you."

She put up a hand as he moved closer. "I'm not interested in talking to you right now."

Her body language was an even more effective deterrent than her words and Derek took a step back.

"I need to take care of some responsibilities this afternoon. I'll see you at dinner."

"Of course." He knew an apology was in order, but he also had the good sense to know it wasn't going to be well received, so he let her walk away.

She'd nearly reached the kitchen entrance to the house when she stopped and turned. "Whatever he once was, that man is not your partner."

* * *

Mark parked the government-issued piece he'd restored in the garage he rented for storage. The thing was a pain to maintain, but it sure did come in handy.

Just like last night.

He'd left the car in a visible place and knew Winchester would take the bait. Backup. *Yeah, right.*

He still couldn't believe how smooth and easy things had gone. The frantic calls, setting up the op. Even dragging Big Al to the warehouse hadn't taken too long. The guy had struggled but he'd managed to subdue him.

Headquarters had taken longer than he'd have liked but all in all, even that went according to plan. Leo had chewed him out for giving Derek intel on the case when the man was supposed to be on leave, blah, blah, blah.

Whatever.

Fortunately the death of Big Al had provided a sizable diversion and the ass whipping had been minimal. His airtight story and the manufactured notes he'd created on the case had helped seal the deal.

Just doing my job, boss. Can I help it Winchester's obsessed with the Frederickson case?

Obsessed was right. And that obsession was going to be the end of Derek Winchester.

He pulled out his phone and hit Sarah's number. The soft strains of her voice lit him up inside, tightening his gut with need. "Did you hear anything? I've been so worried."

"Sorry it took me so long to call. It was a bad night, babe."

"What happened? Is it Derek?"

The ball of need that pulsed for her, desperate to make her his own, morphed into something raw and ugly. "Derek's in trouble, Sarah."

"What happened?"

"He shot the perp. The one we've been after for Rena. Killed the poor sucker."

"What?"

He walked her through his version of the story—the same one he'd shared with the office brass—adding his own concerns about Derek's mental health in this re-telling.

"I don't believe it."

"Come on, Sarah. We've talked about this one. Derek's out of control and his vengeance over that kid knows no bounds."

"Has she been found yet?"

Mark imagined his next stop and caught himself be-fore the smile on his face could reflect in his voice. "No. Not yet. Perp keeps playing us with just enough infor-mation to get excited."

"And now there's no perp."

Her use of the word was a surprise. Normally she shunned any and all police talk, so the question had him stumbling. "No, there's not."

"What about the people he works with?"

Mark forced a light tone, well aware the seething in his gut would come through if he didn't play his com-ments correctly. "When did you suddenly get so inter-ested in this case?"

"I'm not. I mean—" She broke off. "I've just had a lot on my mind."

"Want to tell me about it?"

"It's just…I've been so alone lately. And I can't help wondering if I made a mistake."

"Mistake?" A hard bite edged his words and Mark fisted his free hand on his knee, willing the anger out of his voice.

Mistake?

When the hell had she suddenly changed her mind?

"Well, yeah. I mean, I know Derek wasn't there for me but, well, maybe I was too hasty."

"And his mental health? Are you willing to simply overlook that?"

"Ye… No." She wavered before speaking again. "No, I'm not."

"The Bureau's a tough life when you make it your whole life. Derek didn't put you first, and you deserved to be first."

"You're right. I know you're right." Sarah heaved out a heavy breath, her voice stronger when she spoke. "Of course you're right."

"You want me to come over?"

"Not tonight, I'm tired. It was a long day at school and the kids were a bit out of control with spring fever. Want to meet for a movie this weekend?"

"I'd like that."

Mark disconnected after their promise of where to meet. Although their meeting was a bright spot, her sudden softening over Derek was a concern. He was so close with Sarah he didn't have time for her second thoughts.

An image of Derek where he sat under a street lamp, ensconced in the car with Landry Adair, drifted through his mind. He thought Rena was the key to getting rid of Derek Winchester once and for all, but maybe he'd been too quick to judge.

As he climbed in his car, Mark mapped out his next steps. It looked like Rena Frederickson might be getting another roommate after all.

Chapter 16

Landry paced her sitting room, the wine in her glass sloshing from side to side as she walked.

Babysitter?

Was that really how he saw her? How he saw his time here at Adair Acres?

She knew he was disillusioned about his forced time off from the Bureau and the difficulty with his current case, but Derek Winchester had no right.

No *freaking* right.

She took another sip, surprised to see how much she'd drunk already. She wasn't a lush and didn't view alcohol as the answer to her problems, but, well…a girl was entitled to a bit of a wine bender every now and again. Especially when the cause of said bender was a stubborn, gorgeous, pigheaded man who couldn't see past the end of his very strong, attractive nose.

And when had she decided he had a handsome nose?

Landry glanced down at her glass, then resumed her pacing. Maybe she had had a bit more than she'd thought.

"Hi."

The reason for her pacing stood in the arched doorway that set off her sitting room from her bedroom. Her gaze zeroed in on his nose quite before she could stop it.

Yep. Strong, firm and gorgeous. Just like the rest of him.

"Why are you in here? I had my door closed."

"I figured after the way I left things I should take my chances and just come in."

"Well, you can head right back out the way you came and go away."

"I'd like to talk to you."

"I'm not ready to talk to you."

He strolled into the room, looking for all the world like the king of the manor. She saw where he stopped and lifted the wine bottle from the coffee table, holding it up to the light to see how much was still in the bottle.

"You're welcome to what's left."

"Oh, don't let me stop you."

The thread of amusement underneath his words nipped at her heels. "You can stay or you can go but you will not sit here and laugh at me."

"I'm not laughing at you."

"Nor will you be amused at my expense."

"What if I'm amused at my own?"

She stilled, curious. "What?"

"I realized something yesterday and I was too big of an ass to remember to tell you."

Landry wasn't sure if it was the wine or the sudden tension that gripped the room, but she had trouble catching her breath as his gaze lasered on hers. Those dark, fathomless pools gave nothing away. Instead, they dragged her in and under, holding her still in their spell.

"What's that?"

"I love you."

Landry stilled all the way, her body nearly going numb at his words, until her gaze dropped from his to the wineglass in her hand. A wash of emotions—happy, sad, euphoric, angry—slammed into her from every direction and she desperately sought to grab on to one to find some purchase from the storm.

With surprisingly steady movements, she set the wineglass on the coffee table, then whirled on him in a flash.

"You love me? Because you have a damn funny way of showing it."

"I know."

"And now here I am, half drunk on wine and anger, and you try to tell me you love me? Way to ruin it, Winchester! Where are the flowers? The moonlight? The freaking candles!"

She caught the screech in her voice and dropped it as tears balled in her throat. "And why am I yelling at you when you said the most lovely thing?"

A hiccup had her gasping for breath as another hard wave of tears fell. Before she could say anything else, Derek had pulled her up in his large arms, his hands smoothing over her hair."

"Shhh. Shhh, now."

"You told me you love me and I'm ugly crying."

"You're what?"

"Ugly cry—" She broke off and swallowed around another lump of tears. "Never mind."

"You're beautiful. Even when you cry."

"I'm no—"

Her protest was smothered by his mouth, the tight press of his lips simply stealing her breath.

She sank into him, the moment as powerful as he was. As powerful as the feelings that had sparked to life between them in such a short period of time.

How had it happened? As fast as a blink and as powerful as a hurricane.

And so necessary she needed him the way she needed her next breath.

In some dim, distant part of her brain Landry knew she'd made a muddle of this—as had he—but she couldn't find a way past the crazy, desperate need to kiss him back.

He was safe. And he was here with her.

The endless moments back at the FBI office—and the implications beneath Derek's boss's words—had chilled her to the core. Even the anger and frustration that had carried her inside after their fight had been fueled by something more.

Fear.

It consumed her, the reality of what he lived and worked with. The horror of kidnapped children and murdered criminals that now threatened to pull him under, branding him as a criminal, too.

"Landry?" Derek pulled back, his gaze tender as his thumbs grazed over her wet cheekbones. "What's the matter? You were kissing me back and then you just seemed to disappear."

"They think you did it." Her quiet words filled the room, their power louder than a gunshot.

The mouth that had just moved over hers, so lush and rich with passion, firmed into a straight line. "I'll deal with that."

"*You'll* deal with it?"

"It's my damn job, isn't it?"

"And I'm the woman you claim to love."

"Claim?" Another round of flame sparked to life, filling the depths of his gaze. "Do you think I'm lying about my feelings? Using them to manipulate you? Because believe me, I've been there. I've been the one manipulated and I won't do that. Ever."

She saw the hurt as clearly as if she'd struck him, but filed that away for later. They would deal with the lingering specter of his relationship with Sarah, but not now. Not when there was so much more they needed to discuss.

"I think you struggle to share your circumstances at work out of some sense of embarrassed pride."

"Now you're a shrink, too?"

"No, I'm just a woman who can see clearly. And that clarity, along with stubborn, boneheaded comments like the one you just made, make it more than evident you're too close to this."

"And you think you have the answers?"

"I do know I'm as involved in this as you. I'm here, Derek. And I will help you see it through."

"The case is my job. You're my life!"

Raw truth crackled between them and she nearly crumbled right there—nearly gave in and leaped right back into his arms—but something held her back. For once the fear of being alone had faded, overridden by the fear of being with the right person for all the wrong reasons.

"Yet you push me away and compartmentalize that aspect of your life from me." She took a few steps of her own, backing away from the heat and warmth that beckoned her closer. "You say you love me, yet you want me to know my place."

"This isn't 1952, Landry. There is no place."

"Isn't there? You can say your attitude's modern, but it smacks of trying to protect the little woman."

"This has nothing to do with you being a woman. I'm a trained federal agent. It was irresponsible enough of me to bring you into the city last night. To taint you with the stench of whatever is going on with that case. Hell, with my partner, as well."

He dragged a hand over his head and ran his long fingers over the short-cropped hair at the crown. "I don't know who to believe anymore."

"Believe me. And believe what's between us." She moved back into his space and settled her hands on his shoulders, before slipping them up to cup his face. "Believe in us, Derek. Because I love you, too."

The light in the room seemed to change—soften somehow—as his gaze narrowed on her. Moments rich with emotion welled between them, wrapping them up tight, like the warmth of a roaring fire.

He laid his hands over hers before reaching out to pull her close, pressing his forehead to hers.

"Yes." His lips followed the whisper, soft and gentle on her forehead. "Yes."

Once more his lips pressed to hers. And once more, Landry knew the searing ecstasy of being in his arms.

And as the kiss spun out, pulling both of them further and further into the abyss, Landry couldn't help wondering if it was enough.

Derek crushed her against him, willing everything he felt inside into the kiss. How could she possibly think he'd prey on her emotions to get what he wanted?

Once again, the evidence of her family's dysfunction threw a strange, disturbing set of challenges into how they communicated with each other. And he was determined to break down every wall—every single obstacle she could prescribe—to make her see he wasn't the same.

"I want you." Landry's sultry voice banished the thoughts of her family as she ran a line of kisses down his throat and over his chest, easily accessible from the exposed vee of his shirt.

"Landry—" Her name came out on a harsh breath before he pulled her close for another kiss. "It hurts to breathe I want you so badly."

"Then it's lucky for us we're already in my bedroom." She slipped from his arms, walking backward toward the bed.

Although he'd grown up comfortable, Derek knew the Adairs lived in the rarefied air of true wealth and privilege. While he'd seen firsthand the challenges that lifestyle had created, he had to admit a private wing definitely had its uses. "I do like the privacy here."

"That makes two of us."

She already had the thin silk blouse she'd worn up and over her head, and Derek could only stop and stare. Her full breasts pressed against the pale silk of her bra, and his eyes traveled those lush curves before following a path over her trim waist and flared hips.

"Why, I do declare." Landry cocked a hand on one hip, her smile at odds with the delicate Southern drawl she affected. "I believe you're speechless."

"Nearly." He moved in quick, his arms wrapping around her and pulling her flush against his chest. "Fortunately I still have a few other moves at my disposal."

"Talk, talk, talk, Mr. Winchester."

He flicked the hook of her bra, then slid the material off her arms, making quick work of the piece. "Then maybe I should show you."

His mouth closed over her breast and all he heard was his name, echoing on a long, lingering sigh. It was the last word either of them said for a long time.

Derek ran a lazy hand over her shoulders, delighting in the simple feel of having her in his arms. The night before played through his mind on a loop, and the simple comfort of holding Landry close and feeling her heartbeat went a long way toward calming his roiling thoughts.

Not that he was any closer to the truth.

Was Mark really behind the killing of Big Al? Derek turned that one over, the question lingering even as he came up with a dozen reasons why it made no sense. What purpose would killing Al possibly serve? The man was a low-level enforcer. Small potatoes, even if he was in the running for scum of the universe.

Nothing added up.

Derek didn't want to believe his partner was responsible, and not simply from some misguided sense of wanting to be "right." He cared about Mark. Hell, the man was going to be in his wedding before things had gone south with Sarah. They'd been partners for a long time and he trusted the man with his life.

Had Mark gotten himself into some sort of trouble?

As that idea took root, Derek let it flow, itemizing what he knew about Mark's lifestyle. To the best of his knowledge, Mark wasn't dating anyone. He'd never shown signs of having a gambling or drinking problem, but that didn't necessarily mean anything.

"Mark or Noah?"

Landry's sleepy voice whispered over his chest on a warm puff of her breath.

"Hmm?"

"You're lying here thinking about Mark or Noah. I was curious which one."

At the realization he'd forgotten about Noah in the rush to LA and back, Derek struggled to surface from his thoughts. "It's Mark. And I should have my mind on Noah."

"I'd say both are pretty hot priorities." She patted his stomach before shifting so they could face each other. "And if I were being honest, I'd say I was more than happy for you to get your mind *off* Noah for a while."

"I know." He tightened his arms. "Your family's been through enough. I don't want to add to that."

She swirled a soft pattern into his chest with her index finger. "I know you don't. That makes it easier to bear somehow."

Derek laid a hand over hers, holding her palm to his chest. He pressed a kiss to her forehead, determined to give whatever comfort he could.

"So what were you thinking about Mark?"

His sigh fluttered the soft strands of her hair. "That it doesn't make any sense. And that the longer this case has gone on, the less sense it makes. Al, the man who was killed last night, was a low man on the totem pole. A thug, nothing more. Yet he's somehow the mastermind behind some bigger human trafficking ring?"

"How long have you been following this case?"

"A few months," he said.

"So why hang on to Rena so long? She would have been held temporarily, then processed for whatever horrors they'd planned, right?"

"Sadly, yes."

"So why would she still be held captive?"

"I have no idea. But all our intel has suggested there's

been something about this child they've wanted to hold on to."

"But why? To what end?"

Just as during their drive to LA the night before, Landry was engaged in the discussion. Engaged in what he had going on professionally. Engaged in his life. "That's what's so impossible. I don't know."

"Which is why it all comes back to Mark as the conduit of information."

Derek nodded, the truth not lost on him. "Even if he is, it's no excuse for my forgetting about Noah."

"Let's just say I've done enough worrying for the both of us. In my rush to have our first fight, I forgot to tell you what I found."

"Found where?"

"The papers we pulled at the Bureau the other day. I took them with me and spent most of my time in the hotel going through them."

"And?"

"And I don't think I can pretend any longer that my cousin isn't really my brother."

Derek scrambled to sit up. "Why do you think that?"

"Come on." She sat up next to him. "Let me walk you through it and you can tell me if you see what I see."

Landry laid out the papers she'd organized. She pulled the tie of her robe tighter before pointing at the ones on top of the stack. "Take a look, then tell me what you think. I want to see if your interpretation is the same as mine."

Derek picked up the stack and laid each page out, side by side. She stood back to give him time and reached for the mug of coffee she'd had sent up.

Maybe she was being silly. What had seemed like a

lead after staring at pages all night might be nothing. Sleep deprivation had a way of blurring information and blowing things way out of proportion.

"Here." Derek pointed toward the birth certificate and that last thread she was hanging by snapped.

"Yes. That's the one."

Landry sat next to him and pointed out the details. "Right there. I know the dates are written in the European standard of day, month, year. That's why the birth certificate caught my attention. When I looked closer I could see the dates look adjusted."

"February second, 1978." Derek read the form. "That matches his age, right?"

"Yes, but look at the zero before the month. Doesn't it look like a one turned into a zero, written over with dark ink?"

Derek nodded, his gaze scanning the document. "And here, as well." He pointed to the year. "The last seven on 1977 was rewritten into an eight. Even on this photocopy you can see it."

"So they forged government documents?"

"Where would they have gotten a birth certificate in the first place?"

Landry had wondered the same until the truth slammed into her with absolute certainty. "The baby who died. The one my uncle Sheldon was talking about. That's got to be it."

"This is easy enough to verify. I've got my laptop in my room. Let me get it and log in to the Bureau database and we can check the records."

He'd put his slacks on when they had dug into the records, but she couldn't help being fascinated with the play of muscles across his back when he bent down to grab his shirt. Her gaze was drawn to the hard lines of his shoulders, and sparks shot off under her skin.

He was so strong. So capable. Even with the latest events—and she knew his confidence had been shaken by Rena's case—he was still determined to do what was right to see that a young girl got her life back.

As they'd done since the previous evening, her emotions batted between Derek's case and the situation with Noah. And swung right back to Mark.

Was that part of the problem? Had Mark lived in Derek's shadow for far too long?

She'd have believed one of the most elite organizations in the world knew how to weed out problems, but what if Mark had circumvented the system at the FBI? Toed the line just long enough to gain trust before he did damage?

The questions were still swirling when Derek returned with his laptop. She'd nearly put voice to the most pressing ones about his partner when Derek turned the laptop around in his arms. "You were right. Look here."

She leaned forward and studied the original copy of the birth certificate on the screen.

"Scroll top to bottom."

Landry did as Derek asked, taking in the birth records of a child named Noah born to Emmaline and the late Nicholas Scott in December of 1977. "The child in this record was born in December."

Landry picked up the altered birth certificate and held it up to the screen. "Yet my cousin was born on February second of the following year."

"I did a quick search query on a death certificate." He sat on the love seat, the laptop on his knees. "Let me see if it's come back yet."

Concentration limned his features, reinforcing her

earlier thoughts. He was innately competent, likely to a degree he didn't even realize.

Derek Winchester was a man who knew how to take charge. And for a lesser man, that could either be an inspiration or a threat.

An awful, terrible threat.

Landry took the seat next to him and laid a hand on his arm. "Is anything there?"

"The birth certificate on record for everything Noah's ever done states a birth date of February second. Paperwork. Job applications. His driver's license. All say February second."

"That's the date we've always celebrated his birthday."

"So what happened to the Noah Thomas Scott born on December second?"

Chapter 17

Landry knocked on Whit's door, a wash of nausea coating her stomach. The reason Derek was here—the real reason—had been proven true.

Noah was Jackson. All the evidence added up and a simple DNA test would finalize the results.

Not that they needed one.

Derek had done some additional digging now that they knew what they were looking for, and he'd uncovered flight plans from the night of March first, filed when Noah's grandmother flew a transatlantic flight from Raleigh to Lyon, France.

Derek reached for her hand, linking their fingers together. "We will help him get through this."

"I know. We're all committed to that. But—"

Whit opened the door, immediately taking in what had to be somber visages from her and Derek. "Come in."

Elizabeth slipped from the small study that occupied

the far corner of Whit's wing and stood beside him. "What did you find?"

"What Georgia suspected all along. Take a look." Landry handed them the birth certificate as Elizabeth gestured them back into the study.

Derek walked them through everything they believed, then opened up his laptop to outline the flight plan details. Both a departure to France and a return the following evening.

Elizabeth had laid a hand over her rounded stomach in the retelling and hadn't moved since, her fingers splayed over her belly. "Who would do that? And a parent, no less. Your grandmother stole your father's son."

Whit kept his arm around her, pulling her close. Despite all the pain at the evidence of what they'd found, Landry couldn't help the small spark of joy that filled her. Her brother had found love with an amazing woman and they were bringing a new life into the world.

She glanced at Derek's strong jaw and wondered if they'd ever get to that point. She loved him, yes. And she believed he loved her in return. But they still had a lot to work out. His job. Her dysfunctional family. And the truth of his past. While he hid it well, his failed relationship with Sarah had done damage.

And he still didn't see her as a full partner. She gave him all the credit for wanting to—and believing he did—but in the end, he still saw her as a responsibility instead of as an equal. That wasn't how she wanted to live her life. She'd had the bright, shining example of Reginald and Patsy and she knew what an imbalance of power in a relationship did in the long run.

She wouldn't live the same way.

* * *

Derek linked his fingers with Landry's, a small bedside lamp keeping the darkness at bay as they walked back into her room. They'd stayed late with Elizabeth and Whit, turning the situation over and over until they had a workable solution.

They needed Noah's agreement to take a DNA test. Derek had assured all of them he could get the test done via something as simple as a glass the man had used, but the Adairs were firm in vetoing that approach.

The next step required Noah's full participation.

Georgia had kept a small bit of hair from Ruby's brush in the eventuality of a DNA test, but had kept that news from her stepmother. The risk of getting the woman's hopes up had forced more stealth into the situation than any of them were comfortable with and they refused to do the same to Noah.

He admired the hell out of their approach and respected the fact that it was time to tell Noah the truth. What he hadn't quite reconciled himself to was his future.

It was time to go home.

He'd done the job Kate asked—finding the missing heir—and he needed to move on. Even if a pervasive stain lingered over Adair Acres. Reginald's murderer still walked free and the faceless saboteur who'd used a snake and a blackout as weapons had yet to be caught.

Stay or go?

Derek knew what he wanted to do, but he also knew he needed to get back to his life. Even if Rena Frederickson was never found, there were others who'd go missing.

Others who were already missed.

And it was his job to find them.

He knew returning to LA shouldn't change things with

their relationship, but the reality of distance and his rein-statement in the Bureau would change the dynamics be-tween them. It was only a matter of time before Landry grew tired of his caseload and fieldwork. The travel and the endless hours of not knowing when he'd be home.

Landry fiddled with the edge of her bedspread, her anxiety palpable. "It'll be an early morning. Noah's up at the crack of dawn to get down to the stables and we need to get to him first."

"We'll tell him over breakfast. You'll all be there with him and you're coming clean on what you suspect."

"We're ruining his life." Landry sat down on the edge of the bed. "He went to sleep this evening as Noah Scott and tomorrow we're going to tell him he's Jackson Adair. What kind of people does that make us?"

"The fact that you're this upset and worried about telling him makes you very good people in my eyes."

Derek sat next to her and took her hand in his, the mattress sagging where he sat. He'd recognized it before but it struck him once again how easy it was to be with her. To laugh and love, yes, but to comfort and share the more difficult moments, too.

"That's what will get him through this. You care for him. This is eating you all up yet you're willing to do what's right. You'll do right by Noah, too."

"And what of his mother? Will we just arrest Aunt Emmaline?"

Tension tightened her slim shoulders and he pressed a hand to her back, rubbing light circles. "It's ultimately up to Ruby to press those charges. But at this point I suspect the joy of a reunion will overshadow the immediate need for punitive action."

"He's an adult. Ruby's spent her life missing him. Noah's spent his life thinking he was another man. And

Emmaline's spent her life hiding the truth. What does that do to a person? To all of them?"

"People can grow twisted, Landry. The things they want that they don't have. The dreams they have that go unfulfilled while they're unable to find a new direction or a new goal. The changes life brings, oftentimes that are painful or terribly unfair. It's a thin line to cross before those perceived injuries are seen as punishment instead of what they are."

"Life."

"Exactly."

Myriad expressions tumbled over her face, lining that porcelain skin with any number of concerns. He knew her love for her family. And he also knew the tentative bonds she and her brothers had worked so hard to create since Reginald's death.

Yet all three of them had been in unison when it came to Noah, proving those bonds were stronger than any of them realized. They were a family and the core of that—the core of what made them a unit—would see all of them through the new reality of uncovering the missing Adair heir.

The deep blue of her eyes was nearly purple in the soft light of the room when she turned to him, studying his face. "You see it all. The lowest depths of people's souls, yet you keep on. That's a special gift, Derek."

He waved off her words, uncomfortable with the praise. "It's what I do."

"No." She reached for him, one hand on his shoulder while the other took his hand. "What you do every day. That's real strength. You're brave beyond measure. And you give up your life in service of making others' better. First your willingness to protect my aunt. Now the victims you work so hard for. That's rare, Derek."

Her compliment and the sincerity buried deep in her words touched him on a level he'd never known. Had anyone ever really seen him like that? Understood his need to help others and how it pulsed in his soul, as necessary to his life as the beat of his heart?

Yet she'd seen.

"There are many who would argue it's selfish to those I care about."

"Then that's their shortcoming."

The fresh shoots of love that had been growing for days sprouted deep roots in those quiet moments together. He'd looked for someone to share his life with. Had thought he'd found someone—had believed they'd make a good life—but now that he saw Landry he knew how wrong he'd been.

And just how far he'd missed the mark in all the moments of his life that had come before.

In Landry Adair he'd found a partner and champion. He'd found a woman who believed in him.

The early notes of morning lit up the windows with pale light, visible through a small break in the curtains she'd forgotten to close all the way. She hadn't slept well, and the first signs of morning had her rising from bed, ready to do battle with what lay ahead.

She had another brother.

From the moment her father's will had been read up to now, it was so strange to realize just how monumentally her life had changed.

In addition to a brother, she had sisters now in the form of Georgia and Elizabeth. She had the new reality of a life without her father and—whenever Patsy was eventually caught—likely not her mother, either.

And she had found love.

Derek's breathing was heavy and even where he still lay in bed, and she took a moment to simply watch him as she pulled the tie of her robe around her waist.

Connections.

And they all circled around her father.

Whether the mantle had ever set comfortably on his shoulders or not, Reginald Adair had been the center of AdAir Corp, the heart of Adair Acres and the foundation of their family. Through that connection, Whit found Elizabeth. Carson found Georgia. And they'd all found Jackson.

She turned from the bed and crossed to the window, parting the curtains slightly so she could look out over the grounds. Landry knew she was apprehensive about what was to come. She also knew a strange sentimentality she couldn't quite shake.

It was so odd to reflect on it all now and see how everything had unfolded. Because even in the sad reality of what her aunt and grandparents had done to her father and his family, those connections had been vibrant and strong, iron bands tethering them all together.

Jackson Adair had lived right under their noses, but alive and well. Whatever fear her father and Ruby must have lived with could finally be assuaged. Their baby boy was a grown man.

"You're up early."

Derek wrapped his arms around her from behind, his large body like a shield, protecting her from all that was still to come. "I didn't sleep well."

"It's to be expected. You'll feel better once this is behind you. Once you can begin again as a family."

"Which means you're going to leave."

The statement was out, so simple, really, she hadn't

even realized it was lingering, lying in wait for the perfect moment to leap out.

"I... Well..." His arms tightened before he dropped them and stepped away. "My responsibilities to Kate will be completed."

"And you have a life to get back to."

"You don't have to make it sound like a duty."

"Neither is staying here."

"Landry—"

She wrapped her arms tight around her waist, holding back whatever pain threatened to swamp her. They'd made love. Had even told each other their feelings. But they'd never discussed a future, and it was silly to pretend there was one.

"We can talk later. We need to get downstairs."

That went well.

Landry hadn't stopped berating her impulsive tongue since she reached the dining room. A part of her—the small, petty part—wanted to blame her "state of our relationship" question on sleep deprivation, but she knew that was unfair.

She'd asked because she wanted to know, plain and simple.

And hadn't been prepared for any reaction besides an unequivocal desire to stay.

The large silver urn of coffee that had stood sentinel at the end of the breakfast sideboard for as long as she could remember greeted her as she filled a mug. Landry watched the rich black coffee fill her cup, hot and strong, and wished for a do-over. All at the tender hour of 6:00 a.m.

Maybe if she had enough coffee she might find a way

to put the genie she'd inadvertently unleashed in her bedroom back in the bottle.

She risked a glance at Derek, busy fetching cream from the small fridge the staff kept stocked in the corner. The hard lines of his body had remained stiff as he finished dressing in her room, then left to change into fresh clothes in his own room. He'd donned a buttondown shirt and faded jeans, and she wondered how she could be so attracted to him, even as her thoughts were in a million different directions.

They didn't live that far away from each other. A relationship wasn't out of the question, and it was barely even long distance considering how often she was in LA for her charity work. They could find a way. And if things continued to progress, she could eventually see herself moving to Los Angeles full-time.

Except he hadn't suggested that would be a welcome next step.

The truth slapped at her and Landry busied herself with making a plate of fruit to pass the time until Noah arrived. Just when she thought she couldn't dither over selecting one more strawberry, her brothers' arrival in the dining room ratcheted up the tension several more notches.

"Anyone see Noah yet?" Carson kept his tone casual as he beelined for the coffee, but Landry sensed the notes of unease under the gruff demeanor.

He was a man used to giving orders and expecting them to be followed. Process. Rules. Order. Carson had lived by those principles for his entire adult life. Which made what they were about to do that much harder.

They were about to unleash chaos.

"Everyone's up early."

Noah's voice rang out from the doorway. He looked

comfortable, Landry realized, his usual work outfit of jeans, T-shirt and chambray button-down like a second skin. Yet even if the dress were casual, she knew it was something more.

He was comfortable with who he was. Even the jokes the other day before the baby shower had held more frustration at his mother's insistence on his settling down than any real upset over the matter. He did as he liked and lived as he pleased and by all accounts, Noah liked it that way.

With the truth of his parentage, his life was about to grow considerably more attached, with responsibilities and expectations.

And with the complete annihilation of anything he believed to be real.

"I'm glad you're here." Whit greeted Noah first, slapping the man on the back and gesturing him toward the coffeepot. "Carson, Landry and I have something we'd like to discuss with you."

The pleasant civility ringing out in the Adair dining room had a tense air about it, and Derek kept his position by the French doors that led out to the patio, unwilling to intrude any more than he needed to.

He wasn't a part of the family and they deserved the space to make the proper explanations to Noah. Hell, he was just the evidence man. The keeper of the facts and details that would blow up Noah Scott's world.

Starting with the fact that he wasn't actually Noah Scott.

"Oh?" Noah snagged a mug off the sideboard. "What's going on?"

"We've come upon some information you need to know. About our father."

"What?" Noah stepped away from the coffee immediately, his concern evident as he walked toward his family. "Did you find out something about his killer?"

"No." Carson shook his head. "We found out something about you."

Confusion stamped itself in Noah's gaze—a vivid blue he shared with Landry, Carson and Whit. "Found out something? About me? Like what?"

Landry moved close to him, her hand on his shoulder. At the subtle nods of her brothers, she confirmed what they already knew. "You're Jackson, Noah. You're the one our father spent his life searching for."

"I'm what?" Color drained from his face, leaving a ghostly visage in its wake. "That's ridiculous."

"I know it's hard to believe—"

"You know?" His words were sharp, their bite swift and immediate. "You think you can drop a bomb like that on me and then tell me you *know*? Like you somehow understand?"

"I don't claim to understand, no. But I can empathize that this is a shock to you." She lifted her hand once more but dropped it, her fingers curling into a fist at her side. "A terrible shock."

Noah shook his head, his gaze darting to each Adair in turn. "What could possibly make you think this? I'm your cousin. I've been coming here since I was a kid. There's just no way."

"It may be hard to swallow, but it's true." Landry gestured in Derek's direction. "Derek has the details. The only thing left to do is a DNA test to prove it."

"Details?" Noah's gaze swung from puzzlement to accusation as it landed squarely on Derek. "You've got evidence or something? Is that why you're really here?"

Unwilling to lie any longer, Derek nodded. "That's

why Kate sent me. My expertise is missing persons, and she wanted the Adair heir found. We can do the DNA test but you're Jackson. I know it."

Each word was like a gunshot, and Derek saw how the delivery took Noah apart, piece by piece.

"So it was a lie. The relationship with Landry. Your time down in the barn, buddying up. You were playing me?"

He'd prepared himself for the accusations—knew they'd be a part of Noah's inevitable reaction—but even he hadn't expected how much it would hurt to hear them from a man he'd come to like and respect.

Add on the reference to a fake relationship with Landry and Derek fought to keep his voice level and do the job he'd come to do. "No. It wasn't like that."

"Spare me." Noah stilled before turning on his family. "And all of you. You're in on this. You all knew before I walked in here. Have you been planning this? Plotting to screw up my life?"

Carson stepped forward. "Georgia pieced it together a few weeks ago. After she met you something bothered her. She felt like she knew you. It was only when she remembered a photo of Ruby's father that she put the pieces together. The photo was an image of you."

Landry reached out once more, her voice soothing. "We never meant—"

Noah flung his arm, dislodging the comfort of her touch. "If I meant anything at all to you you'd have told me. Instead, you went behind my back. For what reason? Some misguided sense of protection?"

"We couldn't tell you." Whit hesitated before pressing on. "We couldn't risk your mother vanishing into the wind."

"You think—" Noah broke off at that, landing heavily

in one of the dining room chairs. "You think my mother's responsible?"

Derek stepped forward, effectively taking the burden off Noah's siblings to share the truth. He laid the proof of what they'd uncovered on the table, the flight plan information on top. "Your grandmother was behind it all. She managed the kidnapping and took you to Europe after stealing you from Reginald and Ruby's house."

Noah glanced at the papers before reaching forward to take the top sheet. His moves were ginger, as if he were dealing with a frightened horse, and Derek knew the analogy wasn't that far off. Only now, Noah was the frightened one.

"My mother might not have known who I was. She might have thought I was just a baby that her mother arranged."

"But she was still complicit. Whether she knew beforehand or after, she kept you. There was no way she didn't know who you were."

"But she was pregnant. I've seen photos. Even in the photos from my father's funeral, she was visibly pregnant."

Landry tried once more to touch him and laid her hand on Noah's shoulder. "That baby didn't live."

"This isn't possible. Nothing about this is possible."

"I know this is a lot to digest." Derek took the lead once more, the overt shock and upset in the room in dark contrast to the sun streaming through the windows. "I'd suggest taking a DNA test first. That will give you actual proof and then we can work on next steps from there."

"Next steps?" Noah leaped up at Derek's words, ignoring the papers on the table. "I'm not a project, Derek. Or an FBI file."

"Noah—" Carson reached out but Noah shut him off.

"None of you understands this. You can't possibly begin to understand and I could see past that. If this is true, it's not your fault that you uncovered it. But what I can't see past is that you didn't tell me what you suspected. That you left me in the dark while you played Sherlock Holmes with my life."

Every word hung over the room, noxious clouds of black, before Noah slammed out the door.

They all remained still for a moment, absorbing the reality of what had just happened, when Landry stood up. "Let me go. I'm sure he's at the stables, and we have a special bond over the horses."

"You don't have to go alone," Whit said, already moving to follow her toward the door.

"No, really. Let me try." She glanced in Derek's direction once more before she turned toward the door, the dazed look in her eyes cutting him off at the knees.

He'd known her life hadn't been easy these past months. The death of her father and all that had ensued since had taken its pound of flesh. But what killed him was the sheer absence of hope in her gaze, replaced now with a resigned sense of duty.

The woman he'd come to know was warm, vibrant and full of life.

And the woman who slipped from the dining room looked as if the weight of the world had settled on her shoulders, never to lift again.

The cool morning air whipped around her shoulders as she headed for the stables. Landry's thoughts were a jumble between Noah and Derek, swinging back and forth, one to the other. Her brother needed her, more than ever, and she'd do her best to help him through this trying time.

But she needed Derek. And as each moment passed he seemed to be slipping further and further away.

Or maybe you pushed him away.

The thought she'd tried so hard to ignore wrapped around her with the breeze, whispering in her ear and forcing her to consider her role in what was between them.

She loved him.

After a lifetime desperate for the emotion, it was amazing to see how easily it had planted roots and now lived inside her. And with that love she'd learned something even more significant about herself. Derek's wants were as important to her as her own. Maybe even more so. She wanted what was best for him and believed in supporting him.

So what are you afraid of, Adair?

Grass crunched underfoot as she continued her walk, replaying the morning in her mind. Today was about Noah yet she'd attempted to rush into a conversation with Derek about their future.

Why? To sabotage what was between them?

Or to protect herself from the risk that he might walk away first?

She'd spent so long blaming much of her life on her mother it was startling to acknowledge her own role in what had happened with Derek earlier. *She* had pushed him away. Their focus should have been the meeting with Noah yet she had pushed her fears smack in the middle of their discussion. And when he had been caught off guard, she'd used the moment to pick a fight.

The stables came into view, the tall structure reassuring. No matter how bleak her life had ever seemed, the stable held the key to restoring her equilibrium. She could only hope it did the same for Noah. Or did she need to call him Jackson now? Would he even want that?

Landry sighed and let the thought fade. They'd figure all that out in time. What Noah needed now was their understanding and support.

Then she'd go see Derek and start over. The morning hadn't gone as she planned, but they would get through it. And this time she wasn't hiding behind juvenile emotions that had no place in their relationship.

A wispy cloud floated past her peripheral vision and Landry gave herself a moment to stop and look at it. So simple, a quiet moment enjoying nature.

There was beauty to be found if you looked for it. She could see that now. Even after all she and her family had been through these past months, she could—and should—take a moment to appreciate what she had.

In time, Noah would find the same.

Images of him through the years floated through her mind, as wispy as the clouds. He'd always been as much a brother to her as Whit and Carson. As youngest, she was both family pest and doted-upon sister. She'd been teased to within an inch of her ponytail and championed for whatever she wanted to do.

Yet no matter the circumstance, Noah along with Whit and Carson had always shown a fierce devotion, their concern for her well-being at the heart of their actions.

They were her first loves. She'd spent the past few months determined to help Whit and Carson find their way. Now she'd help Noah do the same. And as she navigated the waters with Derek—no matter the outcome—she knew the Adair men would support her in return.

The welcome scents of the barn greeted her as she stepped through the heavy door. "Noah!"

She strode down the long path toward the back office,

so full of her own thoughts it took several moments to register the anxiety in the horses. Landry stopped, the restless underpinning growing evident just as she heard a loud whinny from Pete's stall.

And felt the distinct kick of adrenaline and fear as Mark Goodnight stepped out of Noah's office.

Chapter 18

Derek refilled his coffee mug, the meaningless action something to pass the time. He'd already drunk enough caffeine to be jittery and on edge, and certainly didn't need any more.

He knew he should be focused on Noah but all he could think about were his clumsy moments with Landry that morning in her room. He wanted to make it up to her—*would* make it up to her—as soon as they got Noah past the upheaval of learning his real identity. He'd already put a buddy at the Bureau on notice for a DNA test and the need for expedited results.

All they needed was Noah's go-ahead.

And then he could focus on the woman he loved. If he'd had any question at all about his future, the past few hours had erased any doubts. He loved Landry Adair and wanted to spend his life with her.

"Did he agree to take the DNA test?" Georgia's

voice interrupted his thoughts, the question giving him a chance to focus on the real reason he was here.

She'd joined Carson shortly after Noah, followed by Landry, had left the room and her husband had filled her in on the details.

Carson shook his head. "He didn't agree to much of anything. And he's worried about Emmaline. You can see it beneath the anger."

"What should we expect there, Derek?" Whit asked. "As you said before, she's complicit in this."

Derek took a seat, happy to have something to focus on. This he knew. Missing persons and kidnapping was his profession and he'd spent nearly his entire adult life understanding the ins and outs of the law.

He also understood the damage individuals could inflict on each other and wanted to prepare them. The shock of the news likely wouldn't assuage Noah's innate need to defend his mother, regardless of the evidence against her.

"We first have to prove she knew. We've all leaped to the conclusion she had knowledge Noah was really Jackson, but it's possible Eleanor could have kept that from her."

"And if she didn't?" Carson's question went straight to the heart of the problem.

"Then Noah hasn't only lost the life he believed he had, but he's lost his mother, too."

At Derek's words, Georgia covered Carson's hand with her own. "I know Ruby's suffered. The pain of losing her son has never faded, even after all these years. And because of that, I struggle to give any sort of excuse to Emmaline. But what sort of madness must that be, to live a sort of half life as a parent? To forever look over your shoulder and know that your child came with a price?"

"What price?" Whit stirred his coffee. "If what we believe is correct, Grandmother stole Jackson from son to daughter. No one was paid."

"It's not the money. She's paid with her soul."

Georgia's words echoed through the room with a grim finality and Derek knew she spoke the truth. No matter how desperately Emmaline wanted to be a mother, the choices made decades ago had to have taken a toll. "Landry mentioned she'd come here, to the ranch, every summer with Noah. But that somehow she'd fade into the background, as if she didn't wish to be scrutinized too hard."

Carson nodded. "Now that you put it that way, I know what Landry means. Emmaline was here, but she wasn't. She just sort of hovered on the fringes."

"Remember the summer she had that fight with Dad?" Whit said.

"What fight?"

"What happened?"

Derek and Carson both leaned forward on that tidbit, their questions overlapping.

"I don't know all the specifics, but it had something to do with AdAir Corp and Aunt Kate's run for VP." Whit rubbed at his chin. "I'm pretty sure that was it. She was upset with how public a figure Dad was with the company. Always throwing lavish parties and doing his level best to get as much PR—even if it was personally related—as he could."

"She didn't like the spotlight on the family, then?" Derek considered Landry's memories along with Whit's, adding another mental tally in the "Emmaline knew" column.

"No. And she hated the spotlight that hit the family once Kate made the presidential ticket and ultimately became VP," Whit said.

"Mom has never liked her," Carson added. "And while that's not saying much, it's the reasons why she didn't like her that have always stuck with me."

"What are those?" Derek pressed Carson, sensing there was yet another level of detail. For all they'd never known about Noah's parentage, it was growing more and more evident there had been signs that all wasn't right, either.

"Mom always felt she was a woman who let the world act upon her instead of making her own choices. Said she had a birdlike countenance that came off weak and needy and way too fragile."

Derek knew circumstantial evidence was just that—more anecdotal than hard fact—but he'd always believed in trusting his gut. By all appearances, the Adairs had borne a traitor in their midst and it was up to all of them to now tread lightly enough to get Emmaline to confess.

"You're all still here?" Noah came back into the room, color high on his cheeks.

"Where's Landry?" Derek was on his feet first, immediate alarm ringing through his system in harsh, clanging waves.

Confusion stamped itself in Noah's blue eyes, still hazy and dull with the news of the morning. "I don't know. I never saw her."

"She came to find you in the stables."

"I didn't go to the barn. I wanted to walk through the orange groves for a while and calm my thoughts. I was afraid of spooking the horses with my bad mood."

The alarm bells that hadn't quieted on Noah's arrival

ratcheted up to a five-alarm blaze. "You never went to the stable at all?"

"No."

"So where's Landry?"

Landry fought hazy memories and the harsh wash of light as she opened her eyes. Pain screamed through her skull and she stilled, focused on breathing through the pain and the sudden panic that gripped her chest.

Where was she?

The air had a dank, heavy smell, like a wet basement or a cave at sea level. She kept her eyelids at half mast and stared at the brownish, water-stained ceiling. Her mind whirled as she tried to piece together where she was.

The anxiety of the morning filled her mind in a wash of memories. The discussion with Derek about their future. She and her brothers' announcement to Noah that he was their long-lost sibling. And the walk to the stables…

Thoughts of her family faded as the reality of what had lain in wait came crashing back.

Mark.

Derek's partner and fellow agent at the FBI was dirty. He'd waited for her to arrive, then taken her—

A sob filled the air and Landry bolted upright at the evidence she wasn't alone. Pain ricocheted through her skull and she held still, eyes closed, willing the agony to subside to a dull roar now that she was upright.

With delicate movements, she blinked open her eyes and stared into a dark brown gaze devoid of hope. "Who are you?"

The child's whisper was raw, as if she hadn't spoken in days, and whatever pain had accompanied Landry upon waking faded against the insistent hum of realization.

"You're Rena."

"How do you know that?"

Fear lit up the dark brown depths of the girl's eyes and Landry tried to quickly reassure her. "I know the man who's been looking for you. He's from the FBI and he wants to bring you home."

"No one's looking for me." The rasp was still there, but her voice now held wisps of bravado. "And the FBI's the reason I'm here."

She knew Mark was responsible, but she hated to think how he'd destroyed any image this child held of law enforcement. So many were working so hard to get her back. Not just Derek, but his entire team wanted to see this child rescued.

"No, sweetie, they're not. They're the ones trying to find you and bring you home."

The heavy metal door to their room swung open and Mark stood in the entryway. Rena pointed toward Derek's partner. "Then why have they been holding me?"

Her pulse spiked once more as adrenaline rushed her system and Landry fought to remain calm. She'd get nowhere if she didn't keep her wits about her, especially since he had the upper hand. Because based on what she knew of the case, Mark had had plenty of time to prepare for whatever it was he had planned.

Derek's partner strolled into the room, the trim cut of his suit at odds with the menace that rolled off him like heat lightning. "Glad to see you woke up. You're surprisingly heavy for a woman with such a hot body."

Landry ignored the insult—only made worse by the leer that traveled over her breasts—and forced a calm bravado she didn't feel into her tone. "What have you done?"

"Isn't it obvious?"

"No, it's not. You're a federal agent. Why are you holding this child?"

"She's a means to an end." Mark walked up and stood over her, that leer morphing into something far more menacing. Madness.

Sheer, utter madness.

"Just like you, Landry Adair."

Derek and Landry's brothers had already raced through the stables as soon as they'd ascertained Noah had never seen her after rushing from the house. Their hurried walk-through past the agitated horses hadn't produced much and he was now back in the estate's security room assessing what he could on the cameras.

The morning's footage clearly showed her walking into the barn and then nothing.

"You find anything?"

"No. Damn it!" He dragged a hand over the back of his neck, frustrated at the evidence that the video feeds had been tampered with once more.

Carson took the seat next to Derek and ran the surveillance footage, his fingers surprisingly nimble and well versed on the keyboard.

"And my contacts at the Bureau haven't gotten any more details on the tampering last week, either. It's like the footage simply evaporated. They've tried tracing it and nothing's worked. All they get are some bouncing shadows that suggest there was footage but it's been thoroughly erased."

"I thought you couldn't do that anymore. Not with digital technology the way it is." Carson tapped a few more keys.

"I thought so, too. And when I say the Bureau team is the best, I mean it. They can do amazing things with the smallest amount of footage. Heck, I saw them re-create an incident off a slivered image from a building's surveillance thirty yards across the street from another building."

"You send them the new stuff from this morning?"

"Yes."

"If they can work with cameras at a distance, what about our neighbor in the sky?"

Derek had his eyes on the screen, willing something to show up when Carson's comment registered. "What neighbor? You've got all the acreage for nearly half a mile."

"I know, but we've also got a cell tower in our back-yard. It's a bit of an eyesore but my father was never one to turn down money. And it ensures we always get out-standing reception here. He camouflaged it in the trees just past the stables."

"Give me a minute."

Derek made quick work of the information and had his Bureau contact on the line in moments. "Can you get at it, Brad?"

The hard grunt and quick tap of a keyboard was all the confirmation Derek received and he knew it was more than enough. In moments, Brad was giving instructions on how to pull up the feed on the house computers.

Derek put him on speaker, then leaned toward the screen, orienting himself to the angle of the cameras. "There, Brad. What's the time stamp on Landry's ar-rival?"

When Brad gave him the same time as the house com-puters, Derek pressed him on. "Good. We're in sync. Go ahead and back it up. Someone got in there and we need to find out who."

Footage whizzed past, nothing visible but the stable

dwelling growing increasingly dark as the time moved earlier and earlier in the morning. As the screen grew darker, Derek worried they'd miss something when an image caught all of them at the same time.

"There," Carson said.

"There it is." Brad's voice smacked of triumph through the speaker. In moments, the man had the image manipulated, using the lights surrounding the barn to maximum advantage. He zoomed in on the individual hovering around the doorway, his gasp evident when a face became visible through his work on the resolution. "I don't believe it."

"I do."

Derek's acknowledgement was grim and devoid of any emotion. Landry had been right all along.

Mark Goodnight was dirty.

Derek worked through the specifics with Leo and Brad as they developed a sting operation. Mark still needed to show up for work, but they couldn't be sure he hadn't created some sort of remote detonation on wherever he was keeping Landry. Brad was given authorization to dig into Mark's files and phone records, but so far he'd found nothing on Bureau assets that was useful.

Although he wanted to leave immediately, the chances were high that Mark was holding Landry in LA. He owed it to Landry's family to fill them in before he left. He kept the updates short, walking them through what he knew of his partner.

Whit spoke first. "And you've never had any signs?"

"None. I've worked with the guy for years." Derek hesitated before the well of grief and regret that threatened to swamp him spilled over. "How couldn't I have known something?"

Elizabeth had been quiet in the telling, her hand on Whit's shoulder, but she moved next to him, her voice warm and soothing. "People know how to hide their true selves and their true feelings. You can't beat yourself up over that."

Derek knew Elizabeth and Whit had cared for each other for a long time, neither admitting to their attraction, but somehow he couldn't see this as the same thing. Their love for each other was something that made each of them better when they'd finally admitted the truth. Mark's deception, on the other hand, was like a cancer, eating away at the core of the Bureau. Hell, at the core of his life.

How much had the man known that he'd never shared? And how much of the recent cases they'd worked had Mark messed with out of sheer spite or ill will? There was no time to go through it now but once this was over—once he had Landry back—he'd find out.

Because he would get her back.

Failure was simply not an option.

Landry had spent the better part of the day calculating what time it was based on the movement of the sun through the windows. Rena had slept off and on and in the child's quiet moments Landry had observed her.

What horrors had this poor young girl seen?

Derek had said she was kidnapped with the intent of using her in a human trafficking ring. Had that happened and Mark rescued her, only to then use her as an expedient resource? Or was Mark a part of that, too?

She shuddered, humbled by a reality she'd never acknowledged before. She'd believed herself well aware of the problems brought on by poverty and lack of opportunity, but did she really have any idea? She'd spent the better part of the past two months feeling sorry for her own personal situation, yet here she sat with a young girl who had nothing.

Landry was entitled to her own grief and pain, but something shifted inside her as the day progressed, one long hour after another.

Reginald and Patsy's inability to love her and parent her in a functional, positive way was on them. She'd done nothing to deserve their lack of care and yet the longer she wallowed in it, the greater disservice she did to herself.

And to Derek.

She'd recognized her error on the walk to the barn, but it was only now, when the risk she might never see him again became all too clear, that she truly understood. Love was a gift. An offering of the heart that shouldn't come with strings. If he wanted to accept her love and share his in return, then they'd figure out their life together.

And if he didn't, then she was still better for having loved him.

Rena cried out from her cot and Landry went to her, pulling her small body close. The child clung to her in sleep, desperate for the comfort and warmth she'd been denied for who knew how long. Landry crooned to her, soothing her with gentle words and soft strokes over her hair.

She let the moments drift, puzzling through the information she already knew. Did she have anything she could use against Mark? Anything she might hold over his head that would get him to at least release Rena?

The loud *thud* of the door woke her, and Landry realized she'd fallen asleep herself while holding the girl. Rena was still wrapped around her but the room was darker than earlier, the light through the window holding the sheen of early evening.

"Get up!"

Rena whimpered awake, her thin arms squeezed tight around Landry's waist. Landry shifted them both to a sitting position, unwilling to cower in the face of Mark's bullying.

Now was the time to get the information she desired.

But as she stared into his eyes, she had to question why he had done this. And how many others had he possibly hurt?

If she could get those details, she might find some way to use them, either to trip him up or to leave some bit of evidence behind for Derek and his team to use.

"You don't have to yell. You're scaring her."

"Kid's been scared for a month."

A month?

A renewed burst of anger filled her chest but Landry held on. "Why did you do this?"

"I rescued her from that human trafficking ring. She should be thanking me and instead all she does is whine and complain."

"Maybe because she's still locked up, away from her family. Her life."

"She's got three squares and a better life here than she would have." Mark's eyes grew dark, the sneer he perpetually wore firmly in place. "But what would you know about that? Miss Overprivileged and Overindulged. Daddy's little princess is now horrified to see the seamier side of things, is that it?"

"The only horror is you. You have a position of honor and bravery and you've thrown it away on some twisted, petty jealousy." The words spilled forth and she refused to hold them back. "What made you crack? Was it the proof that you'll never be as good a man as Derek?"

Mark's face narrowed in anger but he stood his distance. It was curious, she realized. She'd have expected him to strike her for her comments. Instead he stood back, distancing himself.

The impression of cowardice she'd had wasn't far off the mark. Despite his anger and rage, he clearly found it distasteful on some level to exact punishment directly. Other than his rough handling after he'd knocked her out with something in the stable, she was untouched. And she'd gently questioned Rena earlier to find out the girl hadn't been physically harmed throughout her ordeal.

So why was he doing this?

"Winchester's an ass. The office golden boy. Damn protector of the vice president so everyone thinks that makes him a hero."

"He's a good man."

"He's a phony. He acts like he's this big family man yet he never appreciated what he had." Mark slammed a hand over his chest. "*I* appreciated it but could never have it."

Landry stilled as raw fury mottled his face in a vivid red. "What didn't Derek know how to appreciate?"

"Sarah."

"His fiancée?"

"Ex-fiancée." Mark spit the word out on a snarl, the "ex" more significant to him than she ever could have realized.

This was all about Sarah? Mark had thrown his life away—and clearly his sanity—over a woman?

"Does she know?"

"You think I'd taint her with this?" Mark tossed a hand in Rena's direction. "She already thinks brats like Rena take up too much of the job. Too much time and focus and attention. Why would I tell her this?"

Landry couldn't imagine that his subterfuge had come off without considerable time and planning, as well, but she held her tongue. He was obviously riled and now that she had her information, her only goal was to get her and Rena out as smoothly as possible.

"Maybe you would let me talk to her? Sarah."

"Why would I do that?"

Landry forced as much of a bored, rich girl tone as she possibly could into her voice. "I'm the new woman. It'd be easy enough to let Sarah know how right she was and what a good idea it was to walk away."

Interest sparked in Mark's gaze, a small, predatory smile coming to life. "That's not a bad idea."

"Of course it's not."

Mark frowned and Landry nearly thought she'd overplayed her hand when she realized his gaze had slipped away from her completely.

He swore, long and low under his breath, before slamming them all back against the wall. "Looks like your good idea is going to have to wait."

"For what?"

"I need to go kill your boyfriend."

The old warehouse in downtown Los Angeles brought back a series of memories Derek had pushed to the back of his mind. On his first sting after he joined the Bureau, they'd uncovered a flophouse for one of the city's major criminal networks.

The warehouse looked abandoned—purposely so—but the place was used as a transition stop. They primarily trafficked drugs, prostitutes and any young girls they were shipping out of the country, but their capabilities far exceeded simple transportation.

Though the building appeared condemned, it had state-of-the-art security and computer capabilities that rivaled NASA.

He and the team had dismantled the place, piece by piece, securing reams of evidence that had put several criminals behind bars for life and had chipped away at a huge portion of the crime ring's cash flow.

After Brad's cursory glance into Mark's files, they'd spent the afternoon digging more deeply through whatever they could get their hands on that Mark might have touched. The time and forced patience had nearly killed him, but Derek knew they had one shot at this.

One shot to get Landry and bring her home.

Whatever game Mark was playing had come to its end. And there in some obscure piece of paperwork, Derek's patience had been rewarded. As soon as Brad snagged the building file, Derek had made the connection.

It had been Mark's one slipup, but it had been enough for them to put the pieces together. The orders on the building had been signed off on by Mark Goodnight. And when they dug into the paperwork behind the authorization, Derek had found what he needed.

His earpiece buzzed, Leo's voice strong and clear. "Eyes on him. Snipers got a view through the windows. Do not engage."

"They see anyone else?"

"Negative." Leo's voice snapped through the line. "Hold your position, Agent Winchester."

Derek had been through it already and knew the protocols. Mark was armed and if they tipped him off, there was no telling what he'd do.

Derek *knew* he needed to wait for the signal.

But all he could imagine was Landry inside, bound up or—worse—hurt and in need of help. In need of him.

So he held his post, standing sentinel against the battered old door on the back side of the building. He kept calm, tracing the building floor plan over and over in his mind. And he thought about all the ways he was going to tell her he loved her.

How he'd hold her close and never let her go. How he was going to ask her to marry him at the first possible opportunity.

He believed they'd see each other again, willing it with everything he was.

Whether it was the heightened direction of his thoughts or the sharp awareness of seeing this through to completion, he didn't know, but he was already on the move when the door behind him opened.

His body flat against the wall, Derek forced Mark to walk through the door to get a good look at him. Those last few steps were necessary and compelled Mark to expose himself in the open. Despite orders and the snipers in easy range, Derek made his move.

He had Mark slammed against the doorframe, wrestling him against the wall. "Where is she? You bastard! I trusted you!"

The words tore from his lips in a hard cry, words he was barely aware of even speaking. Betrayal layered over anger until all he could see—all he could feel—was the steady slam of Mark's head against the outer wall of the building.

Moments flashed in a blur as screams echoed down the sidewalk, his backup on him in seconds, pulling him off Mark.

And then Landry was through the door and in his arms, saying his name over and over.

"You're okay."

"I'm fine. Shhh." Her arms were tight around his shoulders, her lips against his ear. "I'm fine."

Derek clung to her, amazed she was back in his arms. He'd hoped—believed—she would be, but the reality was so much better.

"Derek." His lips moved over her hair and she said his name again before pressing on his shoulders. "Come here. Come with me."

Time blurred in a series of impressions and he fought to stay with her as she reached for his hand. "Come on. I have someone I'd like you to meet."

Landry pulled him back through the doorway, into the dark, dank space of the building. He nearly pulled her back out, unwilling to have her spend even another minute there, when he saw her.

Rena.

Her tall, gangly body was draped in a T-shirt and jeans, her feet bare.

"We found her, Derek." Landry's voice was quiet as she pulled him closer to the young girl. "She's safe."

Derek fell into a crouch before the girl, unwilling to startle her after all she'd been through.

Landry moved to stand next to Rena, her arm draping those slim shoulders. "He's the one I was telling you about. He wouldn't rest until they found you."

Rena glanced up at Landry, trust swimming in her quiet eyes. And then she moved, all arms and legs, and threw herself into Derek's arms. And as he looked over Rena's head, into the eyes of the woman he loved, Derek knew he'd found his partner. The woman who understood him. Who accepted him for who he was and who he wanted to be.

And for her, he'd do anything. She was his life. His love.

His forever.

Epilogue

"They caught her." Landry snuggled deeper into her robe and wondered why that statement didn't make her feel worse.

Rachel's eyes widened from the opposite couch. "Your mother?"

"Yep. She's being extradited as we speak, ripped from the arms of her European lover, under investigation for the acts perpetrated against Elizabeth."

"Oh, Landry, I'm so sorry." Rachel moved to sit next to her and laid a soothing hand on Landry's leg. Her eyebrows did shoot up in clear surprise. "But a lover?"

Landry wanted to be angry—knew she would have been even a few weeks ago—but she simply didn't have the time or attention to care about her mother's poor choices any longer. "Apparently she's been seeing Raphael for the last year. She was actually with him the night my father was shot so she's cleared of suspicion there."

"I'm still sorry."

"I'm not. She needs to own up to her part in what happened to Elizabeth." Landry thought over the past forty-eight hours. The rescue in the warehouse. Rena's return to her family. Even Noah's agreement to take a DNA test.

All of it was coming to a resolution, and Patsy's extradition was another necessary chapter closed.

Rachel offered up another soothing pat. "Then we'll agree to bury this in the friend vault and only pull it out from time to time if you need to discuss it."

Landry pulled Rachel close in a hug. "You've got a deal."

They drifted to other topics—namely how they'd both gone overboard purchasing baby outfits—when Noah walked into the room. "I wanted us all to be together for this."

"For what?" Landry watched as her entire family trooped in, with Derek closing the line, an envelope in his hands. His gaze was somber as he sought her out, subdued from the brighter joy that had marked him since they returned from LA.

When he came over and took the seat next to her, his hand closing over hers, she squeezed back. She knew that envelope held Noah's future, and she was glad they would share the moment together.

"I should probably get going." Rachel stood but Noah pressed her back to the couch.

"Please stay. I'd like you to be here."

Rachel nodded, her green gaze solemn. "Of course."

"Derek? Please." Noah took the envelope from Derek, his hands steady as he ripped through the thin seal. "I've had some time to think about what's in here. And I've come to accept that you all did what you thought was best."

"Noah—" Whit halted before adding, "You're our

family. You mean the world to us and you always have. No matter what's in there, we're here for you. We're always here for you."

Noah nodded before his gaze landed on Landry. She reveled in the warmth there and the love, always so evident in his gaze. "I know that. And almost losing Landry was a really crappy way to be reminded of how much you all mean to me, too."

Derek wrapped an arm around her and she moved closer to that protection and, to the very depth of her soul, knew Noah was right. Family—the ones you were born with and the ones you made—were what made life worth living. And in a matter of months, she and Derek would solidify their feelings by marrying and becoming a family of their own.

Noah slid the papers out and Landry marveled at how so few pages could change a man's life. He scanned the top page but it was his words that sent shock waves through the room.

"I'm Jackson Adair."

* * * * *

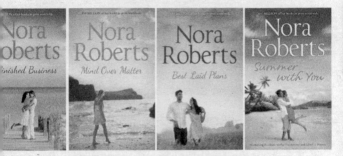

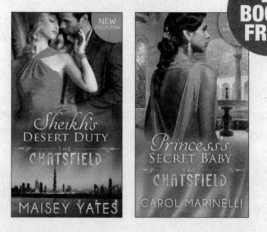